with Dolores DeLuce

Edited by Dolores DeLuce
and Catherine Gigante-Brown

Cover Photo and Design by Vinnie Corbo
Cover Model John Coleman
Author Photo by Vinnie Corbo

Volossal
Publishing

Published by Volossal Publishing
www.volossal.com

Copyright © 2018
ISBN 978-0-9996916-4-9

1

Table of Contents

Prologue	5
Chapter 1 - Noelle's Nightmare	9
Chapter 2 - Sins of the Fathers	13
Chapter 3 - Hit the Road, Jack!	21
Chapter 4 - Noelle's New Digs	23
Chapter 5 - A Grand Feast	33
Chapter 6 - A Big Easy Night	37
Chapter 7 - Sally's Solution	47
Chapter 8 - Same Day, Different Salvation	53
Chapter 9 - No Turning Back	63
Chapter 10 - Holy Roller Murders	69
Chapter 11 - Murdering Religion	73
Chapter 12 - Like Minds	85
Chapter 13 - Noelle Goes to Church	91
Chapter 14 - Missing Sally	99
Chapter 15 - More Shall be Revealed	107
Chapter 16 - Barefoot and Pregnant	115
Chapter 17 - Getting Down to Business	117
Chapter 18 - Dons, Johns and Hookers	125
Chapter 19 - Home Body	133
Chapter 20 - Herbs and Needles	135
Chapter 21 - Back to Noelle's Vigil	139
Chapter 22 - *Flores de Los Muertos*	141
Chapter 23 - Fortune Telling 101	147
Chapter 24 - Self Help Coven	159
Chapter 25 - A Farewell to Catherine	171
Chapter 26 - Esmeralda Schools Tucci	179

Chapter 27 - A Special Meal	183
Chapter 28 - Baby Shower, No Surprise	191
Chapter 29 - A Meeting of Importance	195
Chapter 30 - The Funeral	203
Chapter 31 - Love and Sympathy	219
Chapter 32 - A Date with Destiny	225
Chapter 33 - Second Chances	247
Epilogue	267

Prologue

The light from the late afternoon sun pierced the oppressive black clouds, only to fall on the crucifix atop the tower of Saint Catherine's Cathedral in Jackson Square, New Orleans.

Inside one of the grandest Cathedrals to the Divine, lamps flickered as the Archbishop took the stone steps one by one down to the burial grounds where the remains of the previous archbishops, from the 18th century until today, had been laid to rest.

The Archbishop's footsteps echoed throughout the marbled mausoleum. With a perverse wisdom, he knew it was the perfect altar to take his sacrificial lamb. The Archbishop guided the young deaf and dumb boy slowly down through the dim burial chamber, gripping the small boy's hand tightly. In his other hand, the Archbishop caressed the beads of a pearl rosary.

He stopped to stare into the boy's dark, trusting eyes and slowly mouthed the words, "Matthew, you will be consecrated here tonight." He knew the boy could read his lips. He continued, "When you are crowned, you will be forever one with Christ, our Savior."

The Archbishop stepped to the lower enclave. He led the child around the black marble tombs of his dead predecessors. At the very back of the grand hall, the Archbishop stopped at the last mausoleum. The oldest archbishop was buried there. It was a small, simple altar with a white marble cross that hung on the wall above it. The priest showed the boy how to bow properly in front of it.

On the altar, two large, bronze candleholders rippled a fiery light onto the stone wall. The Archbishop had already prepared everything to his liking, setting the stage as though for a play.

The Archbishop grasped the bronze handle of a wooden chest, which was set before the altar, to nudge it open. Inside were a big, heavy gold crucifix and a gold braided dress complete with white linen skirts. The Archbishop turned the boy toward him so the child could read his lips. He announced to his young, blonde, perfect boy, "As the blessed Infant of Prague, you are to become holy. When it is over, you will be mine."

The boy's eyes widened with the thrill of becoming a saint, sacred, of being blessed. He stood there, perplexed and unmoving as the Archbishop slowly unbuttoned the boy's trousers. When he pulled the white serving vestment off the child, the Archbishop's favorite altar boy was left standing there almost naked except for his undershorts. For a second, the child had a flicker of doubt, but he still stood there, obediently waiting to be robed in the sacred garments.

The priest fingered the white under slips, picked them up and fitted them onto the boy. They wrapped around his slight body like a diaper. Next, the Archbishop covered the under garment with the golden dress, meant for a small male statue much younger than his prey. It fit snugly but it would have to do.

Once fully clothed in the costume, the child grinned from ear to ear, turning round and round in a circle as he surveyed his dress. The priest placed a small crown on the boy's head as he exclaimed, "And now, my child, you are the reincarnation of the Infant of Prague. But with that blessing comes great responsibility."

The Archbishop carefully peeled off his crimson vestment and lifted his long, black, inner cassock to reveal that he was wearing no trousers or underwear beneath them. As he fondled the boy's cheek, he pulled the child's face toward him, pressing it closer to his crotch.

The priest whispered, "This is the greatest sacrament of all, better than Holy Communion. Eat my body; drink my blood."

The Archbishop was startled out of his reverie when he heard heavy steps behind him on the cold, marble floor. The priest felt a sharp blow on his shoulders that knocked him to the floor. He lay there silent, still.

The Avenger placed a blindfold over the boy's eyes and gently held a rag doused with chloroform over his nose and mouth. The child fell into his arms, immediately unconscious. The Avenger gently laid him to the side of the altar. Once he took care of the innocent, he tended to the pressing matter at hand.

The Avenger turned to the priest, who was now weeping. He dragged the clergyman by his thinning white hair to the only electric socket near the altar. Out of his black duffel bag, the Avenger pulled out an electric drill and plugged it in. The Archbishop's eyes were large with shock. He screamed in terror, but only for a moment, as the man quickly taped his mouth shut. The sound of the blaring drill—and the Archbishop's muffled cries—echoed through the catacombs, as the Avenger pushed the spinning drill tip into the Archbishop's chest wall, cutting through his breastbone and exposing his internal organs. Blood spurted and flowed freely onto the oldest archbishop's grave.

The Avenger laughed. The harsh sound echoed throughout the room, only to be silenced by the whine of his drill. The killer pulled the heart carefully out of the priest's chest. To further his fury, with all of his strength, the man grabbed the heavy, gold crucifix from the altar. He held it over the Archbishop's eyes so the priest would know what was coming next...if he were still alive, that is.

The Avenger wedged open the Archbishop's chest where his heart had been. The killer smiled as he drilled into the priest's skull to disengage his rotten, twisted brain. Oh, so cautiously, the man lifted the brain from the priest's split skull.

Suddenly, all was quiet, still. The man unplugged his drill. He placed the Archbishop's brain and the heart into a plastic bag, then into a small, plastic cooler. He pushed the cooler carefully down into his bag, ever so slowly. The murderer checked the boy to make sure he was still unconscious. He was.

As his finale, the killer pulled the Archbishop's body over to the oldest mausoleum and picked up the remains of his victim. He removed the priest's garments and arranged his torn frame on top of the tomb. Lastly, the Avenger took the pearl rosary beads and wrapped them around the Archbishop's shriveled, flaccid penis. He left him there, naked on display.

When he was finished tending to the Archbishop, the killer carried the unconscious boy back upstairs to the cathedral's altar. He did this quickly because he knew it was time to flee. He placed the boy on the altar and wrapped him in the Archbishop's vestments so the child wouldn't catch a chill from the cold air conditioning vent blowing overhead.

Using the priest's blood as ink, the killer wrote something on the marble wall behind the altar. With a flourish, his large, elegant handwriting left a message:

VENGEANCE IS MINE!

Before the Avenger left, he kissed the child on the head, and like the Angel of Death, disappeared into the muggy, back alleys of New Orleans as the sun began to set over the Saint Catherine's Cathedral in the French Quarter.

Chapter One

Noelle's Nightmare

T he dream always started the same way:

Nick Noelle dove into the deep end of the pool to start his workout. After the first few laps, a heavy rain poured down from the dark ominous clouds above. The chlorinated water turned into a murky sludge. Noelle continued to exert himself without making any forward movement as if he were swimming in an infinity pool.

As Noelle swam in place, the waters began to rise higher and higher, taking over the streets of his Houston neighborhood. Hurricane force winds and waves lapped at the windows of his new townhouse where he knew his sweet wife, Sally, was sleeping peacefully unaware of the danger.

Terror struck his heart as the muddy water engulfed his new home. He heard a woman with a strong Mississippi accent calling for help. He realized it was the voice of his mother, Catherine.

She called out his name, "Nicolas!"

He swam toward the voice but the stream morphed into a fast rushing river. Noelle fought the strong current with a herculean effort to reach his mother.

The thunder of insane guffaws and a loud cackle of a woman's laughter stopped his momentum. Noelle knew instantly who it was and was overcome by terror and doom. She was back from the dead.

It was Pamela, the serial killer he had witnessed being swallowed by a crocodile. She was the same twisted, violent she-wolf who almost won his heart and who nearly mutilated his wife. Her dead arm wrapped around his neck and tightened, pulling him deeper into the slime. Noelle bit firmly into her arm and swallowed bits of bone, blood and hair. He saw Pamela's face with her piercing blue eyes literally changing before him. Her body shifted and morphed as her limbs became branches. Her spine straightened and sprouted into a tree. It grew wider and taller with each moment. Her branches covered the sky and blotted out the light.

Shrieks blew and weaved through the branches of the giant evil oak tree. Noelle silently begged the powers that be to free him from this ungodly power.

Noelle's blood chilled when he saw his mother floating and waving wildly. She was surrounded by corpses of the doomed débutantes slain by Pamela. Their bloodcurdling screams were deafening.

Desperate to help his mother, Noelle grabbed one of Pamela's branches that were as sharp as razors. Blood spurted from his hand so heavily that it formed a river in the midst of the muddy quicksand that trapped him.

Noelle cried out to his mother, "Mama, I am coming!" The river of blood that flowed from him built a forceful wave that carried Noelle out of the swamp. Suddenly he was back in his swimming pool again. The waters all around his house had subsided. Beside the pool his mother waited and offered him a towel. She appeared young and radiant. She gently toweled off the blood, slime and murky waters from his shivering body. Once he was clean she comforted him. Nick rested his head on her breast and breathed a sigh of relief.

His mother kissed his cheek and whispered, "Nick, my sweet boy, I have something to tell you. You must come to me for salvation."

Noelle woke up sobbing.

He opened his eyes and saw his wife Sally. She sat up and wrapped her arms around him.

"Nick, you were screaming again!" she told him sleepily.

With a racing heart, Noelle murmured, "I just had that weird-ass dream again."

Sally touched his face and stroked his hair to soothe him. Noelle made the connection between his mother's touch and the loving warmth of his wife. It was the same tenderness he knew as a very young child before his mother remarried Noelle's horror of a stepfather.

Noelle smiled weakly but his nightmare lingered. He kissed Sally then spooned her warm curves until she fell back to sleep.

Once Noelle was confident his wife was out like a light, he carefully stepped out of bed and tiptoed down the stairs. He had a strong need for the Jack Daniel's that he kept hidden in his office.

'Jack' was the only friend who could calm his nerves. That night it took almost the whole bottle of the Tennessee whiskey before Noelle had the courage to crawl back up to bed. Still, he couldn't fall asleep until the sun rose over the house and darkness was gone.

Chapter Two

Sins of the Fathers

The next morning, Noelle rolled over on to Sally's long, red hair. It spread out like a fan, filling the pillow next to his. With a racing heart, he opened his eyes. "I had that nightmare again," he told her.

"I know," she said. "Don't you remember you woke me up in the middle of the night sobbing?"

Noelle felt shame and mumbled under his breath, "Sorry."

"Don't be," Sally told him.

She sat up in their big, brass bed; the one constant in their on-again, off-again relationship. Without makeup and the sun shining across her face, Sally was still beautiful. Noelle never got used to or tired of looking at her.

After he and Lopez had solved the Debutante Murders and Pamela was dead and buried (in the guts of a crocodile), Nick Noelle retired from the Houston Crime Squad and remarried Sally. Noelle took an early pension and bought a new townhouse in Montrose, a budding upscale Houston neighborhood. Sally filled their new home with tasteful modern furniture but had insisted they keep their old brass bed. It had lasted through the worst of their trials and tribulations. The bed did not reflect the new modern lines of her home. She romanticized the bed as a symbol of their powerful lasting love.

As Sally kissed Noelle's head, he smiled, hugging her close. However, the horror of his nightmare lingered. He thought about the passage of time since he had closed the book on those insane Debutante Murders. The events of less than a year ago seemed like another lifetime to him now.

Since he remarried Sally he was trying to wean himself off the bottle and give up the gambling to keep the promise he made to her on their second wedding day. Since he had retired, Noelle's new life lacked purpose and focus while Sally's life had become the opposite.

After her near-fatal ordeal with Pamela, she was struck clean and sober with the help of Narcotics Anonymous. Noelle had made no such commitment, only a promise to try and stop. He felt guilty drinking in front of her, so he did it privately behind her back. It only increased his guilt and shame.

Noelle told Sally what he thought she wanted to hear only to make her happy. He even attended some Gamblers Anonymous meetings but he wasn't about to surrender the whole kit and caboodle. He couldn't abandon Jack...not yet. He needed it more than ever since his re-occurring nightmare.

Although Sally could smell the booze on him, she never said a word to him about it. Noelle knew that she suspected he was drinking a lot. His excuse was insomnia but he knew the truth. He knew he was becoming an alky, just like his loser old man.

Noelle was conflicted. He didn't want to stop drinking but he didn't want his affliction to hurt poor Sally. Noelle knew that if he followed in the footsteps of his deadbeat dad, inevitably it would. God knows, he loved Sally more than life. But Noelle also knew that he was failing miserably at being the man she deserved, the same man she had hoped he would become once they started over again. The question was: could he ever become that man?

Guilt rode Noelle as he realized that his happy, little home was just not enough to make him happy. He missed the chase, the rush of his detective work. He was bored with the empty, predictable, day-to-day life of a retired, married man. He had just turned fifty and suspected that Sally, who was hedging on thirty, wanted much more as well. To keep pace with his young wife, Noelle took up fitness by swimming in their new pool and playing golf, but he still had too much time on his hands. He knew he needed some kind of purpose.

Noelle didn't need his keen gut instinct to know his nightmares were about the unfinished business between him and his mother. He hadn't been back to New Orleans since he put his mother Catherine into an assisted living facility soon after he noticed her slipping into early dementia. Over the years, her letters diminished as did his telephone calls. He only phoned her on holidays and her birthday. All the years he spent crime solving made it easy for Noelle to brush his shaky relationship with her under the table, but lately it had been eating at him.

As Sally made breakfast, Noelle picked through the mail at his desk, resenting all the charities his generous wife gave to, even though it was only ten bucks here and there. It wasn't that he couldn't afford it; he just was cynical. He wondered if the money actually went to the needy.

Noelle remembered how his mother would curse the television preachers when they hit up the holy viewers for donations. It used to make him laugh watching her scream at the evangelical preachers on their old black-and-white television with the floppy rabbit-ear antennas taped down to the set so they wouldn't fall off. It was the only time he'd ever heard his mother use foul language.

As he waited for breakfast, Noelle took a swig of Jack to steady his shakes. He wondered if a trip to New Orleans was in the cards. Maybe, just maybe, the nightmares would end if he went there to face his past.

As they ate, Noelle told Sally that he was going off to play a few rounds of golf with Ted Wilson, one of Houston's prominent "Defender-of-the-Rich-Crooks" attorneys. Ted, like Noelle, had recently retired. But unlike Noelle, Ted was part of the country club set. Although Noelle wasn't in the habit of hobnobbing with the upper crust, and strongly disliked the rich, he tolerated Ted because Ted worshipped Noelle. So, why not golf with the guy? Noelle had nothing better to do with his day anyway.

As he gathered the new set of clubs Sally had given him on his fiftieth, Noelle announced, "I'm taking your advice to stay in shape." He kissed Sally on the cheek and promised to be home in time for dinner.

After an uneventful game of golf, Noelle checked in with Sally to see what she was up to. She told him that she was taking his ex-partner Juan Lopez's wife, Maria, shopping for maternity clothes but that she was planning something special for him and not to be late for dinner.

After her shopping spree with Maria, Sally had decided to take Maria's advice on how to spice up her marriage by cooking Nick a phenomenal meal.

Dressed casually in jeans and a peasant blouse, Sally headed over to Jamail's Grocery Store. She headed right to the butcher's counter and asked for two special cuts of filet mignon.

Sally thought, 'Only the best for my man.' She wasn't going to settle for pre-packaged meat sitting for 'God knows how long'.

At Jamail's produce section, Sally picked out a beautiful bunch of asparagus and thoughtfully chose all the fixings for a spectacular mixed green salad. In the dairy section, she carefully selected an aged goat cheese that would be perfect to top off the salad.

After grocery shopping, Sally put away her purchases and went for a jog around the neighborhood. She believed it was her wifely duty to stay in good shape for her man—and for herself.

Noelle took advantage of his free time and popped into Sam's Gambling Parlor, just for old time's sake. He felt like such a creep lying to Sally and telling her he was going to Gamblers Anonymous meetings when he was actually back at Sam's high roller tables. His wife trusted him so completely and here he was betraying that trust.

As Noelle strutted through the room, people turned to look at him. They shook his hand and patted him on the back.

Solving the most famous murder case in Houston's history had given him a celebrity status of sorts and he dressed to fit the part —compliments of Sally's good eye and good taste. Noelle looked smart in his crew neck sweater, which he wore under a light summer jacket. Although he knew he never looked better, he cringed when he thought of his adoring wife again.

Noelle wiped his sweaty brow and grabbed a seat at one of the poker tables, hoping to fix his gambling itch with one good game. As always, he memorized the faces surrounding him: the do-or-die guy in his late sixties sporting long whiskers and reeking of cheap cologne, the well-dressed lady with a salt-and-pepper bouffant hairdo and an elegant string of real pearls around her slender neck (a sure sign she had money to burn, and "Pearl's" exact opposite sitting across from her. She was a lady he had seen there often. She was a short, plump blonde hiding her wide hips and fat butt under a purple satin tent dress.

Noelle was annoyed by the soundtrack the brazen blonde added to the scene. Her huge, brass, bangle bracelets were stacked from wrist to elbow on both arms. They clanged every time she chugged her whiskey or lifted her cards.

When the hands were dealt, Noelle tried to hide his new, winning smile. (Sally had insisted he take care of his chipped, stained teeth when they remarried. No matter how bright his grin was, he didn't feel like a winner that night even though he held a pair of aces.

He ordered another double shot of his favorite poison, relieved to be among other hard drinkers, including the elegant lady with the pearls who demurely sipped her third martini.

After a four-mile run, Sally took the time to draw herself a bath. She poured aromatic salts into the tub and enjoyed a long, luxurious soak. She slipped into her new dress, the one Maria insisted she buy on their shopping spree. Sally knew it was just the style Noelle loved; subtle yet sexy and innocent all in one.

She paused to study her reflection in the mirror, brushing her long, red hair. It had grown past her shoulders in the ten months since Pamela, the serial killer, tortured her by chopping it all off. As the current fashion trend dictated, Sally now parted it down the middle and wore it poker straight.

She filled in her lush lips with her favorite peach lipstick and brushed blush faintly across her high cheekbones. Next, Sally defined her large blue eyes with liner and mascara. She was pleased at the image of a classy, A-list fashion model staring back at her. For the finishing touch she sprayed the Chanel No. 5 Nick had given her on the nape of her neck.

The clock on Sally's dresser read 7:05. She looked out the window to see if Noelle's car was in sight. It wasn't. Regardless, she walked downstairs to set the dining room table with their best china. She even used the silver candlesticks Noelle's ex-boss had given them as a wedding gift.

Sally had prepped the vegetables and salad earlier and the potatoes were baking in the oven, so there was little left to do. She had the steaks marinating in a Spanish herb recipe she'd gotten from Maria. The only thing left was putting them on the grill. Since they were thick, she turned on the gas broiler so it would heat up, and left it on a low flame.

Suddenly exhausted from her busy day, Sally plopped herself onto the couch. As she waited for Noelle, she flipped through her new magazine on etiquette. The next time she looked up, she noticed that the hands on the large antique clock in the living room were approaching seven thirty.

Certain Noelle was bound to come in any second and apologize for being late, Sally decided to start the steaks. She set the timer so the beautiful pieces of meat wouldn't overcook. (Noelle liked his steak medium rare. When the timer's bell rang, she flipped the steaks to the other side, lovingly basting them with more marinade.

By the time Sally removed the meat from the broiler, her cheeks burned with resentment. It was now eight o'clock and still no sign of Noelle. She put the food in a warmer, sat on the kitchen stool and broke down in tears.

By nine o'clock, Sally's stomach began to heave up the goat cheese she had nibbled off the top of the salad. She blew out the fancy candles and sobbed some more. By ten, she wrapped the food in foil, dumped the salad into Tupperware and stuck it all in the fridge.

Exhausted, Sally dropped back onto the couch and passed out. She was still wearing her new dress. Mascara stained her face.

Hours later, stone cold drunk, Noelle fumbled with his key in the back door. The kitchen light hadn't been turned off. He noticed the uneaten chocolate cake then saw Sally curled up on the living room couch. He stumbled over to her and wrapped his arms around her. Sally opened her big, blue eyes, which flashed with rage, and pushed him away.

"Where the fuck were you?" she yelled.

Noelle slurred, "I had one drink, then another, which turned into three and more." He paused, then tried again, "Sally, please forgive me. I forgot. That's the damned truth!"

Sally howled, "I am trying so hard to accept your drinking. I know you're gambling too. And for all I know, you're probably cheating on me!"

When Noelle attempted to put his arms around Sally again, she screamed, "Don't you dare!"

Noelle mumbled, "I'm sorry. You're right. I have been gambling but I haven't been losing."

Sally snapped back, "Not yet! But if you don't stop, you are going to lose, Nick. You're going to lose me! I don't know how much more I can take!"

"I know I don't deserve you!" Noelle cried out. "I admit, I have been drinking and lying but I'm no cheat! I love you, Sally, more than any woman on this earth." He took a breath. "It's no excuse but I needed something to fix the guilt. I've been haunted by those dreams about my mother. I know I have to take some action but I'm just not sure what."

Hearing this, Sally forgot herself and her heart took over. "Nick, have you ever considered going to therapy?"

"Baby, I don't think that's for me," he admitted. "But I'm seriously considering going down to New Orleans to see my mother. Mending my rift with her could be a start. I won't be any good for you until I can get some answers."

With tears streaming down her cheeks, Sally cried, "Nick, I understand. I'm still working on forgiving my family. That's what all my Twelve-step work is about. I really wish you could embrace the program. But right now, let me go down there with you to see your mom. I can help! I know I can."

Noelle put his arms around her, "Thanks honey, but this is something I need to do alone."

Sally pulled away from him. "Why do you always have to be a tough guy? I'm your wife…you need to let me in!"

Noelle caressed Sally's hair. "I don't mean to be so distant," he said. "But I can't drag you to that place. I never told you but before she married my stepfather, my mother was a prostitute."

Sally told him, "That's all the more reason I should go with you! It will be easier for me to connect with her."

Noelle ignored Sally's comment. "After my stepfather died, Mama let herself go," he said. "When I saw her the last time, she was pathetic, living in squalor and losing her memory. I had to put her into one of those assisted living homes. I've been paying her rent and long-term care but I haven't had the guts to go see her once since then. It might be too much to spring a new wife on her without seeing me first. I promise I'll send for you once my mom and I talk… and mend some fences."

Sally slipped back into Noelle's arms. She kissed him. "You promise?"

They stayed locked in an embrace until Noelle picked Sally up into his arms and carried her upstairs to their bedroom. He went to the bathroom sink, ran hot water over a washcloth then joined Sally back in bed. He knew how she hated going to sleep with makeup on her beautiful, creamy skin.

Noelle gently wiped his wife's mascara and tear-stained face. He laid down the washcloth and ran his fingers through Sally's luscious hair and slowly began to undress her. Noelle carefully placed her lovely dress on the chair bedside the bed and quickly removed his clothes. He climbed into Sally's arms, kissing every part of her slim, sensual body.

For once, Noelle slept through the night without being haunted by his nightmare.

Chapter Three

Hit the Road, Jack!

As Noelle drove his Ford F150 along the Texas coastline, he saw that he was just outside of Baton Rouge, Louisiana. He turned the truck onto an exit where a dirt road led to a gas station. It looked like something out of the nineteen fifties. Attached to the filling station was a small store that sold antiques, cigarettes and alcohol.

Noelle had to pee like a racehorse so he stepped out into the midday humidity. Finding the bathroom locked, he ducked behind a tree. Without the comfort of his air-conditioned Ford, the sweltering heat hit Noelle like a fist as he unzipped his pants to relieve himself.

'No one in their right mind would live in this desolate, unchanging landscape in the suburbs of Baton Rouge,' he thought to himself.

After stretching his legs, Noelle asked the attendant to fill his gas tank. He walked inside the store, put a cold six-pack and two bottles of Jack on the counter and continued to peruse the shelves. Among the cheap antiques was some questionable estate jewelry. He briefly considered getting something for Sally but decided to wait until he got into New Orleans.

Once he paid the attendant, Noelle quickly got back behind the wheel and took a long, soothing gulp of Jack. He popped open a cold one as a chaser, cranked up the AC and hit the road. He was anxious to reach the City of New Orleans, the place of his birth.

It had been a few years since he'd been to the Big Easy. Noelle was fascinated by the sights and sounds as he drove through the Garden District. He ended up just off Rampart Street in a neighborhood close to Saint Mary's Nursing Home. He hoped to find a cheap room to rent by the week instead of staying at some high-priced tourist hotel.

Although not far from the French Quarter, this parish was still slightly on the wrong side of the tracks but not as bad as some of the places he and his mother had lived. Noelle breathed deeply and took in that same atmosphere of the city that reeked of sin, premeditated crime, fish and booze. As the sun baked the busy metropolis, Noelle thought about how the average tourist couldn't even imagine the scum that lurked in the bars and bedrooms of the New Orleans he knew all too well.

As he drove on, the wet, juicy heat stirred his gut, reminding him that he was a part of this hot cauldron they called the Big Easy.

Chapter Four

Noelle's New Digs

Noelle noticed a charming, well-kept mansion, which had probably been a brothel at one time. It had a vacancy sign on the lawn that announced rooms for rent, long and short-term. He parked across the street and went in to check it out.

When he rang the bell, he felt like he might be on a winning streak.

A plump, older woman, perhaps a Southern beauty queen in her youth, greeted Noelle with a warm, welcoming smile. Way past her prime, the landlady swung her large, voluptuous behind as she walked with a sexy air, teetering on leopard print, Spring-O-Lators high-heels. She wore a once stylish, nineteen fifties' era fitted, pink, polka-dot dress.

"How can I help you?" she asked.

"I'm looking for a simple room and bathroom if you have it."

"Yes, I have something. I'm Velda, the owner of this beauteous house."

"Nick Noelle."

"I just need some ID."

Noelle pulled his ID out of his wallet.

When she bent over the reception area counter to examine Noelle's ID, her ample bosom almost fell out of her push-up bra.

Satisfied with his ID, the landlady sauntered up to Noelle and led him to an empty room down on the raised basement level. All the while, she chattered at full speed. "Mr. Noelle, keep in mind, you'll have more privacy down here. We got lots of New Orleans characters staying at my fine establishment, but I assure you, they're all harmless."

Once at the lower level, she led him through a narrow hallway past another locked door that was reserved for storage. At the end of that hallway, Velda's eyes glimmered as she put the key into the lock of the only basement apartment in the grand house. Noelle couldn't tell if she was flirting or trying to win Miss Congeniality in the Miss America pageant.

"Mr. Noelle, once I turn on the lights you'll see how charming this studio can be," she gushed. "The perks of privacy can't be underrated. I decorated it myself with my mama's antiques. That's the reason I need all this floor for storage. There was a time when this grand house was filled with luxury. Some of my old furniture goes back to the days of Master Rhett Butler and Miss Scarlett O'Hara."

When she opened the door to the room, Noelle was surprised to find a very large, clean studio with a small kitchenette and bath. The price was right and the landlady was more than entertaining.

She squirmed, "Mr. Noelle, I trust you are a quiet and respectable gentleman. You're sure to meet most of my other lodgers at the free continental breakfast I host every morning between seven and nine in our dining room on the lobby level."

She smiled, flashing what Noelle guessed were dentures. The big, white teeth had pink pearl lipstick plastered all over them. She gave Noelle his marching orders. "Now I did tell you that breakfast was free, compliments of the house," she stressed. "If there is anything else I can assist you with, please do not hesitate to ask. I'm always available. I'm used to keeping late hours."

Noelle thanked Velda, "I just drove in from Houston so I definitely need to take a little nap."

She took the hint, handed him the keys and practically danced out of the room.

Once alone, Noelle dropped his suitcase on the bed. He noticed that opposite the bed was a large console television almost identical to the one he and his mother had while growing up—rabbit ears and all. Maybe it was a good omen.

As Noelle flipped on the television, he felt nostalgic for the good times of his youth, the few there were. Just like when he was a kid, Noelle needed to adjust the rabbit ears to bring clarity to the grainy broadcast of the five o'clock newscast.

On the screen a detective named Frank Tucci was being interviewed in front of Saint Catherine's Cathedral.

An overly excited news reporter was firing questions at him at a machine-gun pace. Noelle could see that the detective was doing his best to give as little information as possible. Noelle recalled when he himself had played that very same game with the press.

The reporter squawked, "Detective Tucci, what can you tell us about the murder at Saint Catherine's?" Before Tucci could answer, the reporter shot, "Can you confirm that the victim was the archbishop?"

With a New York City accent thicker than a slice of Sicilian pizza, Detective Tucci grumbled, "Sorry to say, it's true, but we aren't at liberty to release any more information at this time. But rest assured a thorough citywide investigation is being conducted to catch the scum who committed this horrific crime. Due to the delicate nature of this killing, if any leads or evidence become public knowledge it will hurt our investigation. I'm sure you can understand that."

The insistent reporter asked again, "But about the church...are they being helpful with your investigation? Is it true you have an eyewitness...an altar boy?"

Tucci was brisk. "Sorry, that's something we can't confirm," he snapped. "But you should be confident that the New Orleans Crime Division is doing everything in our power to find this killer and bring him to justice."

The detective rushed off to his car, leaving the reporter holding the microphone, momentarily speechless.

Although he was glad it wasn't him on the spot this time, Noelle still missed working crimes like this.

Noelle took a long, hot shower to wash the road off his skin. While he dressed, Noelle took a few more pulls from the first bottle of Jack he'd bought. He also helped himself to a warm beer then headed out to find Saint Mary's, his mother's nursing home.

In the hallway, Noelle passed a tall, handsome older gentleman as he headed to the front door. The gent tipped his Panama hat toward Noelle as he stepped out into the stifling heat. Noelle found his fellow lodger's flamboyant dress and manner amusing. More than likely, Noelle imagined he'd run into plenty more characters like this fellow lodger in his new temporary digs —transients who probably rented rooms by the day or the week then moved on.

As he walked the two blocks to Saint Mary's, Noelle's anxiety level was higher than the temperature. Sweat dripped down his back as his obsessive mind took over. His anticipation about his mother's state was more than he could handle. He wished he'd brought Jack with him.

Noelle swallowed hard as he scanned the long block. He spotted a bar right there on the corner with a flashing neon sign that announced The House of the Rising Sun. It brought to mind the traditional song about the brothel of the same name where you could lose your soul. 'How appropriate,' he thought, 'since in its heyday, this neighborhood was known for its upscale whorehouses.'

Noelle decided to get a little more fuel for his journey ahead so he popped in for a drink. Saint Mary's was a block away and wasn't going anywhere, he told himself. The bar was almost empty, except for the few resident alcoholics who kept permanent seats warm. Noelle sat at the end of the bar and ordered a double shot of Jack with a beer chaser. A no-nonsense bartender poured his drink and moved down to a female customer who was starting a loud argument with her boyfriend. Noelle downed his drink and ordered another.

When the bartender returned to fill his glass, he asked, "New in the neighborhood?"

Noelle nodded, "Just passing through. Probably just here for a few nights." He took out a large bill to pay the man. "Buy everyone a round on me," Noelle told him as he gulped his second double shot and finished his beer.

When he cruised back into the heat of the late afternoon, Noelle noticed that the sun was beginning to set in the distance over the tall steeple of Saint Catherine's Cathedral. He walked until he saw Saint Mary's Home. It was just as he had remembered it—a large red brick building, which had probably been a boarding house in its previous incarnation.

Noelle entered the lobby, which sported a shiny, black linoleum floor. He saw a young, black man behind a glassed-in booth. Noelle headed over to the man who smiled, showing off his large gapped front teeth. The man pushed a clipboard with a sign-in sheet through the opening in the glass between them. He said, "Please sign in, sir, and put down the name of the person you're here to see and your relationship to them. I also need to see one form of picture ID."

Noelle still had his old badge from Houston's homicide squad. He had a sudden impulse to show the guy that he still carried some weight in the world. Instead, he humbly handed the man his driver's license. "I'm here to see Catherine Noelle."

The young man looked at the ID photo then stared up at Noelle. "This is you? Nick Noelle?"

Noelle was impatient. "Yes, that's me."

The man smiled again. "You look a lot better in person," he told Noelle. "Your mama's got a whole lot of pictures of you fighting the bad guys. Hey, I hear from your mama that you're some big hero in Texas."

The man was kind and Noelle usually liked having his ego stroked. Except today he was impatient. "If you say so," Noelle shrugged.

The man muttered, "Well, that's what your mama told me when she used to be up and about...back when she had a room on this level and could really talk a blue streak. That's before they moved her to the third floor. She's in Room 305 now. Your mama's a nice lady. I think you might find Sister Theresa with her. It's mealtime."

Noelle made a move to leave. The man called after him, "You're lucky to have Sister Theresa looking after her. She's the best we've got in hospice care. By the way, my name is Eric. If you need anything, let me know."

With a more concerned look, Noelle saluted him. "Thanks, Eric."

"Oh, sorry Mr. Noelle, the elevator's out of order today," Eric called. "So, you'll have to take the stairs over there."

'Could this day get any worse?' Nick Noelle thought to himself. He walked up the three flights of stairs as though he were carrying boulders on a chain gang. He knew he was not that out of shape, but the weight of seeing his mother after so many years required different strength from what he built by swimming and golf.

When he reached the door to Room 305, Noelle peeked in from the hallway.

A young, black nun was feeding a very old lady who spat out her food like a baby. Noelle held back entering. At first, he thought he'd gotten the room number wrong. Then he heard the nun say, "Now, Catherine, you know you must eat to keep up your strength. You won't be happy if I have to give you a feeding tube."

Noelle still remembered his mother as she once was— when she still had her vibrant, red hair and a spirited personality to match it. If the nun hadn't said her name, he wouldn't have known this woman sitting in the bed was his mother.

He stared hard at the old lady and finally recognized her haunting hazel eyes—the one thing about Catherine that remained the same. It was mother all right. Now her hair was white as snow and her once-strong body was failing her—as was her mind. Noelle felt a flash of guilt when he saw that she had become skin and bones. Her high cheekbones were hollow and her complexion was sallow. If ever Noelle felt shame for abandoning his mother, it was now.

When the nun nodded for him to move closer, he walked slowly up to the bed. By the time he reached it, Catherine had lapsed into unconsciousness. Noelle took one of her hands in his. He whispered, "Ma, it's Nick. Ma, are you sleepy?"

The nun spoke up, "Are you Nick Noelle, her son?"

He nodded with tears in his eyes.

"I'm Sister Theresa, the hospice nurse," she said.

Noelle was taken aback. "Is she dying?"

The sister answered him calmly. "We can't say how long she has, but she's been refusing food. That's usually a sign that they're ready to move on. She's been falling in and out of consciousness for the past day or two."

Sister Theresa paused then added, "It's a good thing you came. She keeps calling your name and calling for someone named Brandon, too. Was he your Dad?"

Noelle looked confused. "No, that was not my old man's name. I have no idea who Brandon is. Maybe she had a boyfriend. I haven't seen her in a lot of years. I put her here when she started having trouble taking care of herself. I live all the way in Houston."

"I know," the nun conceded.

"I had no idea she was this bad," Noelle stammered. "I just paid the bills."

Noelle thought he should explain more so he continued. "She never wrote much anyway so I assumed she was just holding steady. She's not as old as she looks, you know? I'm kind of shocked. Mama looks like she aged thirty years since I saw her last. That was maybe about five years ago."

Sister Theresa interjected, "I'm so sorry. She's had a dramatic decline in the past year. When I first got here, she was still quite lively—full of stories."

Holding his mother's hand, Noelle felt her squeeze it lightly. Catherine opened her eyes and in a weak whisper said, "I knew you were coming. I've been calling to you and waiting."

Sister Theresa gently took Catherine's wrist to check her pulse. "Miss Catherine, look. Your son Nick is here. Isn't that wonderful?"

Noelle kissed his mother's frail hand. The delicate, translucent skin was bruised with age spots and dusted with blue veins. "Yes, Mama, I'm here now."

Catherine looked over to the nun. With a sudden burst of lucidity, she cried, "He's the famous detective I told you about! Sister, bring me my scrapbook so I can show Nick how I kept up with him."

The nun smiled and glided over to a dresser. She took out a large scrapbook and handed it to Noelle. When he opened it, he saw that his mother had been keeping track of his career through the news articles written about his murder cases. Instead of feeling proud, Noelle was suddenly filled with more guilt and remorse. All these years, he'd thought his mother wanted nothing to do with him. He turned to her. Just as he was about to speak again, Catherine's eyes grew large then snapped shut. It almost seemed as though she had stopped breathing. She gasped once more then drifted back into unconsciousness.

The lovely, dark-skinned nun checked to be sure her patient was still breathing and crossed herself when she was assured that Catherine was only sleeping.

"That's how it's been for a while," she told Noelle. "It's like she's living in both worlds now—the here and the hereafter. I'm happy you came, though. Maybe now she can let go to her maker and rest in peace. She's sure had a troubled life by the bits and pieces she's shared with me."

"How long have you known her?" Noelle wondered.

"I've only been assigned to Saint Mary's for a little over a year," she told him. "By the way, my name is Sister Theresa but you can call me Sister T or just Terry."

"Thank you, Sister," Noelle said just before she left the room.

He sat beside his mother, who lay there quietly, barely breathing. He kept a hand on her pulse, watching her intently, waiting for something to happen.

When he couldn't take the anxiety for another minute, Noelle fled the room and took the stairs two at a time down to the main floor lobby. That's when he realized that he'd forgotten to call Sally. He asked Eric, the receptionist, where the nearest pay phone was. Eric pointed to a booth just outside the building.

Noelle filled the slot with plenty of quarters and dialed his home number.

Sally answered so fast he imagined she'd been waiting by the phone.

She was relieved to hear from him. Noelle uneasily reported his mother's condition. He told her that the caretakers were pretty certain his mother would pass soon. Sally pleaded to join him, but he abruptly cut her off, lying, "I'm sorry, hon, I'm on the phone at the reception desk and I need to get off. Must be an emergency. One of the nuns needs the line right now. I'll call you when I get back to my room."

Noelle hung up so abruptly, Sally barely had a chance to say goodbye but she held the line just long enough to hear the coins drop into the pay phone's coin box. She knew immediately that Noelle was telling tall tales again. Her first thought was that he had probably called her from a pay phone at a bar. Sally's heart sunk.

Once again, Noelle felt like an asshole. For some reason, he couldn't stop lying to his wife. He nearly ran down the street in a quest to find another bar.

When he drew a long, deep breath of the suffocating, swampy air, Noelle realized that he was starving. He hadn't eaten all day. He sought out one of the many great eating establishments New Orleans was famous for, thinking a rich, seafood gumbo would hit the spot and coat his stomach. He could end the evening at his local neighborhood watering hole for a nightcap before bedtime.

Chapter Five

A Grand Feast

On Noelle's first night in a city known for its culinary indulgences, there were scores of celebrated chefs serving up their specialties. From small street vendors to five-star fine dining halls, you could always count on a good meal in this city —even from a Lucky Dog cart. Near his new boarding house, Noelle slipped into this little hole in the wall known for its excellent gumbo. He took a seat at a booth for two and waited for his server.

Not far from the restaurant where Noelle was dining, an amateur gourmet decided to eat in. He whipped up a special meal in his well-appointed kitchen.

The chef delicately selected his favorite recording of Mozart's *Figaro* from his carefully-alphabetized collection in the antique cabinet. He placed the record on his stereo turntable.

He then proceeded to the Victorian breakfront filled with his best wines and poured himself a glass of *Clos Fourtet*. It was one of two bottles he'd saved from his trip to the south of France. He lifted the gold-rimmed, rose-colored glass to his lips and sniffed the wine's bouquet. It was perfect, delicate.

Still cradling the wine glass, he twirled across the Persian carpet pausing to smell the roses in the crystal Tiffany vase on the dining room table. Swaying to the music, he sipped more wine. All was well in his beautiful nest. This opera was the perfect soundtrack for his solo dinner.

At the kitchen counter, with the utmost care, he opened the packaging, which held the fresh brain and heart. He'd had the foresight to put them on ice and they were still so fresh. He imagined that he could almost feel the heart beating and this thought thrilled him—the thought of holding life in his hands.

From the iron rack attached to the ceiling, he removed a large copper frying pan. It hung among his fine collection of copper cookware. He brushed the pan with olive oil and placed it on the stovetop, turning the flame to medium. From the refrigerator, he took out a stick of creamy butter and picked out fresh herbs and garlic, which he'd already chopped.

As the pan was heating, he took another sip of *Clos Fourtet* and measured two tablespoons of butter into the hot skillet. He added the fresh herbs and garlic then threw in a splash of fine wine from his goblet. His eyes widened in ecstasy as he took a whiff of the heavenly aroma. Very cautiously, he placed the brain and heart into the pan, searing each organ to a rare perfection. He added salt and pepper to taste.

It was almost done. Dousing his orgasmic feast with more wine, he turned the flame down to simmer. It needed to cook a bit longer so that the flavors would marry well.

Once his meal was done to his liking, he placed the rare meat on the antique English china platter and carried it to a small, thoughtfully set Victorian table. He had previously organized a single place setting of his best silver and china. He pulled his Regency chair over to the table and sat like a solitary king on his throne. He bowed his head, but did not say grace or give any kind of thanks to any God. He simply murmured the words, "I eat your mind and your heart, so that your evil will not rot the earth surrounding your grave."

He lifted the silver knife and fork, sliced into the meat, and licked his lips as the blood spilled onto his plate. He was overcome with an exquisite bliss. This was the first time he had ever eaten the organs of one of his victims. The power and pleasure it gave him made him wonder why he had never thought of doing so before. With each delicious bite, his urge for more grew, and with immense satisfaction, he wondered who would be his next meal.

Chapter Six

A Big Easy Night

After his sturdy repast, Noelle thought he had earned the right to do a little more drinking. With excitement, he mused that he might even gamble, too. This was the best way to bury his torturous guilt for double-dealing Sally with his lies, never mind leaving his poor mother alone to die.

Noelle knew the seedy side of New Orleans better than the average tourist, or "Vidalia," as the locals called them. His instinct led him on foot from North Rampart Street to Orleans Avenue, where he passed the monolithic Saint Catherine's Cathedral in Jackson Square. The ostentatious monument of religiosity had yellow tape strung around the front entrance.

He remembered the television newscast earlier that evening and felt gratitude that the macabre crime wasn't his problem to solve. He had enough on his mind. Noelle's inner radar unconsciously took him toward Bourbon Street. In his haste, he nearly passed by a joint called "Lucky Pierre's." It had been his father's favorite spot for degenerate gambling back in the day. Although Noelle was too young to gamble at the time, Lucky Pierre's not-so-secret game room had been legendary among those in the know. He wondered if it was still there.

Noelle stepped under the neon sign flashing overhead at Lucky Pierre's entrance. He moved through the dark, smoky joint, posturing like he belonged there. Plopping down in front of the bartender, in his best Louisiana drawl, he ordered.

"Buddy, I'll have a double shot of Jack, no ice."

Noelle slapped a twenty on the bar and quickly downed his long shot. He requested another. With the liquor bolstering his ego, he asked the bartender where he could find some action.

The burly bartender gave him the once-over. Noelle returned the bartender's intense look while taking in the prominent scar across the guy's left cheek.

The bartender snarled, "Who sent you?"

Noelle took in the guy's gold-capped front teeth. He looked the bartender square in the eye and replied meanly, "Carlo."

It was a name everyone feared and respected back in Noelle's dad's day. He was hoping it might still carry some weight. Carlo Marcello's mob family had run the French Quarter since Noelle was born.

The bartender's eyes opened wide. Leaning into Noelle, he asked, "You mean, Marcello?"

Noelle laughed. "Who else?"

The bartender smiled—his shiny gold caps glistening. He whispered. "You can find the stairs to the back room behind the bathrooms on the other side of that pack of Vidalia." The bartender gestured in the direction with his chin. "Be careful," he warned. "The stairs are old and dark. And you know there's no such thing as a lawsuit against Carlo."

Noelle winked, "Gotcha, Buddy!"

He slapped down another twenty. The dude flashed those gold caps again as Noelle grabbed his drink and headed toward the back stairwell.

When he reached the top of the stairs, Noelle opened the door. A cloud of black smoke hit him like a tsunami. There was an old lady at a small table blocking the entrance with a sign that read "Cash Exchange." Her heavily caked-on makeup made her skin look a sickening yellow, just like a corpse's. Her unflattering, reddish-blonde hair didn't help. She smiled at

Noelle, exposing her floppy dentures that were almost as yellow as her complexion. She asked, "How much chips do you want?"

Noelle took out four crisp fifty-dollars bills and laid them on the crone's table. He stared at her hands as she counted his money, noticing that her right hand had only a thumb, pinky and middle finger. Noelle nodded with silent appreciation for the old gal. She probably had a wicked story to tell but he had no time to listen. He was in a rush to get to the tables.

"Where are the poker tables?"

"There's room for one more player over there," she glared, pointing her thumb behind her.

As he made his way around the other tables, Noelle's eyes stung from the smoke. He nodded to the group at the open table then stood behind an empty chair.

He was amused by the young dealer with a pirate patch over one eye, thinking how Lucky Pierre's looked like a low-rent option to Disneyland with missing digits and absent body parts as the attractions. But "Pirates of the Caribbean" this was not.

With his one good eye, the dealer stared at Noelle and griped, "What you waitin' for? A golden invitation? Sit down, already."

Each player was a character sleazier than the next. The man directly across from Noelle kept rubbing a wart on the end of his nose. To the left of him an old geezer's saliva slid down his chin as he stared blankly at his cards. In the chair directly beside Noelle, a withered booze hound bent to put his cane on the floor. The dealer doled out the cards. With three aces in his first hand, Noelle put on his poker face.

Noelle won that hand and the second round as well. The other players pretended to feel nothing but they shifted uneasily back and forth in their chairs. They were all down and outers and kept their bids low. Noelle felt bored. He glanced at his watch, realizing the time and remembered that he'd told Sally he'd call her as soon as he got back to his room. That had been hours ago.

Reluctant to call it quits, Noelle stood anyway, tossing a fifty-dollar chip to the dealer. He found the old broad, cashed in his chips and gave Miss Stumpy a generous tip.

Pretty drunk by now, Noelle had to concentrate hard not to fall as he made his way back down the dark stairs to the bar. At first, he headed toward the door but couldn't help himself and stopped for one more shot of the Jack with a beer chaser.

The bartender smiled, "So, man, did you get lucky?"

Noelle nodded. "Yeah, I can't complain." He dropped another big tip, took his shot and grabbed his chaser. He shuffled over to a booth across the room. He caught a glimpse of himself in the mirrored wall across from where he sat and quickly looked away. Grotesque shame and guilt stared back at him. He dropped his gaze into his glass. Noelle had only left Houston that morning, yet he already felt dirty and tainted by the city. He looked as if he'd aged twenty years since then.

A couple of cheap suits grabbed the booth next to his. Noelle didn't know a thing about them, but his gut told him they were cops—most likely heavy drinkers, as many cops were. The waiter came to their table with a round of doubles. Noelle continued to drink. At this point, he was starting to see double. If he kept drinking, he might not make it home in one piece. To help slow the pace of his boozing, Noelle eavesdropped on the cops. He was so wasted that he didn't recognize one of them as Detective Tucci from the news.

The suit facing him was short and wiry with black, kinky hair slicked back with lots of grease. Noelle perked up when he heard the guy say the word "murder" in a thick, New York accent.

"This was done by one, sick fuck," the guy said. "The fuckin' heart and the fuckin' brain…some souvenirs!"

Noelle wondered how many times it was possible to say "fuck" in one sentence. He pretended to be absorbed in his own private reverie and avoided eye contact with the wiry cop, except now he was listening more intently.

The guy got even louder. "Jesus-F-IN-Christ, there was more blood in that church than Christ shed on the cross," he said. "I almost lost my cookies! You know me, Melville; I never puke at a crime scene. I've been known to eat a po'boy over a corpse while watching evidence being collected." The other cop just shook his head in disbelief.

"Melville, what's wrong with you? Cat got your tongue?" the loud cop prodded.

The portly detective with his back to Noelle said, "Tucci, I don't think I can handle this. You know I'm a Catholic and if we start poking into Church business it could…"

"Melville, don't let me down," Tucci raised his voice. "I'm depending on you. The whole city's got eyes on us. Ya know, the press won't let up. We have to solve this shit and fast. Or the next thing you know, the feds will be all over our asses."

Melville whined, "I'm sorry, Boss, but seeing that gold cross pushed into the archbishop's chest got me spooked. And that poor little deaf boy—who the fuck put the kid in a diaper?"

"My bet's on the priest," Tucci answered. "No offense to your religion, man, but I went to Catholic school, too. I'm a WOP for Christ's sake!"

Noelle had heard enough. He stood up, wobbling his way over to their booth. Struggling not to slur his words, he extended his hand to make an introduction.

"I'm Detective Nick Noelle from the Houston Police Force," he slurred. "Maybe I can be of some assistance."

Tucci's hand dismissed him. He waved it towards Noelle and barked back, "We don't need your help, Mister. If you are who you say you are, you better go clean up. I'm sure the Houston force would be embarrassed to have you giving them a bad rap…in your current condition."

Noelle dropped his trembling hand and gripped the table to steady himself. Sure, he could argue the point but he knew his appearance spoke volumes about who he really was: a filthy, old, drunken gambler just like his father. Belching uncontrollably, he turned away. Despite his blurry vision, Noelle managed to walk out of the bar, swaying and muttering to himself like a madman.

Weaving his way through the French Quarter, Noelle somehow found his way back to his boarding house using some inner intuition. As he approached the front step, he stumbled, fell, hit his head and passed out.

In the middle of the night, a fellow tenant came along. He bent down to check Noelle's breathing and found his neighbor was alive. The man recognized the passed-out drunk as the man he'd tipped his hat to in the doorway earlier that day. When he searched Noelle's pockets, he found his room key with the number on it. The Good Samaritan gallantly lifted Noelle's limp, heavy body, threw him over his shoulder and carried him inside.

Entering the vacant lobby, the man very slowly brought Noelle down to his basement apartment. Fumbling with the key, he struggled to open the door. Once inside, he laid Noelle on the bed and used a washcloth to clean the minor gash on Noelle's head as best he could. When the man noticed the bottle of Jack Daniel's on the table, he opened it and used the remaining drops of whiskey to sterilize the wound. Noelle winced, still unconscious.

Before the man left the room, he wrapped Noelle's head in a clean towel and pulled off his shoes. Lastly, he covered him with a light blanket. He left hoping his charge could sleep it off.

The next morning, Noelle could barely open his swollen eyes. When he put his hands to his throbbing head, he felt the tightly wrapped towel around it. He made a weak attempt to sit up but fell back against the pillow.

His last foggy memory was gambling at Lucky's Bar but he forgot almost everything after that. Much of the night before was a complete blur.

Noelle forced himself up off the bed but the room started to spin and he fell to his knees. He crawled to the bathroom to vomit. After wiping his mouth on the back of his hand, he pulled himself up by the sink and washed down four aspirin with water straight from the tap.

Gradually, the previous day came into focus. Noelle remembered seeing his mother and calling Sally. The tremendous guilt he felt about Sally surged like a wave of nausea. It was so great it almost hurt. His wife trusted him implicitly and Noelle had lied to her. He'd gone out on an alcoholic and gambling binge instead of tending to his dying mother. He remembered tipping the dealer, cashier and bartender heavily. After that, it was lights out.

Noelle lumbered toward the shower. He had to sober up before he called Sally. He couldn't afford any more broken promises to his wife. She was going to be plenty pissed off and rightly so. Sally deserved better…better than a drunken gambler…better than him.

As he shaved, Noelle studied his face in the mirror, staring hard at the gash on his head. It still hurt like a son of a bitch. Noelle wondered if he'd been in a fight or if someone had mugged him. He grabbed his pants off the floor and felt in his pockets for his wallet. Everything was there. How he got into his room and bed was a mystery.

Suddenly, Noelle was ravenous. With every part of his body aching, he dressed in fresh clothes and went to breakfast hoping it wasn't too late to get something to eat. He locked his door behind him and headed upstairs.

Velda was fussing about in the dining area. Noelle was relieved to see that there were no other lodgers in sight. He wasn't in the mood to make small talk and it would take all his strength to endure his landlady's yammering. She took one look at Noelle and was off and running.

"Boy, Mr. Fletcher was right about you," she gushed. "He said he found you in a bloody heap outside on the stoop last night."

Velda was wearing a pink duster, the kind you put on straight out of bed, and a pair of pink feathered marabou slippers. As she shimmied about, clearing the coffee cups off the tables, she started in again, "Lucky for you, my long-term lodger, Mr. Fletcher, found you. He said you had an awful gash so big you could have bled to death." Velda paused to take a breath. "That would have been very bad publicity for me and my residence! I try only to rent to respectable folks, you know. I'm giving you the benefit of the doubt, knowing that you're a stranger and all. Heavens, you may have been mugged! Do you remember what happened?"

Noelle shook his head; it hurt. "No, I'm sorry, but I don't recall a thing. I went to see my mother at Saint Mary's. I stopped off for dinner and drinks over in the French Quarter. And that's about it."

Velda swished her duster and grinned, "Well, your memory may come back to you but you could have a concussion or temporary amnesia, you know. You might want to go and have it checked out. Ya gotta be careful in the French Quarter. There are a lot of bad men who look to take advantage of someone who's...impaired. Now, I'm not suggesting you were drunk but maybe someone would have rolled you if you were walking around in that kind of condition!"

Noelle wanted nothing more than to stuff Velda's dish rag into her mouth to shut her up. "I assure you, I haven't been rolled," he choked out. He snatched the last beignet off the tray before Velda whisked it away. She poured what was left at the bottom of the coffee pot into a clean mug.

Noelle took the coffee and thanked her. "Ma'am, I'm sorry I'm late but I'll be out of your hair as soon as I chug down this cold coffee."

Velda scolded him like a schoolboy. "Well, Mr. Noelle, that's what naughty boys get when they are tardy: cold coffee... and stale pastry. I warned you that breakfast was over by nine am."

"Oh no, I'm not complaining," Noelle said apologetically. "I'm grateful to you. This beignet is the best I ever tasted. I'm sure thankful to your tenant, too. You'll have to point him out to me so I can thank him properly for taking such good care of me."

Velda was circling around Noelle like a dancing pony while her mouth shot off, "Oh, you can't miss him! Mr. Fletcher's that queer fellow who dresses like a dandy and prances through the lobby on his comin's and goin's. He's a handsome gent. Sure is a pity he's a homo. What a waste of a good man."

Noelle had no doubt that in her day Velda was certainly not the blushing belle she pretended to have been. Most likely, she was some jigged-up whore.

Noelle fought off the wave of nausea that was overtaking him again and stood up. "Sorry to eat and run but I have to call my wife," he said, trotting out of there as fast as he could.

As Noelle rushed back down to his room, he heard Velda holler, "You are welcome to use the pay phone in the lobby. It's a lot cheaper than making a long-distance call from your room."

Back in his room, Noelle puked up the coffee and the beignet then collapsed on his bed. He took several deep breaths before he dialed his home number back in Houston. The phone rang and rang. He almost drifted back to sleep as he waited for his wife to pick up. Eventually, he hung up; glad Sally wasn't there to answer. He knew that his perceptive wife would be able to see his pitiful state right through the telephone wires. He wasn't in the mood for a second confrontation, not that morning.

Chapter Seven

Sally's Solution

Sunday morning, Sally was still stewing with anger over Noelle's abrupt call. On top of that, she didn't hear back from him as he'd promised. She could only guess that he was up to no good. Sally wanted to call her friend Maria to complain but feared that Maria would suggest for the umpteenth time that Sally come to church with her and Juan. Maria really seemed to love Saint Cyril's.

Since Sally had joined Narcotics Anonymous, she knew she needed some kind of higher power, but she had her doubts about organized religion, especially the Catholic Church. But Juan and Maria Lopez had been so good to her and Noelle. She appreciated how their faith made them such kind, moral people and wondered if she should give their church a try.

Sally had been brought up Baptist and hated and feared the "fire and brimstone" thing. The message from the pulpit always made her feel like a sinner long before she'd ever learned how to sin. If it had not been for the transgressions of her father and mother, Sally may have never fallen into a life of prostitution.

In a moment of desperate loneliness, Sally picked up the phone and called Maria, who said she was just heading out to

Saint Cyril's. And as she feared, Maria invited Sally to come along. This time Sally accepted Maria's invitation only because she couldn't bear the torture of another day of sitting home alone waiting for the phone to ring.

Sally searched her closet for something modest to wear and came out with a light jacket to cover her simplest dress. Although it was the most conservative outfit she owned, she worried that the congregation would see right through her. She was still pretty new at the Twelve-Step Program and had only begun to work the steps. Sally knew about the "making amends" step but didn't realize yet that the biggest amends she needed to make were to herself.

The Lopez family pulled into her driveway and honked the horn. Sally raced outside, her thoughts obsessing over Noelle. The Lopez's smiles were so bright and genuine, they immediately lightened her mood. Sally hopped into the back seat with their teenage daughter Dolores and immediately started chatting comfortably. However, when Juan pulled into the parking lot of Saint Cyril's, Sally got nervous, especially when she saw the crowd pouring into the modest, little church.

As they entered the vestibule, Maria whispered to Sally, "Here, we anoint ourselves with the holy water in this dish." Imitating Maria, Sally followed and dipped her fingertips into the bowl. She made the sign of the cross on her forehead just as Maria did.

Sally was impressed with the interior of Saint Cyril's. It was a sharp contrast to the wood shack she attended as a child. Sunlight streamed in through the magnificent stained-glass windows. Colored rays of reflection spilled onto the dark, wooden pews. She looked around in awe at the banks of candles that lined the side altars as hundreds of tiny burning flames flickered in them. Above each set of candles, the Virgin Mary or a saint, held court. The believers offered prayers and donations as they lit the candles with thin, wooden sticks.

To Sally, there was something so soothing and reassuring about seeing these people with such innocent faith. This was the special quality Maria possessed that Sally cherished the most.

She was also in awe of Maria's strong mothering instincts—and secretly envious that Maria was pregnant with her second child.

Sally followed the Lopez family to a row of empty seats and waited as each one genuflected in the aisle. Each made the sign of the cross again before entering the pew. Sally followed the steps as though she were learning a new dance routine. She was determined to give this new "dance" a go.

Once they were all seated in the row, Maria handed Sally a tiny booklet. In it were prayers written in Spanish for the parishioners to follow the Mass said in Latin. An organ played and a priest dressed in golden robes followed by two altar boys in black and white vestments entered center stage in front of the main altar. Sally felt excited, as if she were about to see a show. In a very real sense she was: a show of faith.

Above the altar hung an almost human-sized Christ, crucified. It gave Sally chills to see the ceramic statue of Jesus wearing a crown of thorns, nailed to a wooden cross with blood dripping from his wounds; grotesque and beautiful all in one.

The priest kneeled while speaking Latin. Everyone repeated the responses back to him, in Latin, reading from their booklets. Feeling silly, Sally continued to repeat them. Sensing Sally's uneasiness, Maria showed Sally the back of the book where there was an English translation as well. After a lot of kneeling, standing and sitting, the priest walked to a side podium to preach while the two altar boys took seats at the side of the main altar.

At that point, Sally noticed that she was grinding her teeth. The priest began to read out loud from the Bible, this time in English. *"The Scribes and the Pharisees brought a woman who had been caught in the act of adultery and placed her in their midst. They said to Jesus, 'Teacher, this woman has been caught in the act of adultery. Now, the Law of Moses commands us to stone such women. What do you say?'"*

Sally's face flushed hot pink. She felt as though the sermon was being directed at her. Her paranoia took over. Sally began to imagine that someone must have told Maria about her past years as a prostitute. She feared that she was about to be publicly shamed. Even though her rational mind told Sally that her thoughts were unjustified, the priest in the pulpit morphed into a flashback of her childhood at the Baptist church where the minister screamed about hellfire and sin.

Sally wanted to run down the aisle and out of the church as fast as she could. But when she turned to see Maria and her family so involved with the sermon, Sally knew her fears were unfounded. She knew that her friend Maria, her daughter and her husband didn't plan to punish her—they simply wanted to share their faith with her. Sally remained seated, still fighting herself to remain calm and listen. To her surprise, the words brought her comfort.

The priest continued to recount the Bible story. *"'What do you say, Master?' This they said to test our Lord; that they may have a charge to bring against him," the priest explained. "'Jesus bent down and wrote with his finger on the ground; He said, 'Let him who is without sin among you throw the first stone.' And once more, he bent down on the ground and wrote. They went away, one by one, beginning with the older ones until Jesus was left alone with the woman standing before him.*

Jesus stood up and said to the woman, 'Where are they? Has no one condemned thee?'

The woman said, 'No one, Lord.'

And Jesus said, 'Neither do I condemn you and from now on go and sin no more.'"

Suddenly, sharp tears rolled down Sally's cheeks. A deep, peaceful feeling engulfed her and began to melt her heart. It was a sense of freedom she had never felt before. Yet somehow, the emotion was familiar; it made her feel washed clean like an innocent child—the same child she once was before her father had tarnished her innocence. Out of nowhere, this priest's sermon swept away all of Sally's sins. She hadn't even known how much she'd been looking for forgiveness until that very moment.

At the end of his sermon, the priest invited the congregation to partake of Holy Communion. Sally remained in the pew as Juan, Dolores and Maria joined the others to take the host. She watched everyone file up the altar, still filled with a beautiful feeling of peace.

After Mass ended, the Lopez family invited Sally to a Mexican buffet with some of their friends. The parish priest, Father Bruce, was also in attendance. Sally was pleased to meet this young priest and appreciated how warmly he welcomed her. She was also grateful he didn't come on too strong about joining the congregation. He only invited her to come back to Saint Cyril's any time she liked.

After the wonderful lunch, the Lopez family dropped Sally back home. Maria got out of the car and walked her to the door. She handed Sally a Bible. When Sally looked down, she noticed that Maria had already imprinted the name "Sally Noelle" on the front cover.

"I knew you'd come around...when you were ready," Maria told her.

Sally threw her arms around Maria thanking her for her love and friendship before she went inside.

If Sally'd had a number to reach him, her first reaction would have been to call Nick and share her good news. Unfortunately, she knew he would not understand what she was feeling.

Sally sat on the sofa, hung her head and sobbed, although the tears were bittersweet. She realized that these were not only tears of sorrow; they were happy tears too. Thankful tears for regaining the feeling of innocence she had lost many, many years ago. Sally was crying from the joy she felt surging within her. It was a deep emotion of unconditional love, which had no rhyme or reason. It was pure and simple. For the first time in her life, this feeling had nothing to do with Nick or any other man, for that matter. Except perhaps this man they called Jesus.

Chapter Eight

Same Day, Different Salvation

Noelle shivered at the thought of his pansy neighbor putting him to bed during his alcoholic blackout. But he had woken up with all of his clothes on, so he figured nothing weird had happened. He had to admit that he was grateful he hadn't been rolled. The thought of how differently it could have gone should have been enough to strike him sober.

But unfortunately, it didn't stop Noelle from stopping off at the neighborhood bar. He told himself it was to supplement his courage on the way to Saint Mary's as well as combat his fears when he'd tried to call Sally and she didn't answer. Noelle wondered where his wife could possibly be so early on a Sunday morning. Was she out and about for one of her charities? There had to be a logical explanation. He'd try to call her again after his visit with his mother.

By the time Noelle reached Saint Mary's, he was three sheets to the wind. He greeted Sister Theresa with a sheepish grin. Out of nowhere, rage (and Jack Daniel's) took his senses. He blurted out, "So, how's the old whore today?"

Although Sister Theresa was taken aback, she didn't let it ruffle her feathers. She could see that Noelle was obviously in pain and very drunk. The wise nun had more than her share of handling belligerent boozers so she humored him.

"Well, Detective Nick, I think they prefer the title 'Ladies of the Night,'" she quipped. "Unfortunately, all of our residents here at Saint Mary's have a hard time recalling their livelier days. God is merciful in that way."

Noelle was shocked by his own crassness and felt slapped across the face by Sister Theresa's candor. He apologized profusely, "I'm sorry, Sister. The Devil must have snatched my tongue. Please forgive me!"

"No worries, Detective Noelle, I haven't always been a nun, you know."

Noelle truly felt remorse for his slip of the tongue. He gave a feeble excuse. "I didn't get much sleep last night and had a few drinks on the way over," he explained. "I hope you can let it pass."

"I already have," she said. The young nun pulled a chair close to the bed next to Catherine and waved Noelle over. With love and light shining in her deep brown eyes, she told him, "Your mother called your name a few times earlier. I hope she'll wake up again for you today."

Noelle's depression grew darker. "I'm sorry… I meant to be here earlier."

Sister Theresa smiled sweetly, "Oh, I understand. I'm sure you must have lots of old friends you'd like to connect with while you're in town. At least you're here now. That's what's important, isn't it?"

Her kindness only made Noelle feel more guilt. He felt shame knowing that the nun could smell the alcohol leaching out of his skin and on his breath.

When Noelle took his mother's fragile hand in his, Sister Theresa stood up to leave. "I'm going downstairs to eat my lunch. Can I bring you anything?"

Noelle stared into her warm eyes. "No, thanks, Sister. That's very kind of you," he said. "Look, I really appreciate how good you are to my mother. If there's anything I can do for you or your church, please don't hesitate to let me know." She nodded and left him alone with Catherine.

Noelle couldn't stop the self-pity that oozed out of every alcoholic pore of his skin. He knew he was hurting the people he loved most but he couldn't stop himself.

A moan snapped Noelle out of his reverie of self-pity. He gazed at his mother. Her eyes were open but she was staring into space, smiling at the wall. He whispered to her, "Hey, Mama, I'm here."

Catherine made a feeble effort to pat her son's hand then closed her eyes again. Noelle was frustrated. He wondered how long she would be in this semiconscious state. He had wanted to tell her he was sorry. He wanted to tell her about Sally and all they had been through. A flood of mixed emotions overtook him. He was pissed off, confused and felt sorrier for himself than he did for his poor mother. On top of all that, he felt ashamed for feeling the way he did.

With all of these mixed emotions confronting him, old resentments surfaced. Noelle knew damn well that he hadn't forgiven his mother for not protecting him from his abusive stepfather when he was too little to defend himself. He sat there brooding as he listened to his mother struggling to breathe. He was terrified she might die before anything was resolved. Noelle knew he had to forgive her fast or he'd suffer from guilt the rest of his miserable days. The monotony of watching his mother's labored breathing lulled him to sleep.

An hour later, Sister Theresa woke Noelle, softly whispering, "Detective Nick, it's time for me to bathe your mother."

Startled from his nap, Noelle cried with alarm, "How long was I out?"

"About an hour," she told him. "I'm sorry Catherine isn't more talkative like she used to be." She rustled over to the closet. "Oh, before I forget, I found these in your mother's storage locker."

Sister Theresa bent down to retrieve a large box from the closet floor. "I thought that perhaps they might hold some interest for you."

She handed Noelle a brown, very aged, hardcover diary. It looked like it had been through two world wars.

"This is one of your mother's journals," Sister Theresa explained. "Old Catherine must have lived a very exciting life, judging by the bits and pieces she shared with me before she fell into this state. I only had time to go through one of her boxes in the storage unit. I'll check the rest tomorrow. But you can start with this one." She smoothed down Catherine's sheets and added, "You know, they say it's good to talk to people in a coma...that they can hear you."

Noelle nodded. He scanned the notebook. There were bits of dried mud stuck in between some of the pages. The writing seemed to be that of a child. Had his mother ever been a child, he wondered?

As Noelle was occupied with the book, Sister Theresa unhitched the brakes on Catherine's rollaway bed and wheeled her through the door.

She called out behind her, "I'll bring your mom back after I've bathed her." She disappeared, pushing the bed down the hallway.

Noelle propped his feet on the chair across from him and began to read:

"The Diary of Catherine Lee"
August 1914 - My first writin' day.

Some people will call this a diary but I think it's like I's talkin' to God. I turned 12 last week and Miss Kirkwood gave me this here notebook. She says I have the gift to write and wants me to practice. So, since I been having some terrible thoughts popping up in my head, I figured I'd share em' with You, God. I have to be careful to hide this writing. I probably will bury it out here somewhere because, God, you know that if my daddy ever finds it, I'll be in big trouble.

Daddy has no idea that I hope to get out of Mayville, Mississippi and move to a big city, a really glamorous place where I have a chance to be somebody. I don't know what but I think you created me to be something better than a cotton picker. I know I'm good at lots of stuff like math, reading and writing. I'd read more if I could but the Bible is the only book we have at home. I'm never allowed to bring even a magazine into my house without Daddy saying it's the Devil's work. Seems like everything I ever like has something to do with the Devil accordin' to my daddy.

The question I keep asking myself is, if I'm supposed to fear you and if you be so angry all the time, what's to keep me from doin' what I want to? Seems like with You and my Daddy, there's no pleasing y'all. My daddy, Gerald Lee, is a righteous man but why does he always talk about Your wrath? If Your son Jesus came down to die for my sins, He couldn't of been mad at me, could he? He musta loved me. So why my daddy says it's Your will for me to be punished. It's confusin'.

Today, when I was layin' down on my back on that dry, scorched grass and I look up at the muddy sky, I saw the sun try in' to peek out. I thought about all that is beautiful in Your creation. How could a God who made all that beauty want to punish the folks He put here on earth to enjoy it?

I know I'm not the prettiest girl in town but I do have a fair share of my mama's beauty. Mama got gentle features: sky blue eyes and a strong jaw line. Makes me think that Mama may have had strength like me when she was a girl. I wonder how she looked before Daddy wore her down so. Even the picture of her on her wedding day, Mama already looked tired. I think she was just 16 then. She was round and a bit plump, like me.

No matter how many plain rags I try to cover up with, Papa always make me feel ugly about my fast growin' lady parts. God, You the one that created me this way, so how come I feel ashamed? Maybe one day I can have nice clothes like I saw in those magazines Mrs. Kirkwood's shows Mama to teach her how she wants Mama's alterations on her wardrobe to look.

You know, I really like them pictures in them magazines. Otherwise I would never know what the outside world looks like. I know the world is changing fast, especially now that all the good boys gone off overseas. Folks that are left here don't have enough time to keep the land properly. The only place that looks descent is the Morgan's' property on the other side of the dividing fence between Daddy's piece of dirt and them rich folks' rollin' hills. Their land goes on farther than I can see.

When I was lying there out on the ground, I looked over at that dividing line and I was taken off guard when I saw that handsome Morgan boy. He just popped out of nowhere. He had his jacket slung over his wide shoulders and just leaned up against the barbed wire fence so casual like. I could see his thick, black hair shiny in the sun.

I felt ragged and ashamed as I could tell his dark eyes were leerin' at me. I wondered how long he had been there looking at me lying on the ground.

My heart began to race and a hot fire spread over my face, all the way down to my stomach, and even lower. Then it got worse when he started talkin' to me.

"Take a good, long look, girl" he said. "I'm going off to die for my country. Gonna follow in Bobby and Derek's footsteps like a good Morgan boy. Gotta keep up the family tradition. Girl, you gonna grieve for me when I'm gone?"

I just sat there all red-faced, frozen, not knowing what to say. But that seemed to egg him on. "Be a good girl and come here. Nobody's gonna know just you and me," he said. Then he leaned further over the fence and put his long leg over the top rung of that high fence.

Before I knew it, he was over the fence and coming toward me.

I shot up to my feet and felt my heart pounding as I started to walk away fast. He laughed. "Oh, I get it. You want me to chase you, do ya?"

I don't know what would a happened if I hadn't heard Mama callin' out my name. I could see her fragile figure in the distance, next to our old, rickety barn. As I started to run toward her I could hear the Morgan boy laugh again and say, "I just want to feel you up against me, just once before I go off and die for our country."

I looked back at the boy and he was smiling and the sun was coming down through the clouds in a blaze of glory. I bit my lips and turned back toward my house. He was howlin' with laughter as I ran away.

God, I know it's wrong but I never felt such a strong temptation to sin. It's a good thing that Justin Morgan is going off to war. I hope You keep him safe and forgive me for having such impure thoughts.

Noelle was fascinated by the level of understanding his young mother possessed and was disappointed to find the next two pages glued together with mud but he gently eased them apart and carried on reading:

God, I'm hiding in here before I have to go back in the house. This old barn is so hot and humid. There's no light except in the window perched high above the loft and that is teaming with bugs and who knows what else. This rotting barn makes me feel the opposite from what I feel when I'm out at the edge of the field. Out there is the only space where I can dream.

In this here barn, I feel like I'm trapped in thin air. It reminds me of every breath my Mama takes since her sickness got so bad. Now when she tries to suck in air, she starts coughing so hard it brings up the blood. The barn is like my mama: all broken down from neglect.

When I started my chores today I remembered I had left a gas light on in my room because I was thinkin' so hard about that Morgan boy. I knew my daddy would take a belt to me if he knew I was wastin' gas, let alone messin' with a boy. He been in an awful state since the doctor from Hattiesburg came to see Mama. I overhear what he told Daddy.

He say, "Your wife's body is eating her from the inside out."

I watched Mama bent over in pain holding that tattered, wet cloth over her mouth, spittin' up the blood as the doc say to Daddy,

"She needs treatment and you're going to need money for that." Then he packed his little doctor bag and left.

I told Mama we would find the money but I knew I was lying. I suspect she did too.

As I watched Mama hold that sputum rag to her mouth, she tried with all her might to stop coughing. I couldn't look at her dry, parched lips, all sucked in from where her teeth had fallen out and her blue eyes cloudy with that yellow glaze that drips from the infection.

Out a nowheres, an old tune pass through my mind and I started to miss the radio at Miss Kirkwood's house. I used to listen to it when Mama wasn't too frail to work there sewing her alterations. Mama musta seen the faraway look in my eyes because she set the rag aside, stared me straight in the face and scolded me for day dreamin'. "Now child, I done told you daddy will pitch a hissy fit if he see ya jest a standin' there makin moon eyes at the sky"

My pity for Mama gets all mixed up with feeling shame for even thinking about listening to "If You Don't Like My Peaches" on Mrs. Kirkwood's radio while Mama was in so much pain. I was longing for those days when Mama was strong enough to leave the house to get that sewing work.

God, please don't strike me down for sayin' this but I think it is Mama's lifetime of misery and doing without that has done her in. God, I got to get back into the house now to start supper.

The sicker Mama gets, the more God-fearin' Daddy gets. He say if I worked harder, make the crop better, churn the butter more or if I prayed harder, then Mama would be alright. Whatever money Daddy did have, he already gave it all to that mean, old minister. Today, when Mama was hacking so hard that her face was turnin' purple, he blamed me.

"Now look what you done to your mama," Daddy said. "I'm tired of you a runnin' 'round these backfields half naked. You're gonna start spendin' yore free time helping out Reverend Garsett. His garden needs a tendin'.

I told Daddy that I'm not goin' to that preacher because he scares me. Then Daddy grabbed my arm and smacked me across the face. He dragged me down the narrow, dark hall to the prayer room.

He put me down on the cold, wooden floor and yelled, "Now pray for forgiveness."

My head started a spinnin' when I heard the click of the lock. Then I felt the pain in my arm from Daddy pulling it damn near out of its socket. My face was still burning from his slap.

Noelle simmered with rage by the cruel nature of his mother's father. She was only twelve and already had such a hard life. He couldn't pull his eyes from his young mother's words on the page no matter how sad it made him feel. Reading Catherine's private thoughts was like looking at a terrible car wreck with its victims thrown to the side of the road—but he could not look away. He read on:

Being in that prayer room made me remember the time the Reverend and Daddy had Mama get down on her knees inside that hole. Mama fixed them alright. She started hackin' and spittin blood on the Reverend's nice, white coat. That was the last time they ever forced Mama to pray in there. Makes me wish I was as sick as Mama so I could get out of prayin'. I'm sorry, God, I take that back. I don't ever want to suffer as bad as Mama do.

God, please make Daddy forget about me workin' for the mean, old preacher. I won't have time to spend out in the meadow and get to see that Morgan boy again. I hope they haven't sent him off to war yet.

Although obsessed with wanting to know more, the last few pages of the notebook were stuck together with more dried mud. Noelle was emotionally spent. Noelle had finally seen the other side of his mother. He realized why she had never talked about her childhood much. All she ever told him was that her parents died and that she had no relatives so she was forced out on her own at fifteen. Noelle now understood why his mother would want to protect him from knowing the truth.

Noelle was on the verge of tears when Sister Theresa caught him off guard and wheeled Catherine back into the room. "So, have you learned anything helpful?" she wondered.

"I had no idea how hard Mama had it," he told her. "Did she sleep through her whole bath?"

The nun nodded, "I'm sorry today was a lost day. Maybe tomorrow she'll surface again. Mornings are usually best for her."

Sister Theresa studied Noelle's worried face. "You look like you need some rest, Detective. Don't be too hard on yourself. You've done the best you can.

"Have I, Sister?" Noelle muttered.

"Your mother knows you're here and I'm sure she appreciates it."

Noelle bent over his mother's bed and kissed her on the forehead. For the first time in decades, he did this with a feeling of deep love.

As he walked down the long flight of stairs, Noelle realized that he had been in New Orleans for two whole days and still owed his wife a call. There was no doubt about it—he was a heel. Noelle was sure of this because instead of calling Sally immediately, he opted instead to stop off at the Rising Sun first.

Chapter Nine

No Turning Back

Before Noelle could make that call to Sally, he passed out on his bed after returning from the bar. When he woke up to pee, he made the call thinking it was better late than never. The last thing he needed was Sally pleading to join him. Noelle picked up the phone and carried it into the bathroom dialing the number with one hand as he used his other to aim his pee into the bowl.

Sally picked up the phone. Nick's slurring voice accompanied by the sound of running water jolted Sally out of a sound sleep.

"Where the fuck are you? It's after midnight. It takes you two days to call and you thought now was a good time?"

Noelle proceeded, "Sal, I know I'm an asshole but you have to let me explain. It's been harder to deal with my mother than I thought. I need to stay longer than..."

"Nick, I'm tired of living this way!" Sally cut him off. "I know you're drinking and gambling; that's why you don't want me around. Feel free to take care of your business without me. I'm enjoying the break from your bullshit! The next time you call, try a decent hour."

"I'm sorry, baby. I do miss you, it's just that…"
Noelle cowered.

Sally yelled, "I've had it, Nick!"

She slammed down the phone, leaving Noelle standing there, shell-shocked, dick in hand. He smashed the phone down even harder, forcing himself to shuck off his regret. He searched for his last bottle of Jack. Disappointed, he found it empty, leaving him nothing to mask the fear of losing Sally.

Helpless to cope, Noelle decided to go out into the night for more of the hair of dog that bit him.

In the lobby, he ran into the Good Samaritan dandy who'd rescued him the night before. The man was also on his way out. Reluctantly, Noelle offered the fellow his hand. "Hi, I'm Nick Noelle," he began. "I believe I owe you a 'thank-you' for taking care of me last night."

With a twinkle in his eye, the dandy extended his own hand with a flourish and said, "Oh, I've been wondering how you were faring. Let me introduce myself, I am Christian Fletcher. I live upstairs at the top level. I trust you are recovered from your head wound?"

Noelle was sober enough to know it was still nineteen seventy one even though this gentleman was dressed like an aging matinee idol from the nineteen twenties. He was wearing a coat, once stylish for royalty, with striped tuxedo trousers. A large, expensive-looking ruby ring flashed on his hand. When he shook his hand, Noelle was surprized by the strong firm grip of this effeminate man.

Noelle forced a smile and said, "I don't know how to thank you. If you hadn't come along, it could have been a lot worse."

Fletcher responded, "No thanks necessary, good sir, I was on my way to our local pub. If you'd like to buy me a drink, we'll call it even."

With his flamboyant, flirtatious manner, this queer made Noelle's skin crawl. He was none too excited to be seen in public with Fletcher but Noelle did owe him one. Luckily, The House of the Rising Sun was usually filled with a garden variety of lowlife misfits so they would blend right into the woodwork.

"Why not, but just a quick one. I'm on my way to meet a friend," Noelle lied.

Fletcher smiled. "I see we're both nocturnal animals. I have a date too, but I like to keep him waiting. Don't want this boy to take me for granted."

Fletcher's last remark was more information than Noelle ever wanted to learn about this character, but it was too late to pull out now.

As they walked to the bar, Fletcher tittered, "So Mr. Noelle, what brings you to our fair city?"

Noelle responded with as few words as possible. "I was born here. I'm back to see my mother."

"Aah, a mama's boy. I like that!" Fletcher swished suggestively.

Noelle grimaced, then offered, "Well, I wouldn't go that far. I haven't been all that great a son. My mother is dying." Noelle wanted to make sure the queer didn't get any ideas, so he added, "When the inevitable happens, my wife will be joining me. She's back at our home in Houston. I'm retired law enforcement."

Fletcher responded, "Actually, Mr. Noelle, I already knew that about you. After your unfortunate…mishap, our landlady Velda—a bit of a gossip, you know—took the liberty to check out your credentials. She was concerned about any future trouble in her house. Of course, as is her way, she shared the good news about you with everyone."

When they reached The House of the Rising Son, Noelle took a deep breath of the smoke-filled air. He was grateful for the dim lighting as they took a booth in the back corner.

The waiter soon showed up to take their order. Noelle asked for his usual double Jack with a beer chaser.

Fletcher ordered with an air of sophistication, "A dry martini with two olives."

Fletcher picked up the conversation where he'd left off. "It actually pleased Velda to no end to learn that you were a man of the law. Especially now with that horrible news of the archbishop's grisly murder." Fletcher shuddered visibly then continued, "You can imagine she doesn't get many tenants with your notoriety, even if it's from another state. You're famous for catching serial killers, aren't you?"

Noelle tried to shift the focus off him by asking the weirdo what his interests were.

"Well, I've spent most of my adult life traveling the world," Fletcher answered. "I lived in New York City in my twenties and even spent some time in Hollywood where I tried my hand at becoming a matinee idol."

"How did that work out for you?" Noelle wondered.

Fletcher ignored the subtle sarcasm. "I didn't have the stomach for rejection and Clark Gable was getting all my parts," he sighed. "I decided to shift my focus and travel. I covered most of the romantic European countries but something always drew me back to New Orleans. I first came back here in my late teens. Perhaps you lived here then as well…although I suspect I'm a bit older than you."

Noelle raised his eyebrows. "Just how old *are* you*?"*

Fletcher's voice raised an octave. "Please, Mr. Noelle, a lady never reveals her age!"

Noelle laughed at the homo's blatant admission of queerness. "Some lady you are! You have the shoulders of a linebacker and you're strong enough to carry me back to my room."

Fletcher shrugged. "I like to fancy myself as Florence Nightingale. A girl's gotta do what a girl's gotta do." He fluttered his eyelashes at Noelle. "But seriously, I do make it a point to keep fit. I eat well and get lots of exercise."

Trying to change the subject, Noelle asked, "So, are you retired now?"

Fletcher chuckled. "Oh, Mr. Noelle! I've never done an honest day's work in my life. I was fortunate enough to inherit my daddy's fortune at eighteen years of age and I've been enjoying myself to the fullest ever since."

Noelle was taken aback by Fletcher's admission to being affluent and privileged. Most of the rich sons-of-bitches Noelle knew from Houston always tried to hide the fact that they were loaded.

The waiter arrived with their drinks. Noelle took out a twenty and told the waiter to keep the change. Despite his disdain for the queer, Noelle was somewhat intrigued by Fletcher and turned the conversation back on him. "I'm sure you must have some interests or hobbies."

Fletcher tittered again. "Oh yes! I have had many interests and some fun hobbies. For example, I love antiquing."

"Well, you and my wife have that in common," Noelle replied. "She's a whiz at shopping in those second-hand stores."

"I can't wait to meet her. Since we share the same taste in men, I'm sure we'll get on famously."

Fletcher winked at him when he added, "Mr. Noelle, I hope you will allow me to invite you for dinner one evening."

Noelle could not believe how shamelessly this fag was flirting with him. "I'll be pretty busy with my mother's needs and all," he stammered.

Noelle wanted to bolt for the door but before he could, Fletcher added, "Perhaps once your wife arrives, you'll feel more sociable."

Noelle squirmed. "She's occupied with her charities back home," he lied. "But she'll be joining me to help with the funeral arrangements. If there's time, perhaps you'll meet her."

Fletcher tried to pump Noelle for more information but Noelle was done. He paused to drain his beer and said, "Nice meeting you. And, please believe me, I do sincerely thank you, Mr. Fletcher."

Noelle shook the old queen's hand and rushed toward the door. As he turned to eyeball Fletcher one last time, he noticed that Fletcher was studying Noelle's swagger with a big grin on his face. It made his skin crawl.

Chapter Ten

Holy Roller Murders

Detective Tucci burst through the whirling dervish of a crime scene. He ran up the creaky staircase of the apartment above "The Son of God's Baptist Church." The building was like many others in the poor Ninth Ward District's ghetto. It was so rickety that it looked as if it could be easily blown down by the next hurricane or the Big Bad Wolf.

At the top of the stairs, Tucci pushed past the photographer as his rotund partner, Melville, labored up the steps behind him. Tucci barked, "Looks like our killer's been slumming."

Melville gagged as he slowly bent over what was left of the preacher's body. It had been dragged from the bedroom to the hall. Melville suddenly couldn't control himself and purged his lunch. The partially digested oyster po'boy shot up like a missile and landing on the torn, blood-soaked shroud, which barely covered the decapitated corpse.

Tucci screamed bloody murder. "For Christ's sake, Melville! You just contaminated our crime scene with your puke!"

Embarrassed, Melville stood there, shaking uncontrollably, and stared at the severed head. The mutilated preacher's mouth was open in an endless scream. It was easy to see that his eyes had been gutted out.

Although a hardened crime scene investigator of many years, Tucci had never seen anything this ugly either. "Fuck," he growled.

Melville caught his breath and sputtered, "It's gotta be the same killer."

Tucci stared into the preacher's cracked-open skull and agreed. "Yup, his brain's gone too."

When he lifted the drape from the headless corpse on the floor, Tucci could see the hole in the Reverend's chest. "He took the heart, too. But he didn't replace it with a crucifix," Tucci commented. "Unless we have a copycat killer, this is more than likely the same psycho."

Someone on the forensic team cried out from the bedroom, "Detective, look at this on the wall."

Tucci walked full speed ahead into the bedroom. On the bare white wall, in big, dripping, red letters, it said: "VENGEANCE IS MINE!" Tucci turned away, shaking his head. 'Yeah,' Tucci thought, 'This is no copycat unless it's someone on the force. Nobody else could have known what the murderer wrote at both scenes in their victims' blood.'

Another man on the forensic team nervously announced, "Detective, we found a very pretty prostitute in the stairwell with a lump on her head the size of a soft ball. She was just sitting there at the bottom of the stairs, dazed."

"Can she talk?" Tucci barked.

"I think she's in shock. I called for an ambulance so the paramedics can treat her."

Tucci turned to Melville. "Get down there and see if you can find out what the whore knows...if you can manage that without losing your cookies all over her. Okay?"

The forensic cop continued, "Besides the big lump on her head, we didn't see any other wounds."

Tucci nodded. "Melville, take care of it while I make sure none of these a-holes fuck up this crime scene worse than you already did." Tucci then snapped at the crew, "Look for prints, assholes!" Turning back to Melville, he added, "See if the whore knows any names from the congregation. It seems like our killer is looking for religion."

Melville slowly lumbered back down the stairs still sickened by the murder of the Baptist minister. He found the lady in question now sitting on the dry, brown, scraggly lawn outside the church, waiting to be questioned. Just one look at her and Melville saw how lovely she was, despite the lump on her forehead. He ambled over to her and took out his pen and notebook.

The woman turned to face him. With a pained expression on her face, she grumbled, "So, what do you want to know, *Mr. Policeman?*"

Her sarcastic tone immediately pissed him off because he knew he probably wouldn't be able to scare her into talking. He tried anyway.

"What's your name?"

"Rose," she murmured.

"Well, Rose, did you see the killer?"

Rose huffed and put her hand to the knot on her forehead. "I didn't see him. My back was to him."

"So, he knocked you out first?"

"It was the minister who gave me this lump and after that I don't remember anything," she squawked.

As per Tucci's instructions, the investigation team was thoroughly combing through the crime scene. Everything seemed to be under control. Itching to find out what the prostitute knew, Tucci trotted downstairs to Melville and the witness.

When he found them on the parched lawn, his back stiffened. It was Rose, a working girl he was well acquainted with. She saw Tucci and turned her face.

"Melville, you can go back up there now. I'll take over from here."

Melville protested, "But, Tucci, I just started."

"Melville, upstairs NOW!"

More than anything, Melville wanted to get his balls back but he knew now wasn't the time to try. Melville moved away, forcing himself to climb back up the stairs to the scene of the crime.

Tucci waited until his partner was out of sight before he said a word to Rose.

"So, it was you who was banging this loser...huh, Rose?"

Shivering under Tucci's glare, Rose lashed back, "You might think twice before you tell Rocco about this. He was the one who pimped me out to that freaky pastor bastard. You know me. I'm a good girl and do what the mob wants. What's going on up there anyway? The last thing I remember was my head being pounded against the bedpost. When I woke up I was out here on the lawn."

Tucci laughed, "Oh, c'mon, Rose, what did you see?"

"Nothing! Rose cried. "You have to believe me!"

Tucci forced himself to simmer down. He called over to the paramedics. "Hey, you! Take her to the hospital. Someone from the force will pick her up when you're through examining her. Come on! Right now, you idiots! This woman's in pain."

As he walked away, Tucci turned back to Rose and said sardonically, "Baby, take care. If you remember anything, and I mean *anything*, don't let anyone know, not even Rocco!" Tucci stormed away wondering if this was a mob hit pretending to be a crazy copycat killer.

Upstairs, Melville kept his distance from where the sliced-and-diced preacher's body lay. He knew his job was on thin ice. Frank Tucci was looking for any excuse to get rid of him. Tucci was ambitious all right. From the minute he joined the New Orleans Police Department straight from the Bronx in New York City, it didn't take Tucci more than a "New York minute" to assert his gritty street smarts and climb the ranks to top dog on New Orleans crime beat.

Melville was a native son and had been on the force longer. He could have been a first-rate detective but his diabetes and spastic colon held him back. Also, his morals made him lousy for the job. He'd been rejected for every promotion he was ever up for and kept burying his lack of ambition in more donuts. Now all he cared about was hanging onto his job long enough to take an early retirement with a hefty pension. 'What a hell of a way to live,' he thought.

Chapter Eleven

Murdering Religion

Sally's threats screamed in Noelle's head as he labored in the heat on his walk to Saint Mary's. His thoughts grew even darker as he secretly wished that his mother would just let go and die already.

On the corner newsstand, a bold headline caught his attention: "RELIGIOUS MURDERS." Noelle scanned the Times-Picayune for more details.

The front page story was all about an evangelistic preacher from 'The Son of God Baptist Church' who was found slaughtered in the same fashion as the murder at Saint Catherine's Cathedral.

Noelle bought the paper and jumped into a cab that was parked at the curb.

Although Saint Mary's was just a few blocks away, the luxury of an air-conditioned ride and a newspaper were preferable to sweating in the suffocating heat while Noelle's obsessive thinking did a number on him. He believed reading about a murder would be light fare compared to taking in the diaries of his poor, dying mother—or worrying about his wife leaving him.

As Noelle perused the Times-Picayune's account of the crime, it was obvious that there was a serial killer afoot, or at best, a copycat criminal. The press was spinning the story as a likely revenge motive perpetrated by some disgruntled congregant who regretted giving his life's savings to this randy, young preacher.

Noelle mused, 'Yeah, some preacher...probably lining his pockets to shell out for drugs and hookers."

According to the paper, the New Orleans crime detectives were interrogating the local drug dealers and prostitutes that the preacher supported with his congregation's donations. The one bit of evidence leaked from the crime scene was that there was a possible eyewitness: a prostitute found unconscious near the scene with a couple of one hundred bills on her.

'This is really getting interesting,' Noelle thought.

When the cab reached Saint Mary's, he paid the cabbie and stepped out onto the baking sidewalk. He signed in with Eric, who smiled widely behind the reception booth. Eric was happy to tell Noelle the good news; they finally fixed the elevator. Noelle took it to the third floor.

As always, Sister Theresa was in his mother's room, faithfully tending to the comatose Catherine. The nun greeted him warmly.

"Detective Noelle, you're looking a little more rested," she observed. "I'm sorry to say there's been no change in your mother but I found a whole bunch of those notebooks. They're all here piled in this box on the dresser. I took the liberty of arranging them chronologically. Most of them had the dates entered when your mother started a new book so it wasn't hard to figure out."

"Thank you, Sister."

"My pleasure," she smiled. "So, Detective, I'll leave you to your business here. I, myself, have my own notes and paperwork to catch up on."

Noelle thanked the nun again and pulled up a chair next to his mother's bed. He grabbed another chair, propped up his feet and settled down for a long afternoon.

Before digging into his reading, Noelle stared at his mother long and hard wondering what the hell had happened to her. Where had she gone off to? Was she hiding from the past or the future...or both? He kissed her dry, withered hand then opened the next notebook in the pile from the box on the dresser.

In bold, block print, "BOOK 2" was scribbled at the top of the first page:

It's been so long since I come back here to write to you, God. Since You see everything anyways, I suppose You know Mama is gone from this mean, old world. I hope she's in heaven at Your side. Don't know how she couldn't be with all the suffering she did, especially at the end.

Since Mama's gone, my time is never my own but I can feel her lurkin' around, telling me to hold on, that it's goin' to be alright. It's been two years passed and it ain't gettin' any better. Some folks say I don't look 14. My cheekbones done come out from under all that baby fat and my lips are takin over my face. When I get a quick look in the mirror, I see one of those ladies from Mrs. Kirkwood's fashion magazines, exceptin' I don't have the nice clothes. Just as well. As long as I'm under Daddy's watch, I'd never get to ware 'em anyways. All I ever get to do is clean, cook, go to the schoolhouse or the church. There, I be on my knees either a prayin' or a workin' for that nasty, old Reverend Garsett. Then when I get home, I make dinner and clean up again. And those are just weekdays.

Saturdays I spend more time under the Reverend's roving eye while tending his garden. And forget about Sundays! They say that day belongs to You, God. I wish that were so. I get no rest ever, not even on Your day.

The only job I like to give thanks for is when I get to do some sewing for Miss Kirkwood, just like Mama used to do. This makes me feel close to Mama, too. Without Miss Kirkwood, I'd never get to hear popular music or read magazines.

I wonder why Miss Kirkwood ever moved back here from New Orleans. Once I even got up the nerve to ask her and she said, "Young lady, I've seen and done everything I wanted to see and do. Life is easy here, you know? I'm comfortable." Miss

Kirkwood may be an old spinster but rumors have it that she was pretty wild back in her day.

Daddy don't like me being around her but he sure likes the money I get from her.

Yesterday was one of the worse days ever. Daddy invited the preacher for supper. When he called me down to start the cookin', I had to quickly hide a magazine and a lacy bra and a silk nightshirt that Miss Kirkwood hand down to me. I never had anything so soft and smooth. It felt just like a new pup.

Well, I was in such a rush I got careless and just kicked them nice undies under the bed. I ran down as soon as Daddy called. I didn't want him comin' up to my room to inspect it like he do sometimes.

In my hurry, I almost forgot to take off the stockings Miss Kirkwood give me. I quick hid them under Mama's Bible, which I keep sitting on my end table. Then I ran down callin' from the top of the stairs, "I'm coming right down, Father." Hopin' my respect would satisfy him.

Lately, Daddy been lookin' like those walking-dead folks and he been in just as bad a humor as them, too.

When I got to the bottom of the stairs, Daddy yelled, "You jes git in here and git this kitchen cleaned, ya' hear? The skillet is nigh high in bacon lard from mornin' breakfast, you lazy cow."

I told Daddy I was sorry then I went over to the stove and showed him the casserole I had already started in the oven. When I bent down to put the casserole back, Daddy looked me up and down and growled, "What ya wearin, girl?"

I quick straightened up and tucked my shirt in. Then Daddy told me I was too grown for my blouse and said I had to change it before the Reverend come. Daddy opened the breadbox and said, "Where them sweet buns you baked?"

When I pulled out the cold, fresh buns from the icebox to show him, he snapped," Your mother would never have done that—taking up space in the icebox when we got cheese and milk to keep."

I looked down and polite as I could, told him, "But Daddy, the icebox keeps 'em fresher longer. I saw it in a magazine." The split second the words fell out of my mouth, I knew I made a big mistake. Daddy went red and started yellin' in my face,

"You what? You read it in what magazine? Jes where you keep such a magazine?"

Then he ran straight up to my room and I ran up fast behind him. My heart was pumpin' and my gut was doing flip flops."

I said, "It's not here, Daddy. I threw it out!"

While Daddy was opening my closet door, I put my hand under Mama's Bible and in one swift move, stuffed the stockings up under my skirt. I tucked an edge into my underpants so they wouldn't fall out. Daddy swung around and saw Mama's Bible in my hands. Quick as a whip, I held the Bible like I was swearin' an oath and lied, "I promise to God, Jesus, and the Disciples of the Creed that I threw that old magazine away."

Sorry I lied, God, but I figured I'd rather deal with Your wrath in the hereafter then my Daddy's in the here and now.

Then Daddy came over, shook me by the shoulders and yelled, "Well, ya jes better be tellin' the truth." For a minute, he got real quiet, looked at Mama's Bible fondly and said, "Yep, this was your Mama's Bible. A promise on it goes straight to the ears of God."

Daddy gave me a look of kindness, somethin' I hadn't seen in a long time. It made me almost feel affection for him. Or maybe it was just pity. Then that old elastic on my underpants gave way and them stockings come unhitched. They fell to the floor in front of Daddy.

He picked up them silk stockings in disbelief. "Why you a lyin' and a sinnin'? You got no right to have this Bible or anything else your poor mama give you…"

When Daddy snatched the Bible out of my hands, my heart just about tore in two. "The Reverend will know jes how to deal with you when he git here," he spat. "Now, put on that blue dress with the white collar like I told you while I look around for what else you been hiding from me up in here."

Daddy's eyes went straight under my bed. He dropped to the floor and came up with the bra, nightie and magazine Miss

Kirkwood give me. Daddy was lookin' over my head like he saw an evil spirit hovering there and came at me like blazes. He slap me three or four times. I could feel my face floppin' back and forth like those ragdolls with the wobbly heads. Then, when my neck cracked, his eyes come down from the netherworld he was in.

"You may look like your mama but you got the Devil in you. It's good thing she ain't here to see what's come of you."

Daddy pushed me to the floor, stepped over me like I was trash and turned toward the door. With his right hand, he opened it. In his left, he gripped my silk stockings, bra and nightie like he did to that water moccasin when he caught it in the swamp. "Now, get out of them tart's clothes," he ordered.

By the time the Reverend and his wife got here, I looked like one of them ladies that do missionary work in Africa. But before any food was offered, Reverend Garsett had his work cut out for him to earn his supper. My pa told him what happened and how I needed to be punished.

Daddy led us all to the yard out back. He had already started a nice fire in the pit. The Reverend told me to come to him. When I got up close he squeezed my shoulders, brushing my breast with his hand as he forced me to my knees. Then he begin to blabber. I felt his hand upside my left ear and his thunder preachin' voice a prayin'. "In the name of Jesus," he shouted, "I cast out these unholy thoughts of womanhood from Catherine Lee. She was made in the likeness of the first evil, Eve, and just like Eve, she is a strayin' and covortin' with the Devil. Oh, Father help me rid this sinful girl of her demons."

Then the Reverend slap me upside my right ear real hard. I had to bite my tongue to keep from slapping him back. With my ears ringin', I could hear Daddy and Mary Garsett, the Reverend's homely, pitiful wife behind me prayin', "Amen, Lord. Amen.'"

For good measure, the Reverend slap me one more time, even harder. When I opened my eyes, he was mashing his lips together and lookin' all excited as he prepared to put my stockings, bra and silk nightie into the bonfire pit, talkin' in tongues the whole time.

As the Reverend dangled my unmentionables over the flames, his mousy wife turned away like she was embarrassed. Daddy just looked like a zombie drained of all life, the fire casting a red glow over his hardened features.

The Reverend called out with impatience, "Get them buckets, Gerald. Bring 'em fast! Give one to Mary!" The next thing I knew, the Reverend's hands were on my head. I trembled as I braced myself for more hittin' upside my head as he said, "I ask You to purify this sinner. Send Your blight to ravage any ungodliness that rages through her lustful body."

Next, the Reverend cry out to his wife," Now, Mary! Now!" I felt the freezing water pour all down my head, neck and back. Then Daddy poured the next bucket. More water soaked my clothes, making them cling to me like a second skin.

I just kept my eyes closed and thought about Mama and her dead body lying in the dirt next to the big, old oak tree. I wondered if its roots be growin' around her while she down there rotten' in that cheap coffin.

I thought about dying myself and wondered if this was hell, right where I was on earth.

For a second, I opened my eyes and saw Daddy's cold, dead eyes watchin' me. The last thing I remember was the Reverend's smug look as he took the last bucket and poured it all down my front.

When I opened my eyes again, the bonfire was smoldering and I could smell the rubber from my pretty bra burning. It kind of smelled like the oil from Daddy's truck.

Then the Reverend said, "Now Catherine, you kneel out here until the spirit of the Lord pushes out your evil."

Mary stood behind her husband, her tiny voice wavering as she said, "She'll catch her death....Joshua."

The Reverend held out his hand to shush her. "She needs to learn her lesson."

Then he licked his lips together in anticipation and said, "Ummm, now let's get inside and try some of 'em sweet buns and vittles while they still warm."

Shiverin' in the dark on my knees, I stayed out there, not moving a muscle. I could hear them laughin' while enjoyin' my

casserole and sweet buns. God, I'm not blamin' You for allowin'
this to happen, but if You are everywhere all the time, I can't help
but wonder why You weren't there to help me in my hour
of need.

Noelle heard his mother groan. He quickly put down
the notebook to take her hand. Her eyelids fluttered open. She
looked straight at him and gave Noelle the biggest, warmest
smile. With love in her voice, she said, "Brandon?"

"No, Mama, it's me, Nick," Noelle answered. "Mama,
who is Brandon? You keep calling for him."

Catherine smiled again. She said faintly, "Oh! Nick, my
son, you know." As fast as she awoke, her eyes closed and she
slipped back into unconsciousness. At first, Noelle wanted to run
and get Sister Theresa. But for what? She couldn't change his
mother's condition. He turned back to the diary.

Although it was painful to learn all the horror that his
mother had endured, Noelle was fascinated. When he was able to
forget it was his mother's life, it was like reading a good novel.
Not that he would really know what a good novel was, since he
never read much except newspapers and crime reports. Noelle
grabbed the notebook to pick up where he left off.

After dark, I got off my achin' knees and lay on my back.
I looked up and watched a cloud drifting across the
almost-full moon. I heard a crackle and jumped but realized it
was only the fire refusing to die.

I sat up and I thought about the Morgan boy. How I
hadn't seen him in over two years since that day he say he was
goin' off to war. When I looked back up at the sky again, I saw
that the moon had moved and was now behind the old, oak tree.
Then I heard a louder crackle comin' from behind the oak and
saw a tall shadow in the light of the moon, coming through
the brush.

My heart jumped when I saw it was Justin Morgan.
Maybe I had conjured him up. Maybe I was a heathen witch like
the Reverend said I was. Maybe I deserved that punishment.

Cause the man standin' before me in the flesh was the object of my wicked desire.

"It's okay, it's only me," Justin said. "The Devil." His voice was deeper than I remembered. Justin started to laugh that same old laugh like the first time when he chased me. I felt that same humiliation as I felt two years earlier.

Justin slapped a thick branch from Daddy's woodpile up against his thigh and recklessly put his foot in the middle of the bonfire, crushing any life that was left in it. Only the light of the moon filled the darkness. Just thinking of Justin made me feel all hot and sticky down there. So maybe he was the Devil. But I didn't care.

His eyes seemed darker than I remembered. My impulse was to run but my heart said, 'Stay.'

Justin moved closer and gently put his coat over my shoulders. I looked down at the medals pinned to his jacket. They looked like wings. Then I thought he must be an angel cause he was actin' so kind. Then I remember that even Lucifer was an angel once.

When Justin see me lookin' at his medal wings, he said, "Those are from doing my time in the Air Force. I was lucky enough to come home in one piece."

Suddenly out of nowhere, I begin to cry. Justin moved close and took me in his arms. I let my head drop on his big, firm chest. God, I thought I had to be dreamin' cause this was better than anything I ever thought up about the way we might be together one day.

Then I heard my Daddy talkin' with Mrs. and Reverend Garsett. It sounded like they were going out the front door to the porch. They was talking about how good the maple drink had tasted with the buns they jes had for dessert. I jumped away from Justin and whispered,

"Ya gotta go. If they come out back here to check on me and see you, there's no tellin what they'll do to you."

Justin Morgan didn't budge. He looked toward the light in the house and snickered. "There ain't nothin' that old loon preacher can do to me," he said. "I killed more Kraut souls than he ever saved." Then we hear the Reverend thankin' Daddy for the supper, getting in his fancy car and startin' up the engine.

"That Cadillac he drive was paid for by your old papa and the rest of those poor, ignorant dirt farmers who think there's a better life waiting for them in heaven," Justin huffed. Then he reached in the pocket of his jacket, pulled out a flask of whisky and downed a gulp. He held out the flask, offering it to me.

Although I could hear Daddy walk back inside the house and saw all the lights goin' out one by one, I was still jumpy thinking he might come out back to check on me. But this was one time I was happy my daddy didn't care enough about me to see how I was. I felt Justin's breath on my ear as he whispered, "Have some, sugar. It'll warn your insides out."

I got embarrassed and pushed him away, saying, "No, I can't."

Justin laughed. Something about his laugh took the sting out of the pain and I let him put his hand through my hair, which was still damp. He gripped my head and bent it back, telling me, "C'mon, have some. It takes the hurtin' away."

He held the bottle to my mouth. I closed my eyes and took a tiny sip. When I opened my eyes Justin said, "What'd they get you for anyhow?"

I turned my face away. "Nothin.'"

"What were those 'tools of the Devil' the Reverend was talkin about?" Justin asked. He flashed a big grin and added, "Come on, Cat. I saw and heard it all." He handed me the bottle and this time, I took a long swig, letting it cast out the chill. I started to giggle. Justin looked at me with surprise. "I do believe that's the first time I ever heard you laugh, Miss Catherine."

Justin stretched me out on the ground, touched my bare leg and said, "You know, we could use those Devil tools right about now." He walked his fingers up my thigh. It gave me goosebumps. When I felt his hand go between my legs, I pressed them together real hard to try and stop him. But his hot, whisky breath paralyzed me and even if I wanted to, I couldn't move away.

Justin's dark, brooding eyes spoke to me. I opened my mouth and my legs to let him in. With his other hand, he was

*touching my breast real soft and tender-like underneath that
ugly, wet and cold blue dress. As his finger went up inside me, I
thought of my opening as the highway to hell and darkness. But
the more he probed me inside, the more I got filled with some
kind of heavenly feeling.*

*God, that feeling could not be any better than heaven
itself. With my desire and shame all rolled up in this one grand
feeling, I almost exploded. Then I felt a love pour down on me.
God, it was the holiest feeling I ever felt. If that ain't Your love,
God, I don't know what is. I never felt nothin' like it before.
Nothin' and no one but Justin Morgan ever made me feel so
good. So, even if he be the Devil, then God, You can damn me
straight to hell.*

Sister Theresa entered Room 305. The presence of the
nun brought Noelle to reality. Noelle snapped the book shut and
his face blushed bright red; he was embarrassed to have read
about his mother's sex life.

"Sister, you read any of this yet?" he asked.

"No," she replied. "I wouldn't without you or your
mother's permission."

"Well, if you do, I'm warning you, it's racy."

The nun's eyes sparkled as she let out a hearty laugh.
"Like I said, Detective, I haven't always been a nun."

Noelle smiled. "Well, Sister, then you can drop the
formalities and just call me Nick from now on. You did a good
deed by showing me my Mama's dairies here. There is enough
ammo to keep me hanging in for a while. But I haven't found
any mention of a Brandon. She did wake up for a second and
called that name out again. I sure wish I knew who he was.
Maybe the old girl had a secret lover none of us knew about."

Sister Theresa beamed with warmth. "We all deserve
love," she said.

"From her dairies here, it looks like she had her share
early on, and I'm only up to her teen years. I have to go now."

Noelle stood, leaned forward to kiss his mother's
forehead. He said good bye to Sister Theresa as he headed out
the door.

When Noelle hit the street it was almost dusk. The air had cooled a bit. He was hungry and decided to get some more of that good, old New Orleans cooking the city was known for. Despite all of his problems, Noelle was feeling a little less heavyhearted. Maybe it had something to do with knowing that his mother had found love in the middle of her painful childhood; that made him feel happy.

However, by the time he put down a big gumbo, chased it with a few double shots of Jack, Noelle's dreary thinking started to take him over again.

Chapter Twelve

Like Minds

The bar was packed when Noelle cruised in. He found an open spot. His bartender buddy grinned showing Noelle his gold teeth when he asked, "Still drinking double shots of Jack, no ice?"

Noelle smiled. "Yeah, you remember."

The bartender flashed his winning smile and poured Noelle's poison. "How could I forget?" he said. "You had more than a few last time you were in."

"It appears I might have been overserved." The bartender's scar seemed to glow as he put the bottle back on the shelf. Noelle lifted the glass and downed his drink in one long gulp.

"Hey, Buddy, not so fast," scolded the bartender.

"Keep the bottle here. Pour me another and I'll take a beer, too."

"That's what I'm here for," the bartender smiled, pushing the pint glass of Abita across the bar. "Rumor has it that Carlo might be coming in tonight. You might get lucky and find him at the tables."

"It's been so long he may not recognize me. I was still a kid when he knew me."

Noelle was covering his bases, just in case. "Pour me another. My girlfriend's waiting upstairs."

"Yeah, I heard you made a big impression on Millie," the bartender laughed, referring to the old broad with the missing fingers and strawberry blonde straw hair who guarded the gaming room.

"Big tips tend to make a lasting impression," Noelle answered.

Noelle took his drinks and headed to the back room. When he entered the poker parlor, Millie was waiting right where he left her. Her liver lips quivered a tombstone grin when she saw Noelle put two one hundred dollar bills down on her table. She began to count out his chips with her few good fingers. Millie gestured toward the last table in the back. "Mister, I've been saving that lucky spot just for you," she told him. "It's the only seat left."

Noelle knew the bartender had probably sent Millie some kind of signal when he saw him walk in the door. He knew these gambling joints all too well and how they passed the word around when a high roller was in the house. Whatever the case, Noelle was happy to be getting a warm greeting this time around.

As he approached the table he recognized Frank Tucci, the detective from the TV news report about the murders. Somehow Noelle felt like he knew the guy. Something about him was familiar. Noelle felt it was probably déjà vu, like he'd met this guy before.

Noelle studied Tucci with no conscious recollection of their prior encounter at the bar just two nights before. Tucci glanced at Noelle with disgust, immediately recognizing him as the sloppy, know-it-all drunk he had the displeasure of encountering before. Tucci frowned remembering the scene Noelle had made with him and Melville. Noelle made an utter fool of himself while trying to offer advice on how to solve their murder case. Noelle, however, had no recollection of that unfortunate event because he was in a blackout.

Frank Tucci stared at his cards attempting to avoid eye contact with Noelle as Noelle sat down right next to him and got comfortable in his seat at the table.

Noelle scanned the other players. Across from him was a young, baby-faced kid with a crew cut, probably a soldier home on leave from Vietnam. Next to Baby Face sat a fat, bald guy with a large, bulbous nose that kept leaking. He was sweating buckets, soaking his button-down shirt and bowtie. The old, fat man kept pushing a handkerchief up his nostrils to stop the drip. With the same snotty handkerchief, he wiped the sweat off his face.

It made Noelle want to get the hell out of there but he was too fascinated watching Tucci and the mug who sat to the detective's left. He was a tall, stocky, dark and greasy guy with wide shoulders and shoe-polish black hair that struggled to cover a bald spot. Noelle couldn't help but notice his huge hands covered with flashy rings. The playing cards looked like small business cards in the thug's gigantic mitts. Noelle noticed the big brute give Tucci a nod like they were buddy-buddy. Noelle assumed the fellow was connected to the Marcello's or some other mob family.

As the bets went around the table, Noelle kept his gaze on Tucci, who bid high, as did his rough-looking friend. He watched the detective raise his eyes when it came Noelle's turn to bet. Noelle folded and Tucci took the pot.

With the next hand, Noelle kept his gaze downcast at the three queens in his hand. He placed a high bid on the next go around. In competition with Noelle, Tucci bid even higher. Everyone else dropped out as the big-bucks showdown escalated leaving a pissing match between Noelle and Tucci.

Noelle called it and showed his full house.

Tucci folded and decided to call it quits for the night. Turning to his buddy, he whispered something in his ear. The behemoth threw a few chips to the dealer, rose and went over to Millie to cash out.

Noelle played one more hand before he decided to follow Tucci's lead. He dropped out of the game, hoping to catch up with the detective at the bar downstairs.

Noelle was curious to see if he could learn anything new from Tucci about the murders in the news and all around town . Noelle needed some sort of distraction from his own problems, maybe even a friend who wasn't a nun or a queer. He thought that perhaps the detective might be interested in his experience with serial killer crimes.

When Noelle made it back to the bar, he was in luck. Tucci was sitting alone without his gorilla friend. There was an empty stool right next to him. When Noelle sat, the bartender came right up to him. Without asking, he poured Noelle a double Jack and placed an Abita right beside it.

Noelle winked at the bartender. "Get my friend a round of whatever he's drinking, too."

Tucci looked up and snarked at Noelle. "Did you decide to quit before you got shit-faced again?"

Noelle looked puzzled.

"You know, I am a detective," Tucci continued, "It's my business to keep track of what goes on around here. You and I had the pleasure of meeting two nights ago. You were pretty tight, so maybe you don't remember. But I know exactly who you are, *Nick Noelle*. You're one of Houston's finest. You told me yourself." Tucci frowned, "Fine, I'll have a drink with you but if you go over the line, my buddy Mike here has orders to kick you out and eighty-six you from Lucky's for good."

Noelle was dumbfounded. He was not sure what Tucci was referring to. Mike, the bartender, put his two cents in.

"Detective, Nick's not a bad dude," he said in Noelle's defense. "He just had a little too much the other night. Cut him a break, he knows Carlo. That's how he got in the game."

Noelle relaxed. "I don't have much time to be up to no good," he assured Tucci. "I'm only in town because my mother is dying. A little gambling and drinking takes the edge off."

Tucci softened. "Well, in that case, fine. Sorry about your mom," he growled. "I thought I knew all of Carlo's associates. Although, I leave that work to Vice. It's my job to keep an eye on them in case the lines between Vice and murder blur...as they so often do. I'm sure you know what I mean."

Noelle felt relieved. "I know exactly what you mean. And thanks; it's been hard watching my mother go in and out of a coma. Lonely, too," he admitted to Tucci. "I see that you're up to your ass in two grisly murders now. I have a little experience in that department, as you probably know."

"I do know," Tucci replied. "I took the liberty of calling Houston after we met. I learned you were a hero down there. Fifteen years on homicide plus you solved those baffling debutant murders. You have quite a rep but unfortunately not all good. Rumor has it, you let 'pussy' blind-side you."

Noelle was confused. "How so?"

Tucci plowed on. "They say you were dating the serial killer all the while she was hacking up her friends and lovers." Tucci paused before he zoomed in for the next jab. "Tell me, is that why you retired, Detective? Because you realized that you could no longer trust your instincts?"

Noelle frowned. "You can say that, but it had more to do with having my fill of blood and body parts. When I met Pamela, she was a sweet clerk working behind a makeup counter. I feared she'd be the next victim. I'm a sucker for girls who need protection. How she could have done all that twisted shit fucked me up for sure. She almost got my wife, too. If it weren't for my partner Juan Lopez, it would not have been a happy ending. We got lucky."

Although Tucci didn't like Noelle he took pity on him. "That had to be rough on you. Maybe one day, I'll pick your brain on your theories about serial killers in general. But today's not that day. Normally, I'd let you in on our case but I'm not sure I can trust you, especially if our killer turns out to be a pretty, young girl."

After having let himself be vulnerable and honest with the detective, Noelle was wounded by Tucci's slur on his character. He got defensive and added, "My wife and I were divorced when I met Pamela and I can't say I regret everything since because that mishap in judgment is what brought us back together again. I'm a happily married man again and my wife will be joining me here soon to help me bury my mother. "

Tucci hopped up off the bar stool. "I got to run now. Duty calls," he announced.

Tucci walked to the back of Lucky's where the restrooms were. Turning, Noelle saw him duck into the men's room. He also noticed the thug from the poker game follow Tucci into the can. Noelle guessed that Tucci, like so many other cops he had known, was probably on the take with the local mob.

Noelle sat alone, remembering the rush he used feel when he was working a job. It was the same high he got from gambling. Noelle would be the first to admit that he was a risk junkie and thrived on the edge of danger. If it weren't for his dying mother and the fear of losing Sally for good, he might have even offered Tucci his help. But Noelle thought it best that he didn't get involved, especially if this Tucci was a dirty cop.

Noelle had a lot of unsavory character traits but at least he was proud of the fact that he was never corrupt when it came to the law. While unorthodox, he respected his service as a law enforcer. He also realized Tucci wasn't all that keen on him. He seemed like he was holding a grudge against him. Since Noelle had no recollection of their previous encounter, he decided to ask the bartender. Mike was more than happy to oblige.

"The last time you were here, you were an obnoxious asshole and butted into Tucci and Melville's private conversation. You bragged about how you could solve their murder case better than they could. It's no wonder you blocked it out. Dude, you were pretty pathetic that night. I'm glad to see that you're keeping it together now. You seem like a good guy. Sorry to hear about your mom."

Noelle thanked Mike for his kind words. He wasn't surprised that he had no recollection of meeting Tucci since he couldn't remember how he'd even gotten home that night. Feeling like a fool, he packed it in for the evening. Noelle threw a big tip on the bar, finished his beer and walked briskly back to his digs.

Chapter Thirteen

Noelle Goes to Church

On the way home, Noelle popped into a phone booth outside of Lucky Pierre's. He knew it was still early enough to reach Sally before she went to bed. He dropped enough change into the box to cover a long distance call and dialed his Houston home. The phone rang and rang, on and on. A floozy planted herself outside of the phone booth signaling for him to hang up. After ten or more rings, he gave up and left. The lady of the night cussed at Noelle as he exited the booth.

On his walk home, his mind soared with imaginings of where Sally might be at such a late hour.

He couldn't help thinking of the days when Sally looked a lot like that hooker he just saw at the phone booth. To take his mind off such foolish thoughts, Noelle stopped at the corner newsstand and bought a paper. He stood on Magazine Street and read.

Scanning the news, Noelle discovered a few new facts about the dual murders. Contemplating what he might do to solve the local crime brought him some peace of mind. As Noelle walked on, a plan began to brew about how he might be able to befriend a possible suspect in the first case; the

young priest at Saint Catherine's Cathedral who discove[r]
archbishop's body.

Although the cathedral had been closed to the pu[blic]
Noelle walked in that direction. He moved almost as though his
body were on autopilot as he thought of how he might crack the
young priest and get him to confess. That is, if he could find him.

When Noelle reached the cathedral, there was still
yellow tape barring the entrance, certainly not good publicity for
the Holy Roman Catholic Church. He slipped around to the side
of the cathedral looking for other entrances. As if Noelle had
summoned him with magical powers, a young man wearing a
black priest's frock and a white clerical collar was getting out of
a taxi in front of the clergy residence adjacent to the massive
cathedral. Noelle recognized him as the priest from the photo in
the Times-Picayune.

Noelle walked quickly to reach him. When he
stepped up behind the priest, he startled him. The priest was
understandably jumpy.

"I'm so very sorry to disturb you, Father,"
Noelle apologized.

Now face-to-face, Noelle could see that the priest was
handsome, although worn and troubled by recent events. He
looked no more than thirty at best. Noelle wondered why such a
young, good-looking guy would choose a life of chastity.

Noelle spoke softly, trying to charm Father John. "My
name is Nick Noelle. I didn't mean to frighten you," he said.
"But I was hoping to make your acquaintance. I'm here because
my mother is in the advanced stages of Alzheimer's. I thought
perhaps it would help to talk to a priest."

"Certainly, my son. I'm Father John," he nodded wearily.

On his walk over, Noelle had concocted a good story to
win over the priest. He felt slightly guilty about lying to a man of
the cloth but pressed on anyway.

"Before mom slipped into this last stage, she wrote about
the kind of funeral service she wanted in her will. She mentioned
your church."

Noelle paused.

. n "You see, she was named for Saint Catherine. Since I arri a few days ago, she's mostly been in a coma but occ ally she comes to the surface."

The priest nodded, drawn into Noelle's tall tale.

"It's been difficult sitting with her every day, watching and waiting. I feel like her time could be any moment. I need to be prepared. It will be a difficult loss. Except for my wife, my mother is my only family."

The priest replied, exhausted, "Yes, my son. I'm sorry for your trouble."

"Thank you, Father," Noelle told him, then swooped in for the kill. "Father, I realize you and your church have been besieged by the New Orleans detective squad. I thought you should know that I'm a retired detective from Houston. I have great sympathy for what you're going through."

"I appreciate that, my son," the priest said.

"In my career, I've worked on some very high-profile murders," Noelle told him. "I have first-hand experience with solving serial killer crimes. I'd like to help you out if I could. Off the record, of course. It would be my way of using my skills to be of service and take my mind off my sorrow. I know my mother would be proud of me for doing that."

Father John turned to him, "Mr. Noelle, I appreciate your offer, but I've come to believe that only God can help with this horrendous affair."

Noelle stared into the priest's eyes. "Father, I'm sure the Church would like this to go away sooner rather than later. But the way I see it, there is one very vicious killer out there who could be planning on doing more of the same. I don't know if you've seen the news yet today but it appears as if he's struck another religious institution."

Noelle unfolded the newspaper from under his arm, showing Father John the headline.

"I'd hate to see you become his next victim or any other man of the cloth, for that matter."

After glancing at the paper, Father John looked Noelle in the eye with what the salty ex-detective suspected was mistrust.

"Why are you so interested in these cases?"

Noelle mustered up his warmest smile. "The last big case I solved had the same gruesome style murders. It turned out to be a serial killer's work. My own wife was a victim and would have been killed if I hadn't solved the crime just in the nick of time. It left deep scars on both of us. As a matter of fact, it's a cause of distress in my marriage today. We're still trying to heal."

"Well, Detective, prayer is a wonderful tool. There are many other churches you can attend while we're closed. Is your wife here with you in New Orleans?"

"I wish she was, Father, but she's back in Houston. I'm sure she'll come down for the funeral. Perhaps when Sally gets here, you might be available to counsel us both. Why don't you take the number of my boarding house? If you change your mind about accepting my help, you can always call me there."

Noelle scribbled his number on the back of the newspaper article and tore it off.

Father John took the scrap of paper from Noelle. As he walked toward the entrance of the rectory, the priest noticed that the altar boy's name had been circled twice by Noelle in thick, black ink. Troubled, he turned back to Noelle.

"Detective, I suppose you can't help yourself from trying to solve this horrible crime," he conceded. "I guess it's in your blood. Please, come in. Maybe we can both offer each other counsel."

Noelle followed the priest inside. Father John led him through a long hall to his office. The priest invited Noelle to sit in a chair across the desk from him. He pulled out a pack of Marlboro Reds from the drawer and offered a cigarette to Noelle as he lit one for himself with a solid gold lighter.

Noelle shook his head. "Father, that's one vice I don't have," he said. "But it gives me solace to see that I'm not alone in my unhealthy habits. If a priest can smoke, it alleviates some of my own guilty pleasures."

Father John took a deep drag on the Marlboro.

"Mr. Noelle, I don't know what religion you are, but you should try confession sometime. It does wonders for clearing a guilty conscience."

Noelle knew he was winning over the priest. He took note of Father John's very large hands and thought that perhaps this priest might possess the strength to perform the crimes in question. Except Noelle's gut told him that this gentle soul didn't have the stomach for such bloodlust. That is, until he remembered how he'd also thought Pamela was an innocent. However, she turned out to be the most inhumane murderer he'd ever encountered in all his years as a detective. Noelle knew he'd lost his professional barometer and couldn't trust his instincts anymore.

The priest smiled for a millisecond; it morphed into a grimace. "I've never seen anything so horrible in all my life," he recalled. "I don't think even our Lord Christ suffered as much on the cross as our archbishop did in his death. I must admit, Detective, it has shaken my faith."

Noelle worked on his poker face and made an attempt to sound casual but curious. "Is it true what the press said about the altar boy...that he was dressed in a fancy diaper covered in blood? They say he might have been a witness but that he's too traumatized to talk."

Father John's face went from pale to blush.

"The diaper was part of a costume of Jesus as the Infant of Prague."

Noelle admitted, "I'm not Catholic, Father, so I don't understand the religious symbolism of a get-up like that.

The priest's face turned from pink to red.

"The archbishop had been auditioning the youngest boys to see who could fit into the costume," he tried to explain. "It was a relic from ancient times and our cathedral was in possession of the costume. We rarely used it. The costume was used when an archbishop recreated the ritual."

He paused, noting Noelle's perplexed expression.

"I know it sounds weird but we Catholics are famous for our outlandish outfits. Just look at how the Pope and the Cardinals of the Church dress."

Noelle rubbed his smooth chin like he had a beard, as though this gesture might give off an intellectual air. "Oh yes, I've seen his ruby-red slippers," Noelle agreed. "So, you're telling me that the killer wasn't the one who dressed the boy. Does that mean the archbishop could have dressed the boy up like that?"

Father John crushed out his cigarette in a cut-glass ashtray, gulped a breath of air and spoke.

"I supposed he helped Matthew put on the costume. The boy is deaf and dumb and the archbishop knew how to sign, as do I."

Noelle kept on. "And what about Mrs. Murphy, the cleaning lady? Wasn't she with you when you found the body?"

The priest answered tensely, "How do you know I'm the priest who found the body?"

Noelle quickly covered his tracks. "Oh, I just assumed you were, Father John. The press reported that it was a young priest."

Satisfied with Noelle response, Father John continued.

"The housekeeper thought something was wrong when earlier that day the archbishop told her that he would be holding auditions for the Infant of Prague. Mrs. Murphy assumed he might have shown the boy the church gravesite where the other archbishops were at rest, along with the costume and other relics kept in the crypt. Mrs. Murphy would never question the archbishop, although she confided in me that lately she thought he was losing his good judgment. She had known him for many years. He had been a parish priest here when she was just a young girl, long before he was elevated to archbishop."

Noelle nodded and asked, "So, the cleaning lady thought the archbishop wasn't in his right mind?"

Father John's face went white again. "I didn't say that. She suspected a bit of senility could be setting in. I also noticed that some of the altar boys seemed to hide whenever the archbishop led a Mass."

Noelle questioned, "So, how did you come to find the body?"

Father John looked tortured as he recalled:

"I walked out to the altar, preparing for the evening Mass and saw Matthew with a rag stuffed in his mouth. He was wrapped in blood-soaked, gold vestments. The boy was unconscious, thank God, but breathing deeply. I took the rag out of his mouth but didn't try to wake him. I didn't want him to see all the blood on and around him. Mrs. Murphy came into church early to pray before Mass and saw me at the altar fretting over poor, little Matthew. She noticed that there were drops of blood leading to the basement door. That's when she remembered what the archbishop had told her about the sacred vestments for the Infant of Prague Ceremony in the crypt. They're kept in a chest behind the vaulted graves."

Noelle remarked, "Father, if you're looking for converts to the Church, this story doesn't make Catholicism look too appealing."

Ignoring Noelle's wry comment, the priest lit another cigarette. Looking as though he might cry, he took a long drag and exhaled the words, "I left Matthew in Mrs. Murphy's arms and ran downstairs. How I found the archbishop is too difficult to describe." The priest put his head between his hands, trembling.

Noelle said, "If it's too much, we can stop, Father. But please, tell me one thing: did the archbishop have any enemies? Perhaps an altar boy who had grown up in the parish? Someone with a reason to hold a grudge against the old priest?"

Father John shook his head. "No one that I could think of. But you might want to ask Mrs. Murphy. She knew him better than I did."

Father John glanced at his wristwatch. "It's getting late, Mr. Noelle. I have to be up early to bring Holy Communion to the shut-ins and infirmed at some of our Catholic hospices. Is your mother at Saint Mary's, by any chance?"

"Why, yes," Noelle told him. "Perhaps you've met her." "Perhaps I have," Father John answered. "I don't know most of their names but Sister Theresa, who works with the most advanced patients, is an old friend."

"That's good to know," Noelle said. "She's my mother's caregiver and from what I can see, a real angel."

"Yes, that's our Sister Theresa," Father John smiled in reflection.

Noelle knew that he'd just added to the priest's worries but he'd also managed to cull a great deal of new information about the case. He hoped he wouldn't get caught in the lie he'd just spun for the priest about his reason for being there.

Noelle stood. He paused before he spoke again.

"Can you think of anyone, like a handyman or a church member, who knew where the archbishops were buried?"

"Everyone knew the archbishops were buried in the basement," Father John answered. "It's common knowledge within the congregation. Once a year, on All Souls' Day, we invite our members to view the relics and the graves of the deceased archbishops."

"I'll leave you in peace, Father."

Noelle started toward the door then turned back to the priest.

"One last question. Is there any chance I could meet the boy?"

Father John's icy stare pierced Noelle's eyes. "Matthew doesn't remember a thing," he told Noelle firmly. "He doesn't even remember dressing in the costume. Even the detectives on the case haven't been given the okay to question the boy. Matthew Hannigan's parents just want him to forget the whole thing. I can't say that I blame them."

"I get it. I really do. But what if the killer decides that the boy is a risk and comes back to take care of him, too?"

Father John's tear-filled eyes grew wide with fear. "I'll talk to them again and let you know."

Father John walked Noelle to the door. "I hope to meet your wife one day soon. God bless you, Detective Noelle."

"Thank you, Father John," Noelle told him. "I look forward to our next meeting."

Noelle left with a newfound sense of hope. A frightened Father John locked the door behind him.

Chapter Fourteen

Missing Sally

By the time Noelle reached his boarding house, he was drained. Even though it was late, he picked up the phone. He plopped onto the bed, almost drifting off as his home telephone rang over and over again. He wondered where Sally could be that late, two nights in a row. Noelle hung up and called again, just in case he'd dialed a wrong number. His impatience built to anger after a dozen rings.

Noelle shouted into the receiver, "Where the fuck are you, Sally?!" then slammed it down.

As much as he wanted to believe in the new improved, recovered Sally, his mind dragged him back to the worst thoughts possible. Noelle imagined Sally shooting drugs and turning tricks on the dirty downtown Houston streets where he first met her. He had seen too much to trust that people could ever really change. If Sally had gone back to the streets, he blamed himself entirely for taking her for granted.

Noelle's mind tortured him with grotesque images of what Sally had endured because of his sick obsession with Pamela, let alone the mess he'd dragged her into just less than a year ago!

What Noelle worried about was partially true. Sally was out late in one of Houston's more dangerous neighborhoods and she *was* working among the ladies of the night, but not in the way Noelle feared. What Noelle didn't know was that Sally had found religion, and along with that, her desire to stay sober strengthened. She had decided to fill her empty nights by volunteering at a suicide prevention call center. There, she used her past experiences as a junkie and a prostitute to connect with the young women who were at risk in the streets.

After Sally's first Sunday service with the Lopez family, she had met privately with Father Bruce. She trusted the young priest who had celebrated her first Mass. She was anxious to discuss the possibility of joining Saint Cyril's. He was so warm and welcoming. In that short meeting, Sally made the decision to convert to Catholicism.

Sally made a full confession and shared her entire life story with the priest, including her years of prostitution and drug addiction. She shared her deepest darkest secrets. Secrets she even kept from her own husband about the sexual abuse she suffered at the hands of both her parents.

It was Father Bruce who suggested that Sally's penance could be charity work with other prostitutes. She left her first confession with a new resolve to volunteer at the call center. She even applied for a full-time job at a home for battered women.

Within less than a week, Sally went from being a bored, dependent housewife to a liberated working woman. She hadn't decided what to do about her marriage, but she was grateful for the much-needed break from Noelle's toxic hold over her. Her spiritual awakening brought with it the gift of clarity. For the first time in her life, Sally finally had the resolve to care for herself.

The next day Noelle woke up wishing for a way to escape life as he knew it. He was split down the middle between his responsibilities to his mother and his wife and his new obsession with the "Holy Roller Murders," as the papers labeled them. Noelle drained the last few sips of Jack from the bottle at his bedside. He stood and dragged his aching carcass into the shower while avoiding the mirror above the sink.

When he arrived at Saint Mary's, Noelle found a note on the top of the pile of his mother's journals.

Sister Theresa had written that Catherine had actually been awake for almost thirty minutes that morning and that she kept calling for Brandon. The note just added to Noelle's misery.

Noelle bent over the bed and kissed his mother's forehead. He made himself comfortable in his favorite chair, opened the next diary and read.

Lord, I don't how much longer I can hold out working for the creepy Reverend. Today, when it started drizzlin' I heard a creak, looked up and saw his big, fat, red face behind the screen door, watching me. Folks say he got the gout that's why his face look so ugly. Serves him right for gorgin' himself on all those free dinners he be gettin!

The Reverend be milkin' them poor, especially my dumb daddy who gives him everything. Even me, to tend his garden for free. The Reverend has been nothing but a menace. I saw him gawk at me, like he do at the sweet buns I bake for prayer group every week.

When I see his false teeth chompin' down on 'em like they is his last supper and the sticky crumbs fallin' down his chin, it make me so sick to my stomach that I can't even enjoy my own sweet buns anymore.

Today, he had just come from lunch when he said, "Better get all that weedin' done before the rain come down hard." His eyes looked oily as he watched me kneelin' on the damp earth. I just turned back to the garden, doin' my best to ignore him. I heard the porch door shut and the porch swing creakin.'

This time, when I turned around, I see the Reverend's wide girth just a rockin', himself on the porch swing. It was downright ridiculous. The only pleasure I got from seeing that sight was thinkin' that the old swing just might break and he might fall on his fat ass. My mind got carried away and I even imagined that he could break through the porch floor and put a hole in the earth so large that the weight of his body could propel him straight down to hell. But that didn't happen. Instead, he just sat there a swingin' and a watchin' me doin' the weedin.' Then the drizzle turn to a steady rain and the Reverend got up and went inside. But that old swing kept on a rockin' all on its own. It give me an eerie feelin'.

Next thing, I hear a crack a thunder like nothin' I ever hear before. Somethin' like Noah must a heard when he gathered up all those animals before the big flood. Sure enough, the rains pour down with a vengeance.

I made a dash for the porch and Mary, the Reverend's wife, opened the door, looked me up and down, and said, "You better get home girl and change those wet clothes. I can see right through 'em."

Then her withered, old self just turned away and closed the door on me in the pourin' rain. I thought Christians' supposed to be charitable.

The rain came harder and I started to run toward home. The lighten struck just behind me as I passed through the gate. I feared for my life so I ducked into the big barn the Reverend built with the blood money of his flock. I was too wet and cold out there and feared to git hit by lighten.

Next thing I know, I'm sittin there shiverin and I felt some presence behind me. When I looked around, there he stood like he had been a waitin' on me. The Reverend's eyes were dark and scary. When I move in the opposite direction of where he was lurkin', he swung around to block my way and pinned me in a corner.

The Reverend put his hand under my chin, drawing my face close to his and said very quietly, "Have you given all of yourself this day to the Lord?"

Before I could answer, he grab my shoulders, looked down toward my chest where he fixed his eyes through my soaked clothes, and said, "I mean everything!"

When he touched my clingin' shirt, I pushed him hard and screamed for him to stop but he only pulled me closer. He stuffed his hand down the band around my waist. When I lifted my knee straight up to his crotch, that old Reverend doubled over in pain, crying, "You're the Devil, worse than Eve!"

While he was crouched there moaning, I yelled, "Yeah, and don't suppose you is Adam; you is the snake. You is Satan." Then I run like hell!

By the time I was through the gate and halfway across the road, I heard a car horn, the screech of wheels and the sound of a familiar voice at my back. God, I knew it was him even before I heard him yell, "You trying to get drowned or kill yourself by lighten, girl?"

As I got in Justin's car, I took a quick look back at the barn, and sure enough I see the Reverend. I ducked down out of sight before he could see me. I was shakin' from the cold and out of breath from running but I felt calm when Justin said, "What'd he do to you?" I told Justin to drive out of there, and fast.

Justin laughed and put his foot on the gas. The car sped down the road and flew over a bump. I jerked and hit my head on the roof. Then I thought this reckless drivin' might just kill me even if the lighten and the Reverend don't. I asked Justin to please slow down once we was far away from the church.

He pulled over to a side road. The car wavered and grind over the dirt. He put his foot on the brake just before we hit a tree. When I started shakin' again, Justin said, "What's the matter with you? What happened?"

I just sat there shiverin'. Justin moved close to me and put his strong arms around me to stop the shakin.'

"Come on, baby. It's alright. You're safe now," he whispered. Justin held me like the time before when I was wet and cold under the full moon. Then he said, "You better get out of them wet clothes."

God, I just let him undress me right there in the front seat of his car! When Justin took off my shirt, he saw that torn sheet wrapped tight across my chest that Daddy made me ware to cover my breasts. Justin looked shocked as he unpinned it and peeled it away, especially when he saw the red welt it had left on my ribs from all the years I had worn it.

As his hands freed my large breasts, I felt shame and covered my chest with my arms. Justin gently moved my arms away and held my breasts in his hands like they was precious fruit. Then he slowly sucked on each one of my nipples like a baby. I had never before felt such a wonderful sensation.

Next, Justin took off his warm, woolen scarf and wrapped it around my neck to warm me. He held me tighter while slipping off his thick jacket. He draped it over my shoulders and back to make me even more comfortable. Then Justin kissed me all over and said, "Honey, whatever that old bastard done to you, I won't let him hurt you again."

When Justin kissed my mouth, I melted into his and my breath started to come faster. I was startin' to feel so good that it almost erased the horror and fright of what the Reverend almost do to me. There Justin was again at the right time and place to save me. In that moment, I made Justin Morgan my Savior. I was ready to surrender my all to him. And yes, I did. Again. And this time was even better than that first time.

As Justin straddled me covering my nakedness with his warm body, I looked deep into his eyes and made an eternal vow. 'God, I'll do anything for him...yes, anything.'

Noelle gazed down at his mother with conflicting emotions: pity, shock, remorse. Suddenly, Catherine's eyes snapped open. She whispered in a leathery voice.

"Nick...find Brandon."

Noelle took his mother's hand, desperate, confused and frustrated. Gently, he asked, "Do you mean Justin, your first sweetheart?"

His mother's eyes closed as she drifted back to her other world. Sister Theresa entered the room and asked, "Nick, any new light on your mama's past?"

Noelle smirked, "Just more teen love...and lust. If Mom outlives these romance novels she left me, I'll be ready to take *you* on."

Sister Theresa's brown skin flushed red. Noelle fumbled to take his foot out of his mouth and stammered, "What I meant was, I'll be ready to hear your life story next."

Swiftly changing the subject, Sister Theresa asked, "Nick, where's your wife? Don't you think your mama would like to meet her before she dies?"

"Sister, that's another long, complicated mystery I need to solve. But I'll save it for another day when we both have time to swap stories."

Noelle kissed his mother's cheek, said goodbye and made a hasty exit.

Outside Saint Mary's, he decided to use the pay phone; this time to call Juan Lopez. Noelle dialed Houston Homicide. After two rings, he heard, "Detective Lopez here."

Noelle chuckled, "Jesus! Lopez, you still sound like the Mexican Dudley Do-Right."

"Boss, it's good to hear your crusty, old voice," Lopez cried. "What's dragged you out of hell to reach out to me?"

"I have a new case for you to solve. Do you have any idea where the fuck my wife is?"

Lopez changed the subject. "How is it going with your mother?"

"She's taking her time to die," Noelle told him. "Sally's not answering the phone. I think it's to get back at me for not taking her with me to New Orleans. Has Maria said anything to you? You know how these dames stick together when they want to stick it to us."

Lopez hesitated. "Well… I can't say I know about that."

"I'm getting worried. Can you help a buddy out?" Noelle pleaded.

Lopez paused. "I don't know much. Maria won't tell me anything that Sally confides in her. Especially if it's anything about you. I haven't seen Sally since the morning after you left when she came to Saint Cyril's with us. Sometimes I overhear Maria when she's on the phone with Sally, though. I gathered that your wife had a real epiphany at church and that she's been meeting with our priest. I think Sally's becoming a Catholic."

"A Catholic, Jesus H. Christ!" Noelle snapped. "Lopez, please ask Maria to have Sally call me. She's never home when I try, even late at night. I can't imagine that the churches stay open 'till after midnight. It's not Halloween yet, let alone Christmas."

"I think Father Bruce suggested she do some volunteer work at a women's shelter. She's probably working the night shift. I wouldn't worry. But I'll check it out, Buddy, and give you a call."

"Thanks, Lopez," Noelle sighed. "I would appreciate that. I got my hands full with my mother. Oh, and you'll be happy to know that I have a new friend, too. My wife's not the only one meeting with a Catholic priest. Although my priest is the one who found the murdered archbishop at Saint Catherine's Cathedral. I'm sure you heard about it."

Lopez perked up. "Yeah, this is as big as our last case. I've been following it in the papers. Now there's some Baptist minister too. What are you doing down there? Dabbling in some armchair crime solving?"

Noelle snickered, "Something like that."

"Well, stay out of trouble, Boss," Lopez told him. "We miss you on the force. You know, Nick, no one here can surpass you."

"Lopez, you're too modest. You're doing just fine without me."

"I'll keep an eye on your wife, but now I've got to get back to mine. Maria is due in less than two months. I promised to meet her at Houston Houseworks. I need to do some baby proofing around the house. Dolores will be going off to college next year and here we are starting all over again with the new baby."

Noelle nodded. "There are big changes everywhere… well, I don't want you to keep the old ball and chain waiting." Noelle laughed, "Just kidding! I should have taken marriage tips from you, buddy, before I got Sally all pissed off at me. Give my best to the family."

Noelle hung up the phone filled with mixed emotions. He was not too happy his wife had found religion but relieved to know that at least she wasn't living out his worst fears. Or was she?

Chapter Fifteen

More Shall be Revealed

Sister Theresa inserted a tube directly into an open port in Catherine's stomach. Noelle stood back, watching the liquid mush run through the large hose and into his mother's body. It made him queasier than any crime scene he'd ever witnessed.

"Sister, that is one gnarly job," Noelle told the nun. He knew he didn't have the guts for it. Nick Noelle was a lot of things but he was no saint.

Just seeing Sister Theresa's wide, lovely smile as she patiently performed these acts of mercy for his mother made him feel terribly guilty. The nun smiled again, this time at him.

"Detective, it is my calling to tend to the sick," she told him simply. "Just as yours was to catch murderers. How are you today? You look troubled."

"My wife's not answering my calls," Noelle stammered. "I think maybe she's had it with me."

The nun stared up at him beatifically.

"Before you start jumping to conclusions, there might be more to it."

"Oh, there's more to it all right. You couldn't imagine the half of it," Noelle snapped.

"Maybe I could. I'm still a woman underneath this drab habit. I know how my gender thinks. Try me."

Her accidental innuendo made the nun redden but Noelle ignored her unintentional comment.

"Sister, you'll be happy to know that my wife has found religion. Now she's a working woman, working day and night for God, I suspect. Just like you. I need my wife back, not some saint."

A stern look came over Sister Theresa. "Nick, you should try taking your troubles to God; it wouldn't kill you to open your mind a bit. With God lies the answer to our biggest mysteries. Or at least that has been my experience."

Noelle plopped down onto the other chair beside his mother's bed. "It's easy to understand how someone like you can have a strong faith, Sister. But my wife has another story... and I'm damn well sure the Lord gave up on me ages ago! From what I've been reading in my mom's diary, let's just say, the apple doesn't fall far from the tree."

Sister Theresa finished cleaning up after her chore. Her eyes shimmering with faith, she replied, "I know another saying: 'Scratch a sinner and you'll find a saint.'"

Noelle laughed, "So you're trying to say there is hope for me?"

Sister Theresa moved toward the door then turned around to face him. She winked.

"You're off the hook for now. I have other patients to feed."

As she stepped into the hallway, she added, "Oh, Detective, Father John was in today. He told me all about how you shared your mother's wishes for her memorial at Saint Catherine's with him." The nun winked again. "Don't worry, I didn't suggest that I knew anything different," she assured him.

Sister Theresa rushed down the hall, leaving Noelle to ponder his many deceits to himself as well as others. He wondered if his mother had finally found that peace Sister Theresa spoke about. He stared down at the frail woman in bed and watched her breathing shallowly. He picked up the third diary, glad Sister Theresa had the good sense to number them.

He wondered if she'd read any of them. The way the nun went on about his mother, it seemed Sister Theresa knew more than she was telling.

Noelle hadn't had his morning dose of alcohol. His hands trembled as he carefully parted the pages, concerned about causing more harm to the brittle notebook paper. He started reading:

God, I ain't seen the Morgan boy and my heart been achin somethin' awful.

The day after the storm, the Reverend sent word to Daddy with a side of pork to thank him for loanin' me out to the church, and he wouldn't be needin' me for a spell.

Only You and me know why he really sent that pork—to appease his guilty conscience for what he tried to do to me. But my daddy thought it was just for the good works I done. Daddy was mighty grateful to the Reverend for his gift and he get to take the credit for it since he think he own me. I wanted so bad to tell him the truth but. And even if he believe me, he would just say it were my fault, that I musta tempted the Reverend.

After supper, I got this awful nausea feelin' again. It's been happenin a lot lately. I'm prayin' cause I ain't had my ladies' time and that's got me real scared. I know Justin love me since he told me, so if what I'm fearin' is true then he will take me away from Daddy's house and do the right thing. That's if he knew.

When he left me off after the storm, he leaned in to kiss me and said he might be goin' down to New Orleans for business. After one long, sweet kiss, he said, "Girl, you were put here in this place in time just for me."

Since I ain't seen him since, I'm fearin' maybe he had to go do more flyin' since the war ain't' over yet. God, I don't know what I do if something bad happen to him. It's been more than a month and I ain't heard no gossip even from Miss Kirkwood or anything about his family either.

I ain't ever been in the Morgan house but I'm thinking I just might go over the other side of the fence one of these days. I was thinkin' all kinds of ways to get in there. Pretend I was looking for a service job or some such thing, to see what I could find out about Justin.

Today Daddy said something that got me thinkin' he's suspicious. While we was eating supper, he looked at me funny and said, "What's wrong with you, girl? You used to work twice as hard and ate half as much."

I put down my fork and put the extra pork chop back on the serving plate. Next, Daddy said, "In no time, you'll be out of the school and then I'll get some real help around here. Ya need to mend them clothes, child. You bustin' out of 'em. Now clean up this mess and don't eat all of Tuesday's pie jes' cause ya fixed another one for tomorrow. The Reverend and Mrs. Mary is comin' for supper tomorrow and we need it."

When Daddy left and I stood up to take the dirty dishes to the sink, my stomach almost come back up in my mouth. I ran upstairs to the washroom and missed the toilet. My supper was all over the back of the seat, down my blouse and on the floor. I sat and cried for the first time since Mama died.

As I was bendin' over weepin' and wipin' the toilet and floor, I was thinking I had to face Justin and make him take responsibility, before everyone be noticing my belly growin.' I quick-tailed it into my room and reach under my bed for the old, battered suitcase that Mama left me. I felt my heart beatin' and my hands tremblin' but I calm myself with good thoughts of Justin. 'He'll marry me...' I told myself. 'I know it! No more lying, no more sinnin'...I'll be able to love him and nobody will be able to say Jack Rat for any of it!'

I got myself so worked up as I rushed to get out of there before Daddy got home. I rummaged through my clothes to find just the right skirt and the prettiest blouse I had. I threw the rest of my rags, along with Mama's Bible, into the suitcase and hightailed it out of my daddy's house for what I hoped would be forever.

As I walked to the Morgan house, I was no longer feelin' the sickness in my stomach but I was nervous. The house was bigger than any building I'd ever seen, all white with huge pillars and everything.

God, I wondered how long it would take to walk from room to room in a house so grand. Even though I was trembling, I tiptoed around the side to peek some more at it. But then I tore my skirt on a rose bush. I thought I heard music and laughin' comin' from inside as I made my way around to the back. Something in my gut started to rumble and I wished I hadn't come.

In the back of the house, I could see the kitchen was all lit up. The rear door was open so that the light from inside shone through the screen. My heart was thumpin' so loud, I feared they could hear it as I quietly pushed the screen door. Radio music was blaring from down a long hallway. I walk toward the sound and that's when I heard a woman laughing. Right after, I hear Justin's voice say, "So, I told my buddy to get down, and WHAM a Sopwith Camel swung by like an avenging angel and nailed the Kraut bastards!"

The woman's laughter was like little bells tinkling. I didn't know how I managed to get the courage to go up to the door and knock. But I did, even though I was filled with terror, thinking I am a pitiful wreck.

I mustered up my courage and opened the door when no one answered my knock. Justin turned his head and looked dumbstruck when he caught sight of me. A woman with long, black hair and long, silky legs dangling over the chair spoke up as her clinking gold bracelets chimed.

"You got a visitor, Honey-Love," she said. Then she took a sip of her drink and laughed that tinkle laugh again.

Justin smiled a sheepish grin at the lovely lady as she gave him an odd look. Then she stared real curious at me. I looked down, ashamed at my clothes and the rip in my skirt. Justin swigged the drink in his hand. The ice cubes clattered like old bones in his glass. The sound of it was chillin'. I felt a stab go through my heart and straight down to my stomach.

I turned quick and started to run back down the hallway. As I tried to make it out the screen door, I tripped over a fancy table. I heard steps on the hardwood floor and Justin's voice at my back, commanding me, "Wait!" He caught up to me and turned me round to face him. He still had his drink in his hand.

He took a big gulp and said, "Ah, Cathy, c'mon. Tell me why you're here."

"I needed to know where you been and why I ain't seen you. Now I got my answer."

"It's not safe for you to come here. You know that. Where's your ol' daddy anyway?"

"Choir practice," I mumbled.

Justin smirked. "And why are you not there with him like a good girl? With your daddy and your crazy reverend friend?"

"And who is your friend? Who is she, Justin? I asked." Justin began to laugh a cruel laugh. "That's none of your business. I can't believe I'm being interrogated by a 15-year-old red dust farm girl."

I was shocked by his snotty air. "You never used to say mean things. I thought you loved me."

Justin touched my chin. "You used to be a sweet child, Cathy."

I blurted out, "Justin, I ain't no child and you're going to be a daddy. You got to marry me."

Justin looked more frozen than the ice cubes in his drink. He gulped the rest of it down and started to laugh. "Then you're old enough to know that lust got nothing to do with love, and marriage."

My stomach started turning sour. I took my fists and started pounding his big, hard chest. "You gotta marry me. What will I do? My daddy will kill me."

Justin stood rigid and looked like the Devil himself. The same Devil he joked about that night I made him my Savior.

Justin roared at me, "For all I know, that old Reverend, or maybe even your own Daddy done you. It's your problem and there ain't nothing I can do about it. So don't even try to put the blame on me. Folks will just laugh at you, girl, knowing a man like me, a war hero would never touch the likes of a dirt farm daughter like you." When I begin punching him more, Justin yelled, "How ridiculous you are…us getting married!" And he laughed that mean-hearted laugh again.

I tried not to look into his black vacant eyes. Then I heard the dark-haired woman's delicate voice behind me. "Oh, not another one, Justin," she sighed. "It's a good thing you going to inherit your daddy's money to pay off all those little girls...I thought you learned your lesson after that dishonorable discharge?"

I took one last look at evil personified and ran out of there, out into the night.

As I ran, I could hear the woman's tinkling laughter and her saying, "Now what was that little gal's name?"

As I bolted through the bushes that hung over the creek, a tree branch whip me in the face. I wanted to die. I didn't care what time it was or if Daddy was home yet. I didn't care about nothin'.

When I reached the edge of the field, I could see the light on in the kitchen and when I opened the door, Daddy was standing there by the sink with the Bible in his hands. He snapped at me, "Where you been, girl?"

When he saw my torn skirt and the blood on my cheek, he let out a cry of disgust, "I knows where ya been. Out sinnin' again but you can't hide it anymore. Your sin been showin' all over you!" I said nothing, just cowered in front of him.

Daddy screamed, "You don't think I know. Well, I knows. Ain't no sinner gonna marry ya either. So ya come on back heah thinkin' I'll jes take ya in."

Then Daddy sat down with his Bible and said, "Ah been knowin' fer some time, so I went to the Reverend's and we decided that ya gonna marry Ezekiel Garsett. Ezekiel's willin' to take ya bastard and discipline yore willful ways."

I looked Daddy dead in the eye and with my new-found courage said, "You cain't make me marry that old man."

Then Daddy grabbed me by the shoulders and hollered, "Yes I can, girl, or I put you in that grave next to your Mama if'n you don't. I ain't gonna feed you and that bastard. Your suitcase is already packed so best you keep on goin! I want you out of heah! First thing in the mornin, Reverend and Ezekiel be waitin on you at the church."

*Daddy turned away and went up to bed. I done somethin'
awful after that. I took Mama's precious Bible from my suitcase
and I threw it against the wall. I don't know why. I suppose the
Devil made me do it.*

Noelle choked up and slammed the notebook down on
the table beside his chair. He finally understood everything–
his mother's prostitution and why she had cursed those TV
preachers. What a terrible life she'd had!

Just then, Sister Theresa returned. She found Noelle with
his head in his hands. When he sensed her standing there, Noelle
lashed out, "Do you know your God deserted my mother when
she needed Him most?"

"I'm sorry for your pain, Nick, but if I..."

"I don't want to hear it," Noelle cut her off. He sprung
up and cried, "Don't worry, Sister, I'll be back tomorrow for
more punishment. That is if it's God's will, as you holy folk like
to say."

Noelle let out a sardonic laugh and darted down
the stairs. 'Damn!' he thought, 'I'm pissed at a God that doesn't
even exist!'

He headed to the closest liquor store to quell his rage.

Chapter Sixteen

Barefoot and Pregnant

Back in Houston, Sally was finishing her first week at her new job. Feeling proud of herself for a productive start, she cleared her desk at the women's shelter, grabbed her big, straw purse and made her way to the elevator. Just as the elevator door opened, Sally bolted in the opposite direction and ran into the woman's bathroom.

Over the toilet, Sally vomited the full contents of her stomach. This was the second day in a row she had been overtaken by a wave of nausea, ending with her head over the bowl.

She had no other flu-like symptoms, only this strong urge to vomit. Sally washed her face and sat on the small sofa in the woman's restroom. She was caught off guard when tears filled her eyes. She was confused about why she was overrun with emotion. Despite all of the horrible things that had happened in her life, Sally had a strong constitution. She hardly ever got sick. True, she cried easily over her feelings for Nick, but these tears were different.

When she put her feet up on the sofa to relax, it suddenly dawned on Sally that perhaps the miracle she had been praying for could finally be happening. She went back to her desk and made a call to the family planning clinic.

If her suspicions were right about Nick—that he was drinking and gambling again—she feared the worst for any child the two of them would bring into the world. Yet Sally wanted a baby more than anything. But did she still want Nick? If this had happened in her past, she would have had no hesitation and hitchhiked straight to Mexico for an abortion. Sally knew in spite of Nick's affliction, it was most likely her last chance to become a mother and if she were pregnant, she knew as a Catholic, killing this gift from God was unthinkable.

Sally needed guidance now more than ever. She knew Father Bruce was the one person she could confide in. He would keep her secret, even from Maria, who might not be able to keep it from Juan. Juan would never be able to keep this news from Nick. The last thing Sally wanted was for her husband to find out before she sorted out her feelings.

Chapter Seventeen

Getting Down to Business

Noelle showered and shaved before he headed out for more recreational gambling. Just as he reached the door, his telephone rang. When he picked up the phone, it was Father John with good news. "Matthew's parents agreed to let us talk to their son," he said. "But only if we can get over there in the next hour, before Matthew's dinner and bedtime."

Noelle forgot all about Lucky Pierre's for the moment and bolted up the stairs to the main floor. He slipped past Velda, who was at the counter, collecting rent from one of her unusual suspects. Noelle hurried toward the exit, hoping to avoid one of his landlady's typically intrusive conversations. Velda loved to discuss the local murders with him but Noelle wasn't in the mood for her trash talk. He didn't have the time for it.

Almost in the clear, he cursed silently when he saw Fletcher standing in the doorway, holding it open for him. It was just Noelle's bad luck to be going out at the same time. Fletcher smiled as Noelle thanked him and rushed through the door. Fletcher caught up and attempted to make small talk. "On an urgent mission, Detective?" he wondered.

Not wanting to reveal his hand, Noelle shrugged, "No, not really. Just the same old same old: a visit with my mother before her bedtime and then some dinner later in the Quarter."

Fletcher replied, "Do allow me to make some suggestions. The list for great meals is endless. For a sure thing, there's always Brennan's. They've been around since the nineteen forties. It's over on Royal Street, a robust walk from here. Brennan's has that wonderful turtle soup. Or if you have plans to get frisky after dinner, I highly recommend the oyster soup. Best to save that option for when you're wife arrives. But either choice will not disappoint."

Fletcher wasn't done; he took a breath and continued his impromptu restaurant review. "For a main course, their gumbo is divine with that marvelous Poche's andouille sausage. Or, if you're fond of organ meats, the pan-roasted veal sweetbreads with the truffle grits and sherry bacon is just to die for!"

Noelle smiled and said nothing. Anxious to rid himself of Fletcher, he quickened his pace. Undaunted, the older gent managed to keep up with Noelle. Fletcher smiled as he kept on talking. "I like to think I know a bit about fine dining," he admitted. "I'm a decent chef, if I do say so myself. I wish you had time to accept my dinner invitation. I don't often invite guests for a home-cooked meal but your profession intrigues me, Detective. I was wondering if you've been helping our local police with their mounting bodies in the morgue."

Noelle quickened his pace even more. "You forget, I'm retired. My wife would divorce me if she caught me getting close to any new murder investigations."

Fletcher finally got the hint that Noelle was in a rush and wound down the conversation.

"Well, I'll leave you to your evening constitution. Perhaps after your mother's passing you'll be in need of good Southern home cooking to soothe your grief," he conceded.

"Thanks," Noelle nodded. He turned the corner and headed in the direction of his Ford.

Swiveling back, Noelle noticed Fletcher waving his arms wildly, like the pansy he was, in an attempt to hail a cab. He couldn't believe the queer actually had the nerve to keep trying to get him up to his place for a date. 'Some chance of that ever happening,' Noelle thought as he jumped into his truck.

When he arrived at Saint Catherine's, Father John was waiting outside. The priest hopped in and gave Noelle an address in the Garden District. It was an upscale neighborhood not far from where they were.

The priest fidgeted as Noelle drove. He was relaxed for the first time in days. That fifth of Jack Daniel's he'd downed before he left his room burned warmly inside of him. Noelle was surprised he felt confident and happy. He suspected it had to do with the fact that he was on his way to question an eyewitness to a murder. This was something he deeply understood and was good at, even though interviewing a child wasn't one of his favorite tasks.

Noelle took note of Father John's anxiety and suspected the priest feared the detective might uncover something the Church didn't want anyone to know.

When they arrived at the boy's home, Noelle parked his truck in front of the sprawling house. The front door opened and a handsome young couple stepped out onto the porch. Noelle and Father John walked along the winding stone pathway and crossed the big, lush lawn. Beautiful, colorful flowers lined the path to the Hannigans' doorway. The couple greeted Father John with extended arms—they must have known the priest rather well, Noelle surmised.

"Welcome," the woman said. "We are so honored to have you visit our home."

'Obviously the Hannigans were good Catholics and rich ones too', Noelle figured.

Father John hugged Mrs. Hannigan. "Margaret, I'm so sorry it has to be under these unfortunate circumstances," he told her. "This is the retired detective from the Houston Police Force I told you about: Detective Nick Noelle."

Mr. and Mrs. Hannigan turned to Noelle and welcomed him almost as warmly as they had their priest. The boy's father introduced himself as Paul and said, "Matthew is waiting in the game room. We don't want to make this a serious discussion, so perhaps you could join him in a game. Our son is quite bright for his age. He's already learning how to play chess. Can you believe it?"

Noelle responded, "Well, it's not my best game but I'll give it a shot."

Mrs. Hannigan asked Noelle, "What games do you prefer? We have checkers and Monopoly, too."

Noelle laughed, "I don't suppose your boy knows poker."

"Not yet," she admitted, laughing.

Noelle and Father John followed the Hannigans through the well-appointed hallway. Noelle hadn't been in a home this sumptuous since his investigation of the Debutante Murders.

As they made their way down the long hallway, Noelle's eyes popped at the lavish art and gorgeous tapestries lining the walls. He counted five doors that led to other rooms on the first floor. One of the doors was cracked open. Noelle took stock of the library filled with leather-bound books stacked high on mahogany shelves. He practically drooled when he saw the bar at the back. 'Books and bar...nice...a great place to 'get lit,' he thought.

His smile widened as he again recalled the Jack he'd left unfinished at home. Yes, the Hannigan home was very grand. Noelle and Father John followed the Hannigans down a few steps that led to a very large family room.

In the middle of the room sat Matthew. He was a handsome, golden-haired, seven-year-old boy playing a card game by himself. Noelle noted how excited the child was to see Father John.

Matthew ran over to the priest and threw his arms around him in an affectionate hug. Noelle couldn't help feeling suspicious of the priest. After all, Father John seemed to know Matthew a bit too intimately.

When the boy looked up at Noelle, there was hesitation in the child's eyes. His dad signed to Matthew to explain who this stranger was.

"This is Nick, a good man who wants to play a game and maybe ask you some questions, too," Paul Hannigan signed as he spoke.

Noelle sat on his haunches in front of the child. He introduced himself by amiably holding out his hand for a handshake. "I'm Detective Noelle," he said slowly. Then added, "Hey, I'm pretty good at cards. How about you?"

Noelle had been told to speak slowly so the boy could read his lips. Matthew, who was small for his age, grabbed Noelle's hand. The child proceeded to trot over to the shelf where the board games were lined up.

Noelle smiled, "Yes, I hear you play chess. I'm pretty sure you can beat me easy. I'm more a checkers man."

Matthew grinned and signed something to his dad. Noelle assumed the kid probably called him a dumb-ass or something of that nature. The boy pulled out the checkers' box and set up the board. His dad sat on one of the cushions nearby, watching. His mother stood over the boy protectively. Father John and Noelle sat across from them on a low sofa.

As the boy took the red checkers, he handed Noelle the black ones. He smiled and noted, "I knew you were bound to take the red. That was my favorite color too when I was your age." The boy gave a small smile. The game began.

They had made several moves before Noelle began his query. He said softly, "Matthew, I was wondering if you remember anything about the night you were crowned the Infant of Prague."

Margaret signed the question, even though she could tell by the look on her son's face that he understood exactly what Noelle had asked by reading his lips.

Matthew signed back to his mom and she translated his reply to Noelle. "I remember the shiny, gold crown and how it fit perfectly on my head. But the baby diaper was too tight for a big boy like me."

Father John laughed uncomfortably. Noelle stared at him for a moment, moved a checker, then asked, "Did the archbishop wear a crown, too?

Once again, the boy signed his response to his mother. She said, "No, the archbishop didn't even have his hat." Matthew moved a red piece.

Noelle continued, "What about the other man? Do you remember him?"

Matthew was still for a moment. He looked to his mother as if a jolt of lightening hit him and signed excitedly, "Black. That man was wearing all black clothes."

After Margaret translated Matthew's words to Noelle, she turned her face away from her son so he couldn't read her lips. "This is the very first time he has ever acknowledged that he saw this man," she whispered to Noelle. "Whoever that killer was, at least he had the decency to hide his evil deed from my boy's eyes."

Noelle looked straight at Matthew and asked, "Was he a big man? Do you remember?"

Matthew signed back, "I don't know. His hands were big. He touched my cheek when he pushed something into my mouth. After that, everything went black." All the while Matthew and Noelle were pushing red and black pieces across the board.

Knowingly, the detective said, "Like these black checkers, huh? Did you see anything red too?" The boy just nodded his head no. A smile flickered across Noelle's face as he looked up at Father John to gauge his reaction to the boy's memories returning.

Again, Matthew seemed excited as he signed. His mother translated, "Matthew said that the man had a fruity smell, like strawberry bubble gum or mom's perfume."

As seven-year-olds do, Matthew suddenly grew bored. He stood up and signed to his parents, "I'm hungry. Can we have dinner now?"

Margaret put the brakes on the interrogation. "That's all Matthew knows and it's time for his supper," she said. "He needs to get ready for bed soon. It's a school night." The game and the interview were abruptly over.

Margaret signed to her son to go wash his hands for dinner. She waited for him to clean up while Paul escorted the priest and Noelle out of the family room. As they went back through the hallway to the front door, Noelle took note of a photograph on a hall table of what was most likely Matthew's

First Holy Communion day. It had been taken outside of the cathedral and showed the boy posing with the archbishop.

At the door, Noelle asked, "Paul, if Matthew recalls anything else, would you please call me?" He handed him a slip of paper with his phone number scrawled on it. Paul said that he would.

Father John hugged Paul affectionately—no handshake, Noelle noted. The priest asked Paul to say goodbye to Matthew and Margaret as he and Noelle walked out the door.

Just as Noelle and the priest were getting into the truck, Noelle noticed Detective Tucci and his partner Detective Melville pull up right behind them. Noelle was sure that Tucci and Melville got a good look at him and Father John as they drove off. Noelle noticed Paul looking apprehensive on the porch as he waved a greeting at the two detectives as they approached his house.

On the drive back to the cathedral, Noelle had lots of questions for Father John but he kept them to himself. They drove mostly in silence. A block from the rectory, Father John said, "Thank you, Nick, for not grilling the young boy. You led a very gentle investigation."

Noelle said, "No, thank you, Father. Thanks for your help. Tell me something...do you have any idea why the detectives were there? Did you let them know that the parents had given permission for the boy to talk?"

Father John shook his head. "Why would I?"

The priest switched gears. "I'm very fond of Matthew and as much as I'd like to see the murderer apprehended and brought to justice, I think it's a blessing that Matthew doesn't remember anything, don't you?"

Noelle pulled up at the cathedral's back entrance and watched the nervous, fidgety priest get out of his truck. As Father John moved toward the door, he turned and called out, "Oh, Nick, don't forget. I'll be praying for you—and your mother's soul, too."

Noelle thanked Father John again and drove off. After a long, productive day, he headed straight to Lucky Pierre's. He believed he'd earned it.

Chapter Eighteen

Dons, Johns and Hookers

After winning a few hands of poker, Noelle called it quits. He had a new mission, so getting a good night's sleep could go a long way in retrieving his mojo for crime work. He also didn't want to let down Sister Theresa, who had grown to expect him daily. Noelle didn't think his mother even knew he was there given the state she was in but the pretty, young nun was another matter. He couldn't help wonder if she had a crush on him. The thought was a nice distraction from his fragmental thinking.

Thinking back, Noelle regretted his harsh tone the last time he'd left Sister Theresa. He knew that he had to keep friends like her close but he didn't want to slack off on getting to know his enemies either.

Noelle didn't think he'd been in town long enough to make any enemies…unless he counted Detective Tucci. The guy was tricky and not the least bit friendly.

At the high roller table after visiting Matthew Hannigan, Noelle spotted Tucci's mobster thug friend. The fellow had been there the night he'd first met Tucci in the poker game. Tonight, when the mobster left the table, Noelle observed him stealing off into a corner near the restrooms. He noticed the man conversing with a very striking beauty. She had long, jet-black hair and wore a sexy, gypsy-style hippie dress. Noelle couldn't help but notice a small lump on her forehead. He wondered if the thug had slugged her.

Noelle was captivated by this raven-haired beauty. He loved his wife above all women but that didn't mean he was dead. Like admiring a piece of art in a museum, he saw no harm in looking even if he wasn't looking to buy! This babe was something else!

Noelle excused himself from the game to use the men's room, with the intention of getting a better look at 'Beauty' and the 'Beast'. As he passed the brut and the exotic woman, he could see that they were having a heated argument. Noelle observed a hint of terror in the girl's wild eyes. He popped into the men's room, staying close to the door, hoping to hear their conversation.

Most of what they said to each other was blotted out by the ambient noise of the many conversations going on in the gambling room. Noelle could only make out a few words here and there. Suddenly, the volume of their voices rose above the din of the crowd. The only sentence Noelle heard clearly came from the thug when he shouted, "If you don't lift that curse off the family, there'll be more blood in the streets!"

Noelle pressed his ear to the door but there was only the sound of the gamblers mumbling and the occasional winner's exclamations. By the time Noelle took a leak and headed out, the mobster and the mystery girl had disappeared.

Noelle cashed in his chips with Millie. He dropped another good tip then hurried downstairs to see if the couple was still in the bar. There was no trace of them. He was uncomfortable asking Mike, the bartender, about them because Noelle suspected they were involved with the mob.

As nice as a guy Mike was, Noelle knew he still worked for "the family," as do all bar and club employees at some point. Any reported snooping around could lead to Noelle lying dead on the bottom of Lake Pontchartrain. For the first time in a long time, Noelle used restraint over his impulses and went straight home.

Back at Velda's boarding house, Noelle entered the lobby to a big surprise. He couldn't believe his bad luck when he saw Detective Tucci engaged in what appeared to be an intimate conversation with his nosy landlady, Velda. They were drinking port in cut crystal glasses. When Noelle passed through the lobby, Tucci's greeting was so friendly it immediately put him on edge. "Noelle, my buddy," Tucci beamed. "Come join us for a night cap. We need to talk."

Caught off guard, Noelle forced a smile. "How did you know where I lived?"

Tucci grimaced back. "Like I told you, there's not a whole lot that goes on in this town that I don't know about. Your landlady and I go way back. Right, Velda?"

"Yes, that's true, Detective Noelle. There was a time when I ran my business with the full protection of our fine men in blue," she admitted. "But that was long ago." Velda went on expansively, as only she could.

"Mr. Tucci was no more than a twinkle in his daddy's eye back then, not the great detective he is today. Despite the ugliness that exists in the world, I feel safe just knowing a big, strong lawman like him is protecting my home—and the citizens of our beautiful city. You never know when crime could be lurking right under your nose."

Tucci finished his drink and stood up. "Noelle, I know it's late but like I was telling Velda, I need to discuss some aspects of our double homicide with you. They fall under your area of expertise. Do you think we can go to your room for a little privacy?"

Noelle smirked, "Velda has a rule about late-night visitors but if it's okay with her, it's fine with me."

Velda gave her blessing.

As the two men started toward Noelle's basement apartment. Tucci turned to Velda. "Sweetheart, you are one beautiful broad," he told her. "Thank you for the drink."

Velda almost swooned in ecstasy. She plastered a Halloween pumpkin grin on her face, which Noelle found frightening. Velda preened, "Always the gentleman and such a flatterer. Thank you, Mr. Tucci. Now, remember, I'll keep the light on for you anytime you need to pop on by." Although Noelle knew he was in for a very unpleasant conversation, he laughed silently to himself, fully enjoying Tucci's grimace after Velda's love song to him.

As soon as Noelle locked the door behind them, he offered Tucci a drink from the fresh bottle of Jack in the bag he carried. Tucci accepted. Noelle poured them both generous shots. As they took seats across from one another at the dinette table, Tucci wasted no time getting down to business, "Look, Noelle, I don't know what you think you're up to but I don't appreciate out-of-town, retired cops honing in on my crime beat."

Noelle tried to speak but Tucci stopped him.

"I don't give a shit that you're some celebrity dick or whatever the fuck you are. I don't want you interfering in New Orleans police business. It can only lead to trouble for you and more than likely fuck up my leads. You have some balls going behind my back and getting the priest and the kid to talk to you. Who do you think you are?"

Noelle did his best to settle the detective's fears. "Look, Tucci, I didn't mean any harm. I actually met the priest because of my dying mother. She's requested that her final service be held at that cathedral. So naturally, I went to Father John to see if he knew how long the place would be shut down and under investigation. He was very kind to me about my mother so it felt natural to offer him help. I guess I wasn't thinking straight. I've been hitting the booze heavy lately. It's horrible to see my mother dying this way. But I swear, I didn't mean to step on any toes—I was just playing armchair detective to distract myself. I hope you understand. I won't do it again, I promise."

It was hard for Noelle to keep the smile off his face with his bold-faced lie.

Tucci stood up, unappeased. "I hope not," he snapped at Noelle. "Because the next time, this won't be a friendly call. We have our own ways of doing things down here. It's not Houston. Got it?"

Noelle walked Tucci toward the door. "Got it," he told him.

He shut and locked the door behind him, leaning up against it. Noelle knew there was something more than fishy going on with Tucci's code of law. He also knew that Tucci wasn't kidding when he said things here were done differently than in Houston. New Orleans had a flavor all its own and it wasn't filé gumbo.

As Noelle poured another drink, he realized he wasn't tired. As much as he wanted to sleep, it would take the whole bottle of whiskey to knock him out.

His mind twisted and turned over the psychology of serial killers. The one similarity they all had in common with a gambling man was that they thrived on the edge of danger. The more Noelle thought about the encounter he'd just had with Tucci, the more pissed off he got.

He finished the bottle of Jack but still, no sleep. Noelle considered the reasons the detective wouldn't want Noelle's help on the case—other than Tucci's grandiose ego, of course. The mobster at Lucky's immediately came to mind. The big thug seemed so buddy-buddy with Tucci. Maybe one of the mob families had something to do with the first murder. Of course, the Marcello and Carlucci families were Italian and Italians are Catholics—at least they were for appearance's sake. Noelle ruminated on the idea that one of those mob goons could have started out as a sweet altar boy until he lost his faith. Maybe it took being molested by some pervert like the archbishop. That certainly was a good enough motive to kill a priest with the grandiose ritual of writing 'Vengeance is Mine' on the church altar. But what grudge did the killer have towards the Baptists? With his mind racing, Noelle thought about the scene of the first crime.

Feeling energized, he decided to pay a visit to his new friend, Father John, to do more probing.

When he'd left Father John earlier that night, it was obvious the priest was upset. Noelle was sharp enough to realize that if Father John knew the archbishop was a pedophile, he'd feel an obligation to hide it from the public, even in spite of the murder.

It was already past two in the morning but that didn't stop Noelle from driving his truck over to the rectory. He rang the doorbell several times but no one answered. Just as he was about to give up, a woman in curlers and a housecoat opened the door. He figured this was Mrs. Murphy, the housekeeper. Noelle could tell she wanted to read him the riot act so he apologized.

"I'm sorry to disturb you at this hour," he cowered, "but it's urgent that I speak with Father John tonight. Could you let him know Detective Noelle is here?"

Mrs. Murphy scolded, "I can't help you. Come back during business hours. Father John is out on church business."

Noelle raised an eyebrow. "At this hour?"

Mrs. Murphy huffed, shook her head and slammed the door in his face. Noelle headed back to his truck and was about to take off, but he decided to sit and think things over while doing some surveillance from the driver's seat. Noelle thought long and hard about how serial killers often haunt their victims' turf just for the thrill of it. From his vantage point, he looked up and down the streets surrounding the cathedral. The residential neighborhood was empty of any pedestrians.

Noelle heard a noise and saw the rectory door open. He ducked out of sight behind the steering wheel and lifted his head just enough to see a dark figure dressed in black street clothes slipping out the door. 'Damn,' Noelle thought, 'the man looked like Father John.' He shook his head in disbelief; it was the priest.

Noelle waited until Father John walked in the opposite direction, and then started to follow him on foot. Why was the priest going out at this late hour? Why had Mrs. Murphy lied? Now that made her a person of interest too. He wondered what was under those curlers in her head. 'Who the hell are these lying, sneaky Catholics,' Noelle wondered.

He suspected Father John knew he was being followed because the priest began to walk faster, almost jogging now. Afraid of losing him, Noelle picked up his pace but he couldn't afford to get too close. Father John was almost a full block ahead of him when the priest turned a corner, heading back toward the French Quarter. Noelle did the same.

The street was buzzing with locals and tourists. The happy, carefree laughter seemed incongruous with the news of double murder in the air. The gruesome killings didn't seem to deter any of them from partying up a storm. Noelle spotted Father John just beyond a gaggle of young women, one of whom was puking up what Noelle guessed were too many Hurricanes.

He tailed Father John as he barreled down Bourbon Street, jostling through the mass of drunken humanity. When a cluster of Japanese tourists pushed in front of Noelle, he lost sight of the priest in the crowd. Damn! Noelle had no other choice but to search the bars.

Noelle weaved his way in and out of Fat Tuesday then into the crowded Saints and Sinners. He did a quick sweep of The Famous Door and Lafitte's Blacksmith Shop but still saw no sign of Father John. He gave up and went back out into the streets, searching down Decatur to the Mississippi waterfront, then tracked back to Bourbon along Dumaine, checking pubs along Chartres and Royal. But his search came up empty. The priest had disappeared.

Pissed off, Noelle sprinted back to the cathedral. Plan B was to catch Father John returning to the rectory. Noelle drove his truck a few blocks away from the cathedral, parked and walked back. He hid himself behind the tall bushes lining the path between the cathedral's stone wall and the rectory's walkway. In frustration, he whispered a harsh, "Fuck it!"

As ominous clouds began to cover the cathedral's steeple, the night turned black, burying the thin slip of the moon suspended in the sky. Noelle nodded off but was suddenly awakened by a loud crack of thunder. As his eyes fluttered open, he saw lightning bolts slash through the night. In seconds, a heavy downpour drenched him. Noelle sprinted back to his truck and drove it closer to the church so he could continue his night vigil.

Again, he fell asleep, this time hunched over his steering wheel.

Chapter Nineteen

Home Body

In the wet, juicy night, the makings of another murder was brewing in the stewing cauldron they call the Big Easy. 'There was nothing easy about New Orleans,' thought the killer who loved attention but was wise enough to know how to keep a low profile. He had to fulfill his life's mission: the hunt, the torture and the killing of truly evil beings.

He was an extravagant avenger but he disguised his wealth and true nature as best he could. He selected a neighborhood in which to live that facilitated his calling. Although rather cheap, he created a palace within thin walls.

Along with his pursuits, the only thing he cared about was comfort. When not on the prowl, he was a homebody.

This particular evening, with every new and vintage item in its proper place, he eyed the beauty of his domain. He strode through each room assessing the beauty of his burgundy velvet couch, his Regency chair and his Victorian cabinet. He lingered and admired the stock: his best wines, antique glasses, goblets and fine English china.

He had also managed to find the perfect antique Persian carpet. He successfully haggled with the vendor in Afghanistan and managed to get it for a steal. He successfully covered the scarred wooden plank floors with this thing of beauty.

Sniffing the fresh freesia in the Tiffany crystal vase, he played a recording of his favorite opera, Mozart's *The Marriage of Figaro*. Swaying to the music, he delicately sipped wine from one of his rose-colored, gold-trimmed goblets, humming along to the overture.

He moved slowly to the bedroom and placed the goblet of wine on a small Chinese lacquered table where another vase of flowers bloomed—fragrant magnolias. The light of the Tiffany lamp caused a shadow to play upon the wall as he circled his Louis V chair. After taking another long, luxurious sip of wine, he removed his silk robe and draped it over the chair. He sighed, as he propped up his almost-naked body on the soft down duvet, which covered his queen-sized bed. He draped a satin throw over his body, caressing its texture as he rubbed it over his muscular skin.

With his hands itchy and heart pounding, he thought about the time fast approaching when he would make his move on the next target, the pleasure of the kill and the great release he would feel when done. He drifted off to sleep, lulled by the most delicious thoughts of death and destruction.

When he woke from his brief nap, the moon and stars were shrouded in heavy darkness and sheets of rain were dousing the city streets. But that would not deter him. He knew it was the appointed time. He knew the worthy recipient of his sacrament was waiting. He rose and dressed appropriately, all in black, and covered himself with a long rain tarp. He was off for his next date with destiny. He had prepared well and knew the habits of his next sanctified victim. He smiled. He knew just where to find him at that hour.

Chapter Twenty

Herbs and Needles

Zambo's ropelike, black dreadlocks were strung with beads and jewels. They swayed and bobbed as he danced around an altar covered with a brightly patterned blanket. On the blanket sat skulls, colored glass bottles and doll heads. They were carefully arranged around a wood, straw and cloth stick figure of a person pierced with pins and needles. An elderly man, who must have been handsome in his youth, stood shivering in the dark corner while the voodoo master zapped him with an electric stick. The victim shook in pain and terror.

Zambo gripped a lit torch and moved closer to the frightened man.

The light from the torch illuminated the gold rings stacked on each of Zambo's long fingers. The voodoo prince's large earlobes drooped from the weight of giant ruby studs. The torch's light illuminated the areas on the victim's body where the electrical wand had caused bright red welts to sprout. Zambo pushed his wide, flat nose, pitted with acne scars, inches from the man's wrinkled, white, pasty face as he chanted, "Oh, infinite spirit, Nsambi, we ask that this son of a whore named 'Corruption' be returned from where he came. May he live as one who works only for me!"

A high practitioner of the Bizango Vigilantes, a voodoo cult respected by the Haitians who emigrated to New Orleans, Zambo and other priests like him enforced the laws over their cult's criminals. The police turned a blind eye to their crimes because even they were spooked by the Bizango's curses. This same sect of practitioners was also feared for their barbaric methods of retribution. These so-called crimes could be anything they deemed evil, from coveting a man's wife or his chicken to robbery and murder. There was no rhyme or reason to the punishment of a Bizango in New Orleans. Zambo took it upon himself as the one Bizango who would keep the law of the cult as *he* saw fit. Whatever caused Zambo to have a bad day was fodder for murder—or zombiism.

The victim that day just happened to be a very unfortunate, wealthy, white man who was a new member of their cult. Zambo resented him for his success in business. He had spread rumors among the Bizangos that this man had ties to the New Orleans mafia. Zambo had built a solid case against him until his followers believed the old man was the Devil himself.

Zambo methodically began his victim's slow demise with the basics of Voodoo 101. He merely pushed a few pins and needles into a straw doll figure made to represent this enemy. Practitioners of the black art believed that this technique would weaken and ultimately dislodge the soul from the body.

On this night, Zambo decided to take his revenge to a more severe and *fulfilling* level.

His aide in the ceremony was Phara, a sister priestess. She was stately and beautiful with warm, brown skin, high cheekbones and thick, rosy lips. Phara laughed at the shivering man as she tied him to the altar, securing his arms behind his back. With her long, painted fingertips, she held his mouth open while Zambo forced potions of herbs down his throat. Zambo wanted the man to experience the humiliation of knowing that he would become Zambo's eternal slave.

To accompany the force-feeding, Zambo spoke a prayer. "We will render this subhuman to a state of inanimate existence. He will become a zombie, without even the desire to escape his circumstances."

Just as Zambo was adding the final potion, the candles in the room flickered. The torch he had left burning suddenly blew out. Utter darkness fell over the room. Outside, a heavy downpour fell. Sheets of rain washed the storefront windows.

Zambo was unalarmed. He assumed a lightning strike had hit the power lines. Before he could continue his damning incantations, a heavy weight hit him squarely on his back. The powerful black man fell onto the altar. Blood gushed from his spilt chin and splashed all over his 'zombie-in-the-making'. The assaulter held a cloth drenched with chloroform over Zambo's victim's face. The man slumped into the arms of the avenger as he laid the old man down and out of his way.

He calmly went about his business with Zambo. Phara tried to run but was stopped by a small, weighty, voodoo icon that struck her head.

Grasping her beaded braids, the attacker yanked Phara's head backward and slashed the woman's long, graceful throat.

Next, the avenger pulled Zambo's body by his feet. He wanted Zambo to feel the torture he had planned for him. Zambo tried in vain to fight his attacker but the man was too quick and strong. In the end, the voodoo priest was stilled with one, swift punch.

Barely conscious, Zambo heard the whir of an electric drill but he didn't start screaming until he felt the pain slashing through his chest. The sound of splintering bone echoed through the room, eerily accompanied by the cracks of thunder and flashes of lightning outside. The killer pulled out Zambo's heart, carefully slipped it into a re-sealable bag and placed it into an iced cooler propped beside the bloody body.

Like a skilled surgeon, the avenger used his saw to slice through Zambo's decorated skull as the jewels, beads and cowry shells flew everywhere. He took care not to bruise the brain.

When he was finished, the avenger placed the brain into a plastic container and laid it beside the heart in the cooler. He closed the lid, securing his prized possessions.

The avenger paused. He made a last-minute decision to take the heart and brain of Phara, too. This had not been part of his plan but in the moment, he decided to take the extra organs just in case he craved the delicacies before he got to his next kill.

The avenger then took a needle from his kit and pushed it into the already-dead Phara's arms. After draining her blood, he poured some of it onto his gloved fingers. Using blood as a macabre ink, he scrawled on the wall behind him in big, garish handwriting: "VENGEANCE IS MINE!"

After burning all traces of evidence, the avenger made sure to put out the fire. He grabbed his cooler and exited the blood-spattered scene through the store's back entrance and stepped out into the refreshing rainstorm. He whistled as he walked. Flipping up his raincoat lapels to cover the sides of his face, he smiled.

Chapter Twenty-One

Back to Noelle's Vigil

He didn't wake until the rain stopped and he saw the sun rise to the east of Saint Catherine's.

"What?" Noelle exclaimed as he saw the priest swaying down the street, headed toward the rectory.

Noelle jumped out of his F150, calling out to Father John. The priest's face flushed when he saw Noelle. An excuse sprang out of his mouth, "Detective, I'm no saint, just a man like any other."

Itching to ask where Father John had been, instead Noelle gave him a stern warning. "Father, you should be careful," he told him. "I'd hate for you to be the killer's next victim. He could still be lurking around in the area...and you know how he feels about men of the cloth."

Noelle contemplated Father John's whereabouts. 'Where had he been? Could he possibly be a killer?'

However, after his fuck up with Pamela, he wondered if he would ever be able to trust his own intuition again?

Father John didn't fit the part. To the contrary, he appeared to be spooked.

"I know my behavior appears strange, but the truth is, I've been working all night," he told Noelle. "I counsel a group of at-risk prostitutes. I'm trying to get these ladies of the night off the streets." The priest took a deep breath, visibly shaken. "The stress and pressure around Saint Catherine's is taking its toll on me. I look forward to the work I do off campus. After the group session was over, I met a friend for a few drinks."

Noelle smiled as the priest reeled drunkenly. He offered Father John his hand and helped him to the door.

"Father, I'm the last person to judge anyone's morality. You know what Jesus said, 'Let he without sin, cast the first stone.'"

The priest laughed, "Detective, I'm impressed. Quoting scripture to a priest."

Noelle couldn't help but chuckle himself. "I only know the good parts where Jesus hung out with hookers and other unsavory characters," he admitted. "My kind of people. You know Father, when you finally get to meet her, I think you'll really like my wife. You two have a lot in common. She's also working nights to save those poor girls from the streets."

Noelle was itching to know what the priest was really up to and he would press further when the time was ripe. By the looks of him, Father John was exhausted. Noelle decided to let him get some rest. For now, he was pleased that he'd succeeded in building a little more trust with the priest. He knew it would come in handy later.

Noelle waited until after the heavy rectory door closed and Father John was safely inside before he headed home to sleep for a few hours. He needed to gird his loins with forty winks before his next visit to his mother.

Chapter Twenty-Two

Flores de Los Muertos

On his way to Saint Mary's, Noelle took deep breaths of the clean air left from the heavy rains of the night before. Exhilarated by the hint of fall and the cool morning air, Noelle stopped a street vender and picked up two bunches of yellow roses. He thought about how Sally would love the idea of Noelle stopping to smell the roses. He was feeling upbeat after getting a little rest and as he walked, Noelle's gut told him his luck might be changing. Suddenly the lyrics of the song, "The Yellow Rose of Texas" popped into his head and he recalled how his mom used to sing that song when he was little. He saw the flowers as hope that he would find her awake. He never forgot that song because he associated it with the few times his mother seemed really happy. This would be the first time he was not dreading the impending visit to Saint Mary's.

Noelle carried the cheerful flowers into Catherine's room only to be greeted by a crestfallen Sister Theresa. She said quietly, "Nick, I'm so glad you're here. Your mother took a turn for the worse. We had quite a scare during the storm when the power went out on her ventilator. I thought we'd lost her but suddenly, she came alive and started asking for you over and over."

Noelle's bubble of hope popped and he handed the flowers to the nun. "You might as well have these then. I'm sorry I missed her again; seems like my timing is always off."

Sister Theresa accepted the flowers and said, "Don't beat yourself up over it. You can't be here 24/7. The flowers are beautiful. I'll get a vase and put them on her dresser. Don't lose hope, Nick, she might come awake again."

"When I saw these yellow roses I took it as a good omen. They reminded me of how happy my mom was when she sang that song, "The Yellow Rose of Texas."

Noelle plopped down in the chair next to Catherine's bed. Sister Theresa sniffed the roses.

"That's interesting because I always had a fondness for that song too but probably for a different reason. I bet your mama, or most white folks for that matter, never heard that song before it became a pop hit in the nineteen fifties. When I was in high school I loved history and I wrote a report on a book about the original 'Yellow Rose' of Texas. Turns out she was a black woman, Emily West, who inspired the folk song written in eighteen thirty-six during the Texas independence war from Mexico. Over the years there's been a lot of controversy over the true story of the "Yellow Rose". If you're interested I'll see if I can find that old book for you."

Noelle just smiled and said, "That's alright sister, I have enough controversial reading to keep me occupied right here."

"Suit yourself. I'm going to find a pretty vase for your mother's flowers."

When the nun left the room, Noelle kissed his mother's forehead and stroked her thinning hair. He sat back down and picked up another notebook from the side table. He was almost afraid of what he was going to find out next. He didn't know what else to do except continue to read. Just watching her lie there was painful and it made Noelle feel helpless. Although Sister Theresa had said Catherine could hear when people spoke to her, even when she was unconscious, Noelle wasn't comfortable talking to her. Instead, he read:

God, I feel like I'm stewin' in a steamin' cauldron of pork, probly since pork is Ezekiel's favorite. I keep hopin' if I keep him satisfied in the kitchen, he leave me alone in the bedroom but no such luck. Why they say what You put together let no man put asunder? I just grit my teeth until I birth this baby and then one day I'll hightail it out of this forsaken place. When I walked up to the porch, he followed me and put his scrawny arm around my protruding belly. I felt his sicknen' hot breath on my ear when he whispered, "Aren't you gonna kiss your husband?"

Instead, I pulled away and went to get the plates down so I could serve up the pork stew. Soon as I fix his plate, I held my back and slowly begin to head up the stairs so I could lay down a bit. The bigger my belly get the more my back pained me. Then my husband start his whining,

"Hey now, jes where do ya thin you goin'? Ya jes sit down heah and eat with me."

I told him, "Ezekiel, I'm bone tired and I got to put my feet up."

"Not before you have lunch. You eatin' for two so you gonna sit and eat proper in front of your husband!"

That was the only thing that could curb my appetite lately: the sight of his old, crinkled-up mouth slurpin' up my pork stew. And even worse, the thought of his withered mouth with his half missin' teeth puckered up and suckin' on my breasts in the middle of the night made me so sick I had to hold the sink for a spell before I could put some food on a plate and sit down.

Since the day Daddy made me marry Ezekiel, I just want to join Mama in the grave. I do feel sorry for the poor, old geezer, though. It wasn't his idea to be my husband but he sure is taken a-liken to it. He's bald with nasty moles on his face. The Reverend's kin, Ezekiel never seemed to have enough of anything and he complains all the time. When I see him hobbling on his cane, I do pray to feel some compassion cause I know I can never love him. Even though my baby's daddy turned out to be the Devil, I'm still glad I got to feel what love is even if it was lust. I suppose it's tricky to know the difference.

There's a rumor about old Ezekiel that after his first wife died, he tried to hang himself and the Reverend come in and save him in the nick of time. So he been beholding to the Reverend ever since.

Just when I was startin' to feel sorry for Ezekiel, he up and said, "Guess what? No choir tonight and no prayer group. We've got a night alone. How 'bout that? I'll get the porch swing oiled up when I get back from Mayville."

He squeezed my hand, got up from the table and added, "I gotta go to town to tend to some business."

Ezekiel grabbed his hat and cane, then limped to the door. I thought I was free and clear for a few hours, but he turned and give me that nasty smile and blow me a kiss.

"Now you jes be ready at six, ya hear, girl!"

As soon as I heard his engine turn over, I went to the trash bin and turned my plate of simmered pork over in it. Soon as I couldn't hear that engine puffing down the dirt drive, I reached in my hiding place under the pots and pans (a place Ezekiel would never look) and pulled out my diary.

Please, God, let my time come soon and please don't let it hurt too much. I know You sending me a boy. I can feel his kickin'. He's strong and I'm glad 'cause he going to have to help me rid myself of these men holding me back from livin. I know thinking these bad thoughts ain't fitting a mama-to-be. I should be thinking only good things—I don't want the sad in me to hurt my child none.

At first, Noelle thought that it might be possible that he was the baby mentioned in his mother's diary until he realized that the numbers didn't add up. He had vivid memories as a toddler of the house where he and his mother lived. Those memories were actually the good days in Noelle's life.

Noelle was born in a whorehouse, for sure, not a farmhouse. The baby in his mother's story couldn't have been him. But this meant that Noelle had a sibling.

Suddenly, Catherine opened her eyes. She smiled, "Nick, you're back. Did you find Brandon?"

'Could Brandon be…his mother's original sin? Decades later, still haunting her?'

Noelle took her hand and moved closer.

"Mama, do you mean my brother?"

"Please find him," she said faintly.

Noelle grabbed her hand tighter.

"Where, Mama? Do you have any pictures?"

"Mississippi..."

She closed her eyes and nodded off.

Sister Theresa came into the room with the golden roses, beautifully arranged in a large, plastic water pitcher.

Noelle looked up at her, "Sister, I just learned who Brandon is. Apparently, he's my older brother. Now I have a new mystery to solve. It will be a miracle if I could find him before my mother…"

"…moves on," Sister Theresa offered.

"I'm going to do my best. I'll just take this notebook with me if that's okay with you?"

"Of course, Nick, they're yours to take. I wish you luck. I'll call you if there's any change in your mother's condition."

Chapter Twenty-Three

Fortune Telling 101

Noelle wandered out into the late-day heat with his mind spinning in every direction. The thought of drinking and playing cards didn't appeal to him. He considered going to see Father John, but knew it was too soon to pay the priest a visit after their sunrise encounter. Noelle felt lost. He was longing to talk to Sally but realized she wouldn't welcome his call. He found himself wandering about aimlessly and ended up in Tremé, a bad neighborhood adjacent to the French Quarter.

Down a side street, Noelle stopped at a rundown storefront. The sign in the window advertised palm readings, crystals and fortune telling. He had never before in his entire life considered such nonsense but was feeling just that desperate and confused. 'What the hell?' Noelle thought, 'Why not give it a shot?'

He pushed open the door. As he walked inside, a long, beaded curtain hit him in the face. Noelle passed through it, kneading the beads as he did.

The space was small and lined with black velvet curtains that blocked out the sunlight and separated the back area from the tiny front of the store. There was a counter and a large glass case filled with a cornucopia of all sorts of things having to do with religion and the occult.

The case was secured by locked sliding-glass doors, which allowed a browser to look but not touch.

Noelle perused a few different brands of tarot cards and crystals of different sizes and colors. He examined scented candles as well as those embossed with images of the Virgin Mary, Jesus and the saints. Another shelf had several expensive-looking sets of rosary beads, gold and silver medals, and rings with images of saints carved into them. Below that shelf was another, lined with bottles and small boxes of herbs and potions claiming to cure anything from warts to heartbreak.

Noelle thought perhaps he could use some of the latter. His eyes stopped at the very top shelf, which held paraphernalia that looked like voodoo ritual items: dolls and Day of the Dead skulls and such.

Noelle imagined that this funky gypsy store was a front for more than fortune telling. It was a virtual smorgasbord of holy bullshit.

Since there wasn't anyone to help Noelle, he continued to browse the store. He heard a noise, then turned. Popping up from behind the counter was an extraordinarily beautiful woman.

Noelle couldn't believe his eyes—it was the same raven-haired, gypsy beauty he had seen at Lucky Pierre's. She was the woman arguing with Tucci's gorilla. He noted that the bump on her head had healed, making her even more lovely than he remembered.

The gypsy queen flashed Noelle a heartwarming smile.

"Oh, sorry, to keep you waiting. I've been taking inventory. I didn't want to lose count. What can I help you with?"

Noelle didn't let on that he'd seen her before.

"Interesting place you have here," he said. "I'm new in town and was just browsing. Your storefront looked like the kind of place where I could find the gypsy with the gold-capped tooth."

He received no reaction from the beauty, so Noelle persisted.

"You know, the one who sells those little bottles of Love Potion No. 9."

The woman laughed graciously at the song reference and added, "We don't carry that particular brand but I'm sure I can suggest something to perk up your love life, if that's what you are looking for.

'Glad she has a sense of humor,' Noelle thought.

"Where I come from, you don't find anything so exotic."

"Oh? And where's that?" she asked.

"You tell me. You're the fortune teller?" Noelle grinned.

"Oh, that's not me," she admitted. "I'm Rose. I just manage the shop for my mother, Esmeralda. She's the gypsy with the gold-capped tooth. No just kidding, Mom is really a good psychic. Are you interested in tarot cards or a palm reading? Maybe something more involved like a healing or a curse removal? She can even do past life regressions."

Noelle laughed, "I have enough trouble in *this* life without delving into my past ones, if there are such things. Like I said, this stuff is all new to me. I could use some help though. I'm looking for a missing person. I just found out I have a brother I never knew about. What do you recommend for that?"

Rose thought for a moment.

"Why don't you start with a thirty minute reading and see where that takes you?" she suggested.

"How much will it cost me?"

"Only thirty dollars...and for an extra ten, you can get some healing too."

The heat from her hypnotic smile lit up Noelle's body and spirit. He slapped a fifty-dollar bill down onto the counter.

"Take me to the gypsy!"

Rose took his cash and began counting his change. He stopped her.

"No, the twenty extra is for you," he said. "You healed me the moment I set eyes on you."

Rose thanked him and ushered Noelle into an even darker room behind the curtain. She gestured to a small table with two plastic chairs arranged around it.

"Please, take a seat," Rose offered. "Mom will be right down. She's just finishing up her lunch."

At the New Orleans Crime Division, Detective Tucci sat at his desk with a stack of papers and the grisly photographs of the third murder laid out before him. He was fried and stumped. He got up to use the bathroom where he took a long rest on the pot. It's where Tucci did his best thinking.

Afterwards, he scrubbed his hands as vigorously as Lady Macbeth. He turned on the cold water and splashed it onto his face as if he could erase that damned spot. He slicked back his hair and returned to work.

When Melville lumbered in, Tucci hit his partner with a shitload of questions.

"Since you couldn't get anything from the traumatized zombie victim, did you have the good sense to canvas the neighborhood? There has to be other witnesses?"

Melville looked like he was on the verge of tears.

"I long for the days when I was an innocent boy and the only blood I ever saw in a church was the blood of Jesus hanging on a cross. At least that one didn't happen in a real church."

"Well, at least your religion was good training for your job. Too bad you're such a loser at doing it, though. I'm warning you, Melville, you better get over this depression quick or I'll have your badge!"

Back at the fortune teller's shop, Rose's gypsy mama was about to get to work. Noelle smiled when he saw the short, heavy-set woman with long, salt-and-pepper hair knotted into a bun. She slipped through the black curtain and introduced herself to Noelle.

"Good afternoon, sir. I'm Esmeralda," she told him, easing herself into the chair across from him. "I understand you're looking for your missing brother." She looked at Noelle intently. "Do you have any objects he might have touched?"

Noelle shrugged, "I've never seen him. Maybe this?"

He held up Catherine's notebook, the one he had yet to read. Unconsciously, he'd been carrying it under his arm since he'd left his mother's side. Esmeralda placed her right hand over the notebook. Her fingers and wrist were covered in rings and bracelets. She closed her eyes tightly and asked him to close his eyes, too. Noelle did.

Esmeralda instructed Noelle to concentrate on what he wanted to know. As he expected, she uttered some mumbo jumbo. For the rest of the time, she talked about a lot of things that made no sense to him at all. Esmeralda told him that in nine months' time, he would not recognize the man he had become. She also said the baby was a girl and that Noelle's child would be a doctor when she grew up.

With her eyes tightly closed, Esmeralda went on to say that Noelle was very lucky in love and in cards. He thought, 'Well, she's half right on that one.'

Suddenly, her tone became ferocious and a worried look crossed her face. With a furrowed brow, she cried, "Beware of fancy pants and chainsaws!"

Just as suddenly, Esmeralda came out of her fake spell, looking more like a hardened hooker than a fortune teller.

"That's your time. If you want me to look further, it will be another thirty bucks."

Noelle was polite. "No, that's okay; maybe next time."

The room was so dark, he nearly got lost on his way through the black curtains toward the front room where he was further disappointed when he found no sign of Rose.

He left the store and backtracked through the rundown neighborhood. Noelle passed another anonymous storefront which stood out from the other shabby, wood-framed structures on the block. It had yellow crime scene tape blocking off the entrance. Noelle took note but continued straight to his boarding house. The crime tape didn't faze him. He assumed that most likely, there were plenty of crimes in this poor part of town. Tremé was notorious for them.

In the rooming house's lobby, he saw Velda all in a twitter. She was talking excitedly with Fletcher about another murder at some black magic church. Velda turned to Noelle.

"It was on the five o'clock news." She put her hand to her ample chest and continued. "Oh, I'm sick to death with worry. What happened to the days when it was safe to attend a house of worship?"

Noelle looked confused.

"Perhaps you didn't hear the news yet. There's been another horrific murder in Tremé this time!"

Before Noelle could reply, Velda babbled, "I'm sure in no time Detective Tucci will be calling on you to help him out. The newsman said it's pretty certain that New Orleans has a serial killer. Isn't that right, Mr. Fletcher?"

"I'm afraid so, Velda," Fletcher conceded. "It certainly appears that way. Makes me glad I've never been a religious man. Seems like whoever this killer is, he has issues with churches and he's a non-denominational killer." Fletcher tipped his hat. As he moved toward the door, he winked at Noelle, "I'd love to stay and keep y'all company, but, alas, I have a dinner date. I know Velda will feel safe now that her star detective is on the premises." He raised his hand and waved. "Have a good night, y'all."

The last thing Noelle needed after a long day was a gossip session with Velda. He politely excused himself.

"Velda, I'd love to chat, but I too, have dinner plans," he lied. "I just popped in to freshen up and change my clothes. I had a difficult day with my mother. It won't be long now."

"Oh, I'm so sorry to hear that. If there's anything, anything I can do to relieve your stress, please don't hesitate to call on me," Velda chirped.

"Thank you," Noelle said.

"Anything, anything at all!"

He rushed down the stairs to escape.

Alone in his room, Noelle felt his wretched loneliness more than ever. He turned on the television just in time to catch a report on the new murder. Noelle recognized the building immediately. It was the same one he'd passed; the one with the yellow crime scene tape around it. Once again, there was Detective Tucci on the scene being hounded by TV reporters.

When the news ended, Noelle turned off the tube. He needed Sally. He tried to tell himself that he didn't, but he couldn't lie to himself. Noelle grabbed the phone and dialed his home number and once more, the phone rang and rang and rang to no avail. He felt like a pressure cooker, ready to blow.

Noelle knew he had sabotaged their marriage. Since he'd been in New Orleans, he had discovered that he was sicker than he'd thought and traced it back to his poor upbringing. But at this point, he could no longer blame his mother. He knew she could do nothing more than what she had done. She was a woman trapped by her situation. Noelle's rage brimmed over. He pounded the pillow on his bed. It was GOD! God was to blame for his troubles with his mother and Sally! He thought, what a joke. He didn't even believe in this God yet somehow he could blame Him for his fucked up life.

Noelle struggled to pull himself together. He made a mental note to call Lopez and ask him where Sally worked. Maybe Noelle could catch her off guard if he called her there.

He took a quick shower. While dressing for dinner, he thought he might go back to the fortune teller again to see if Rose was at the shop. Noelle fantasized about asking her out for dinner, 'just for company'. Maybe he'd do a little investigating at the same time. After all, the latest murder happened in her neighborhood. Noelle assumed those voodoo folks all shopped for their shit at Esmeralda's store.

With new-found energy, Noelle headed out. This time, he took his truck. He planned to remain cool and calm if he was lucky enough to find a friend in Rose. As he drove toward Tremé, Noelle thought about how he knew better than to start fixating on a beautiful, young woman. He learned that lesson the hard way with Pamela....or had he?

Noelle longed for the comfort of his wife but Sally was punishing him and he deserved it. In his twisted mind, Noelle rationalized that it would be healthier to have dinner with Rose than to do more gambling and drinking, especially on an empty stomach. He made a feeble attempt to deny that he had a drinking and gambling problem, telling himself that anyone in his position would do the same thing; or worse. But Noelle knew better. He had the classic alcoholic mind that could come up with an excuse to tell him that any risky behavior was okay when it clearly wasn't.

When Noelle arrived at the fortune teller's store, he parked across the street. This time, when he reached for the door, he literally bumped into Detective Tucci.

Obviously annoyed at the sight of him, Tucci barked, "Noelle! Goddamn it! Why is it that you always pop up whenever I'm about to interview a potential witness?"

Noelle played dumb. "Witness to what? This place was recommended to me for a psychic reading."

Tucci frowned. "Psychic reading, my ass. I don't believe, for one minute, that you haven't heard about the murders down the block. This is my last warning to you. Stay off my fucking turf!"

With that, Tucci went inside, slamming the door behind him. Noelle left with his tail between his legs.

With Plan A crushed, Noelle went on to Plan B. He needed a drink, badly. He hopped back in his truck and stopped off at his friendly, neighborhood liquor store to purchase two fifths of Jack. His plan was for an early evening at home, then bed.

In his room, Noelle poured himself a big water glass full of Tennessee whiskey. He picked up his mother's notebook. More Jack and more reading seemed to be in the cards that night. With a sigh, he opened the notebook:

So much has happened I don't know where to begin. A few days ago, the Reverend keep me late to type up his Sunday sermon. With all these words from Leviticus, I'm getting good at typing. But I wonder why the Reverend always be usin' the Bible to talk against the female sex. It like we be the cause of evil.

As I sat sucking on some taffy, I heard footsteps. I look up and see the Reverend leanin' against the doorframe. He scared me cause I's thinkin' he was havin' his supper with Mary and my baby boy down in the big house. All of a sudden, he pop up like Satan to Jesus in the desert.

"Why you settin' there in the dark?" he asked me.

And I say, "I just finished your sermon and I's about to

go home. You know, Ezekiel and my boy's been sufferin' from the long hours I's been keepin here."

"Work for the Lord is never finished "besides Ezekiel's got the negra gal to help and Brandon's doin' jes fine. You need not fret over him tonight. He's goin' off with Mary for supper at the Jones's. They the church's biggest donors and got a gang of youngins for your boy to play with. Mary's gonna drop him off later so ya got plenty of time to tend to your husband needs once I's done with ya."

I felt a tight pain in my chest. That sweet taffy turned sour in my mouth. I let my words come up instead of what was in my stomach.

"Reverend, I been working overtime for months now," I said. "I wanna take my boy home so's I could be with him before his bedtime."

Just then, I could hear Brandon laughin' with Mary out in the back yard. I hear her sayin,

"Come on, my precious boy, let's put on your jacket. It's gettin' kind of nippy." Then I hear the car door shut and the engine start up. I knew it was too late.

I snatched up the sermon and tried to give it over to the Reverend. He took the paper, put it back on the desk and said with authority,

"Remember, God didn't rest until the seventh day. So, the way I sees it you's still on the clock. And I got somethin' to keep you busy right here."

I knew I was doomed even before he pushed me up against the wall. I yelled, "That's not my God!" I tried to push him off me. His face turned beet-red and he raised his hand to slap me, yellin' that I was a blasphémer.

Then he started to undo his belt buckle to use on me. I made a quick move to the door but felt my head snap back as he grab hold of my hair and pulled me real hard. Then he pushed me down and locked the door.

I jumped up and kicked the Reverend hard then tried to snatch the key off him. But he grabbed my ankle and the breath went out of me when my head hit the floor. He started fumblin' with my clothes as I grab that key. I unlock the door and run but *only made it down a few steps before he tackled me again right there on the stairs. I tried to push him off but he just laugh as I bounced down a few more steps. When he kick me real hard on my side, I felt the lights go out. Next, thing I know, he's draggin' me back up to the landing at the top of the steps.*

When I opened my eyes, the Reverend was standing over me, takin down his trousers and screamin' that he was gonna fuck the Devil out of me real hard. Then he get on top of me and started lapping at my face and neck like a crazy ol' cat. And he's still babblin' in tongues whiles he's lickin' me.

The Reverend's distorted face, with those big, yellow, false teeth and his tongue snakin' out of his mouth, made him look like the Devil. Then his ugly little thing pop up between his legs, under his fat belly. I swear it looked like the Devil's forked tail. Then he put it inside me. The shock of all that ugly comin' in me made me want to scream Your name, God, and ask for help. I couldn't cause he had his foul-tastin' tongue down my throat and was sweatin' and slobbering all over me. But I prayed to You in my heart.

I guess You heard me, because out of nowhere, this strength come over me. I lifted that big, fat, son of a bitch up off of me and pushed him real hard. I watched him tumble down the stairs. When he hit the bottom, I heard something crack from the weight of him and it made a ringin' sound in my ears.

I stood paralyzed for a spell then grabbed up my clothes. I stepped over the Reverend's crumpled body and without a second thought, reached down around his ankles and into his trousers, took out his wallet and snatched the cash in it. Since he call me a whore, I thought it fittin' I get paid for my services. Well, I took that blood money and left him layin' there in a heap to die and I didn't look back. Not even once.

I walk calmly through the fields, planning to hide out and wait to snatch Brandon when Mary bring him back to the house. I couldn't think straight or find a good reason to explain to Ezekiel why my clothes was all torn up so I just hid behind the tree and quietly dug up the little money I been stealin' from my husband and saving. I knew I had to leave everything behind and wondered how's I goin' to get my boy. Then I had a worse thought—that I might have to kill Mary and Ezekiel too to get away with my child.

I waited for what seemed like hours but Mary never bring back my boy like the Reverend said she would. Then one by one, I see each light go out in the house.

I started to think the worst. The longer I waited, the more scared I got about what would happen to my boy if I was caught. The more I thought, the more I knew what I was going to have to do. I had to run without my Brandon.

Once I's sure Ezekiel were asleep, I tiptoe inside and take his keys off the hook. Then I tiptoe out and stole the truck. I drove out of there as fast as I could and I didn't stop until I was just outside the first big town away from Mayville where they had a train station. I waited by the tracks cryin over what might happen to my boy and then I hopped the first train that come by, not even knowin' what direction it was headed. So, God, that's how I ended up here in New Orleans. I keeps readin' the home newspapers and obituary to see if they mention the Reverend dying but so far I ain't heard no news.

Chapter Twenty-Four

Self Help Coven

Noelle drained the last drop of his bottle as he turned the pages, bleary-eyed, reading his mother's diary until he could no longer contain his rage. The alcohol hadn't helped one little bit. Noelle had no other cure for this new kind of torture—his mother's and the anguish from Sally's abandonment. Without Sally in his life, Noelle could find no comfort or relief. Sex with his wife had been the only healthy thing he knew to ease his pain. He had fucked that up now and his desperation made him consider reaching out to Father John for help. Other than Sally and Lopez, Noelle realized that he had no real friends. He hadn't put in the effort to make any. The pity party played in Noelle's head, running over and over the same obsessive thoughts.

In his foggy state, Noelle drove to the rectory of Saint Catherine's Cathedral. Just as he was parking, he caught Father John sneaking out into the night again. His investigative instinct took over and Noelle remained in his truck and slowly tailed Father John. If he couldn't get counseling, he might at least learn what this priest was really up to on his late-night crawls.

To avoid being detected, Noelle stayed a block behind. He followed the priest all the way to Tremé, the same neighborhood where the Voodoo Murders had been committed the day before. This really aroused Noelle's suspicions about Father John. He stopped his truck and watched the priest enter the fortune teller's storefront. The idea of Father John and Rose possibly being involved in those murders sobered Noelle right up.

New Orleans was a network of hidden alleys and secret entrances. Noelle put on his detective hat and found a way to get around to the back of the fortune teller's place. He was surprised to find the shop's rear door unlocked. Noelle quietly entered and hid behind the black velvet curtains. As he did, he heard Rose greeting others who were coming in through the front door. Within minutes, he heard furniture being shuffled about. When he peeked through the curtains, he could see that a bunch of chairs had been arranged in a circle. He counted about eight women filling the seats.

As Rose lit candles, Noelle feared that he might have walked into a witch's coven or some weird shit like that. When his eyes adjusted to the added light, he could make out the heavy makeup and outfits of the poor hookers styling more trash than class.

Father John took his seat among them in the circle and began.

"Welcome all. It's meeting time. As most of you know, I'm Father John, your facilitator. I think I see a newcomer here tonight. Would you like to tell us your name and a little about yourself? "

Noelle heard a childlike voice speak up hesitantly.

"I'm Tiffany. I'm fifteen. My mother turned me out when I was twelve. Last night, my pimp beat me up real bad because I had a slow night." The girl paused, her voice tight with emotion. "Rose told me I could get help and protection if I came. So, here I am."

Noelle was relieved to learn that Father John was indeed running a support group to help prostitutes. He remained quiet, listening to the women in the circle share their sad stories one by one. Each had a similar tale of pain and abuse. Finally, Rose's turn came to speak. She talked about her fear of retribution from her ex-pimp, Rocco. "He just won't believe that I never saw the killer in the act of slaughtering my trick, the second victim in the Holy Roller Murders. He even had his buddy, that SOB, dirty cop interrogate me for hours. But Rocco keeps still accusing me of hiding something. Now he's making my life worse than usual. If it hadn't been for him pimping me out to that freaky minister in the first place... talk about being in the wrong place at the wrong time. The whole thing smells fishy. Sometimes I think Rocco sent me there on purpose. In the past, he's been known to watch me from a peep hole. All I know is that while I was on my knees sucking off the trick, someone came from behind and covered my eyes and chloroformed me. Now Rocco's pissed because I'm not earning for him. After that, nothing could get me back on the street," she told the group. "Nothing."

Father John concluded the meeting by telling the women that he couldn't promise complete protection unless they moved into a shelter and cut off all ties with their pimps as well as other girls still working the street.

He stood and blessed the ladies with holy water as he made the sign of the cross on their foreheads. The meeting was over.

Noelle held still in his hidden spot until everyone except Rose was gone. As she blew out the candles, he desperately wanted to approach her but he knew it would freak her out. According to her story, the poor woman had endured enough trauma for one life .

Moments later, Rose let herself out the front door and locked it behind her. Noelle quickly left out the back door. He reached the street in time to follow her in his truck as she walked in the direction passed the voodoo church. She didn't even glance at the storefront with all the yellow tape around it. Noelle drove slowly, keeping his distance, but still keeping Rose in sight. He watched her stop as a white Cadillac pulled up to the curb.

Noelle couldn't believe his eyes as Rose leaned into the open driver's side window. 'Was she hooking so soon after she swore she'd never go back on the street?'

Rose walked around to the passenger's side of the car and got in. Knowing that old habits die hard, Noelle was not shocked to see that Rose could be still turning tricks. He wasn't surprised, just disappointed. Sorry for this lovely girl who was so self-destructive. Although he knew a lot about that subject.

The Cadillac peeled out into the street. Noelle followed as it turned onto a deserted block and parked. Noelle found a spot for his truck almost a full block away. Bending down, he snuck out of the Ford and slipped behind the bushes on the side of the road to get closer to the action.

When another car passed the Caddy from the opposite direction, its headlights shoned brightly, illuminating the windshield. This gave Noelle a good look at the driver in the front seat. It was none other than the very same thug Noelle had witnessed Rose arguing with at Lucky's. It was all falling into place now. Noelle was sure that the dirty cop Rose had mentioned was none other than Tucci. He'd bet his right nut on it. This was a dangerous position for an ex-hooker to be in and Noelle began to worry for Rose's safety. At the same time, he wondered if she was playing double agent with Father John and the mob.

Noelle was close enough now to hear their voices rise in the Cadillac. The pimp brutally struck Rose across the face. Helplessly, he watched as the large man pushed Rose down on the front seat. From Noelle's position behind a storefront pillar, it looked as if the guy had his hands around her throat. That was about all Noelle could take.

He sprinted to the Caddy, grabbed the door handle and caught the thug by surprise with one solid sucker punch to the nose. The huge man's blood rained down onto his white silk shirt. Noelle felt pride that he still had the fire in him to take down a mobster. For good measure, he gave the creep one more punch in the jaw to make sure he'd be laid out for a while.

When Noelle looked up, he saw Rose bolt out of the car and start running toward Orleans Street. Quick on her heels, Noelle cornered her at the entrance of a dark, shuttered bar. Rose had fire in her eyes as she tried to push Noelle away.

She screamed, "Asshole, what are you trying to do? Get me killed?"

Noelle held onto Rose's flailing arms. "No, just the opposite. Please, Rose, relax. That guy looked like he was hurting you. Or worse."

Rose sneered, "Rocco? That's a laugh. He only likes to play rough. I can deal with it. Giving him a little taste now and then is my family's insurance policy. Believe me, he's not going to kill me. I'm worth too much alive. He only wants to make my life a living hell."

Rose shook her head and slumped back against the wall. "*You're* the one who's in trouble now," she sighed. "You better hope he didn't get a look at you before you knocked his lights out."

Noelle was taken aback by the tough talk from Rose. All of her warmth and grace was gone. She was cold and hard. The exact opposite of the sweet, amiable shop girl he'd met at her mother's store that afternoon.

Rose asked, "What were you doing around here? Slumming again?"

Noelle couldn't let on that he'd been spying on her or that he'd heard her story at the meeting. Instead, he pulled the dumb tourist card and replied, "As you know, I'm new in town. I got lost on my way to the French Quarter."

Rose smirked, "Yeah, I heard that story already."

Noelle ignored her snarky comment and continued.

"I got out of my truck to see if I could read the street address on a storefront. That's when I saw what was going on in the Cadillac. Are you sure you're okay? I can give you a ride to wherever you need to go. My truck is just down the block." Then, for good measure, he added, "You might consider reporting the attempted rape to the police."

"Get real!" Rose laughed wildly. "Like I said, it wasn't rape. Even if it was, the police could care less about what happens to a gypsy hooker in Tremé. I'll just go back to my mother's store, thanks. I'll spend the night with her."

She started walking.

Noelle asked, "Aren't you at least a little bit concerned, knowing that two of your neighbors were murdered on your block last night?"

Rose shrugged it off. "I've lived in Tremé my whole life. Knife fights, gunshots and crime go with the turf. Although I have to admit my mom's been pretty spooked about those murders. She knew the victims. They shopped at her store."

Taken off guard, Noelle slipped up. "So, that's why Detective Tucci was coming into the store today."

Rose gave Noelle a funny look. "How does a tourist know anything about Tucci?"

Noelle tried to cover his screw-up. "I read the papers and I've seen him on the news. He's a pretty memorable character."

"Yeah, but he didn't come into the shop until long after you left. Who are you, one of the feds? Are you stalking me?"

Noelle swallowed hard and told Rose a half-truth.

"Okay, you got me. After I left your store, I went and had some lunch. While I ate, I read about the Voodoo Murders in the paper. Then I got to thinking about you and how lovely you are. I thought I'd swing back around to see if you might want to have dinner with me. Being a tourist can be lonely. That's when I saw Detective Tucci going into your mom's shop, so I gave up and went home."

As Rose held back a smile, her eyes sparkled, "Oh, so it was just a coincidence that you *happened* to get lost again in my neighborhood tonight? For all I know, you could be a bigger creep than Rocco."

"Yeah, but you have to admit, I'm better looking." Rose just laughed, "Even an orangutan's ass is better looking than Rocco."

With that, Noelle laughed too. "Okay, I'll come clean. The whole truth is I'm an amateur detective and I was curious to check out the scene of the crime. And I confess I was hoping to bump into you again."

At that point, Rose and Noelle were in front of her mom's shop. She took out her key.

"Well, thanks for nothing, Mr. Noelle. You can always come back during business hours for another reading. It seems like you have a lot of questions you want answered. We're open from eleven am 'til seven pm."

Rose opened the door and stepped inside the shop. She slammed the door in Noelle's face. He waited until he saw her turn on the lights then walked back to his truck, frustrated.

Noelle was at a loss as to what to do to quell his impending nervous breakdown. Not only did he attack a well-connected mobster, he had promised to find his missing brother, Brandon, before his mother died. It was a tall order even for him on a good day.

Noelle stopped at a phone booth to call Sally again. Once more, he got no answer at home. He thought to call the Catholic church she was now attending to see if they had her work number at the hotline where she volunteered. When he glanced at his watch, Noelle saw it was way too late to call anyone except for a suicide hotline. Hell, he was desperate. He probably *would* need a suicide hotline if he hadn't been such a coward.

Noelle just stood on the street, stumped, with his stomach grumbling. He couldn't remember the last good meal he'd had—and here he was, in a city world-renowned for its outstanding cuisine. But Noelle was so worked up, he knew that a heavy meal would only fester in his gut.

Across the street was a street vender with his cart. The air was fragrant with the scent of fresh beignets frying in a vat of grease. Noelle couldn't resist and bought three to go.

On the way back to his room, he picked up a fresh bottle of Jack. He figured at least the deep-fried fritters would soak up the alcohol he was about to consume. Noelle was being pulled beneath the surface in an undertow of loneliness. He knew this dejected feeling required more than an ocean of booze to drown it out. But for now, Jack and beignets would have to suffice.

Back at the boarding house, Noelle entered quietly, going straight to his room. After locking the door, he poured a long drink. He devoured the powdered sugar-encrusted fried dough while jotting down ideas for ways to find this brother Brandon. He really didn't have a clue. He thought it was a pity that he couldn't believe in God because he was going to need a supernatural power for that task.

Eventually the whiskey got Noelle's wheels spinning again. Although he thought it would be like finding a needle in a haystack, he figured his best course of action was to start looking for Brandon in Mississippi by calling the town sheriff. Maybe the law would have some idea of his brother's whereabouts.

Noelle let the words roll off his tongue, "Mayfield, Mississippi... ." It sounded old, archaic. He called information for the number of the police department in Mayfield and had the operator place the call while jotting down the number.

As the phone rang, Noelle imagined a crummy, hole-in-the-wall with a single cell jail. It probably had no more than two cops on the beat for the entire town.

Giddy with Jack Daniel's, he snickered when he pictured a scene from the Andy Griffith television show. Andy was a widower sheriff in Mayberry, North Carolina, where he lived with his son Opie and his Aunt Bee. When Andy's bumbling idiot of a deputy sheriff, the neurotic Barney Fife, came to mind, Noelle laughed until he cried.

If only his mother had lived such an innocent, 'white picket fence' childhood, he wouldn't be the screwed-up man he was today.

Finally, someone picked up the phone in Mayfield. The southern drawl of a good old boy barked into the receiver, "This better be an emergency. You got any idea how late it is?"

Noelle imagined that the guy had been taking a nap in the cell when the phone woke him up.

"I'm so sorry," Noelle apologized. "But I'm calling from out of state and I wasn't sure if you were open twenty-four hours like the big city precincts."

Noelle knew his remark would strike an envious chord in the police officer.

He continued, "I'm Nick Noelle, a detective working on a serial homicide case. I'm looking for information on a baby boy born in Mayfield sometime after the First World War."

"Buddy, you've got some..."

"Look," Noelle told him. "I know it's been awhile but I thought there might be a few senior citizens still alive today who may have known his mother. I would have checked Mayfield's Hall of Records, but I know he was born at home."

"Well, if you know the mother's name and the child's name, I could ask around. But it will have to wait until tomorrow."

Noelle took a moment to shuffle through his whiskey-addled brain. He wasn't sure if his mother used her maiden name of Lee or was the child registered as Ezekiel Garsett's son on the birth certificate.

"All I know is that her first name is Catherine and she named the boy Brandon. Although the child might have been adopted and given a different name since his birth mother ran away without him. He was only two years old then. My guess is that some preacher and his wife took him after that. Their last name was Garsett."

"I'll see what I can find out."

The alcoholic haze momentarily cleared and Noelle suddenly remembered another name. "It's possible his real father was a big shot named Justin Morgan. His family owned half the town back then. Maybe they still do."

"Thanks. I'll do my best but I can't promise much," the cop said. "Call me between four and six tomorrow. It might take some time to ask around. Mayfield isn't the horse and buggy town it was in those days."

"Who should I ask for? I didn't get your name."

"I'm Officer Billy Bob Barton. If I'm not here, leave a message."

Noelle hung up the phone feeling a glimmer of hope. He poured another tall drink to celebrate the possibility that he might have some answers about his brother soon. He finished off half the bottle and got into bed, hoping for the soothing comfort of sleep.

Early the next morning, Rose woke in her mother's bed to a loud pounding on the door. She stumbled downstairs in her robe to see who was making such a racket.

Rose couldn't imagine that any of her regular customers would be so rude—everyone knew Madam Esmeralda never woke before ten.

Rose unlocked the door to see Rocco staring her in the face. He was sporting a big, fat shiner and his already long, crooked nose was now even more bent out of shape. It was black and blue and twice as swollen.

"Okay, bitch," Rocco yelled. "Did you see who did this to me last night?" He pushed Rose up against the wall just inside the store and leaned into her.

Rose tightened the robe around her body and tried to move away even though she knew it would get Rocco even angrier. Cornered, she felt his hot breath on her face.

"All I saw was a big fist out of the corner of my eye. You were on top of me, blocking my face, so I couldn't see anything, she cried. "I got so scared that I jumped out, ran and never looked back. Can you blame me after what I've been through. I thought whoever it was, might have a hit out on you, and would not want any eyewitnesses. So I ran as fast as I could and didn't look back. I'm sorry. It looks like he got you pretty good…but at least you are alive."

Rocco threatened Rose with his frightening, black eyes. He roughly wedged a finger under her chin, lifting her face to his. Rocco's putrid breath made Rose want to vomit.

"You better be telling me the truth, Rose. If I find out this has something to do with that faggy priest you've been hanging out with, he could easily end up like road kill...worse than the archbishop."

Rose was stone-cold scared but didn't show it. Rocco had done a lot of things to her but he had never threatened a priest before. He was a good Catholic, well for a wise guy that is.

Rose spoke up, "Father John could have never done that to you. He's half your size and doesn't have an angry bone in his body. From the size of the fist I saw and the thick upper arm, this was no skinny guy that clocked you. Besides, Father John doesn't know anything about our relationship."

After his beating, Rocco's left eye now had a speck of black on its white pupil. Rose stared at the mark while trying to hide her fear.

Rocco appeared even more dangerous when he cocked his eye and smiled.

"Rose, since we were so rudely interrupted last night, you still owe me that date you promised," he said.

Rocco grinned and whispered in her ear. "Don't worry doll, I'll be gentle, but you *will* give me what I crave. And I'll make you dinner. My Bolognaise sauce has no competitor," he winked. "Now, where's that sexy smile?"

Rose forced a grin.

"I know you love it when I cook for you. So be hungry, baby. I've got some business to tend to now but I'll pick you up later. We're gonna eat early because we'll need all night to play."

Rose gritted her teeth, "Okay, Rocco, I'm looking forward to it."

Rocco pushed his thin, pale lips onto Rose's soft, plump ones. When she tasted his rancid saliva, she wanted to wretch. The sight of his big, ugly, broken nose made her sick.

He put on his black sunglasses and squeezed her cheek hard. He spoke like an Italian grandma, "Ma quanto sei bella."

Rocco emitted a laugh of pure evil and headed out the door. Rose slammed the door hard, leaning against it in relief.

She looked at herself in the shop's mirror. Rocco's pinch of affection had left a red mark. She knew it would bruise. Rose knew it was a dangerous fine line she walked with this monster. All she could do was pray that his karma would catch up to him someday and that Rocco would end up like one of his own victims.

Chapter Twenty-Five

A Farewell to Catherine

That night, Noelle was tormented by the same dream that brought him to his mother. In that dream, his mother was always calling him. And he could never save her.

The sun had yet to rise when Noelle jolted up out of his nightmare. His eyes flew open and he shook fiercely. At first, he thought he was still asleep because he couldn't believe what he saw. The room was brightly lit and he found himself shivering from the icy, cold air. It looked almost as if a cloud had opened.

Standing there before Noelle he saw his mother Catherine. She loomed larger than life and flew over him to land at the foot of his bed. His first impulse was to scream until he laid eyes on this beautiful, innocent, young presence. It was Catherine before life had taken its toll, before young love betrayed her, before she was attacked, before she was forced to give up her first-born son, before poverty perverted her spirit.

A great ease took over Noelle and he felt incredibly relaxed. He smiled at Catherine who was dressed like an innocent bride, all in white. Her long, red hair was blowing in a breeze. She stood as if she was challenging the wind.

For a brief second, Noelle thought this vision could be Sally. But no, it was definitely his mother. Catherine stood there for a few moments, sweetly smiling at him. She blew kisses with her lovely, graceful fingers. In amazement, Noelle watched his vision of Catherine float closer to him until she was seated at the edge of his bed. As she leaned forward, her arms circled him, holding him tightly, she whispered, "Brandon is closer to you than you know. Look in the unlikely places." Noelle felt the most glorious sense of love engulfing him, a feeling he had never known.

Suddenly, without a word, Catherine smiled, stood and began to back away. With each backwards step she took, her body became more transparent until she disappeared altogether.

Once the apparition was completely gone, Noelle began sobbing uncontrollably. Never could he recall a feeling of such incredible bliss, of such peace, then followed by deep sorrow. The tears just kept coming. Noelle hoped this was a dream but he knew he was awake, wide awake. Noelle pinched himself, just to be sure. It hurt. Yeah, it hurt to be alive.

In awe, Noelle realized that he had just seen his mother's spirit. Before this experience, he wasn't the sort to believe in ghost stories but now he was a true believer. 'This is some sort of an omen,' Noelle thought. He knew in his gut that his mother must have passed during the night.

By the time Noelle showered and dressed, the sun had come up. He drove slowly to Saint Mary's to face the truth. When Noelle arrived at the home, the receptionist was coming on his shift. Eric waved, "What a surprise to see you at this ungodly hour! What'd ya do, pull an all-nighter? You know officially, visiting hours don't start until nine, but you can go up. I'm sure Sister Theresa has started her breakfast rounds by now."

Noelle nodded distractedly. His mind was on his mother only. Like a robot, he took the elevator to the third floor. The hallway was cloaked in silence, as if it too knew a secret. Today there were no patients wandering about or bumping into the walls with their wheelchairs. Today, there was nothing.

Through the doorway to Room 305, Noelle saw his mother sleeping peacefully with a sweet smile on her face.

172

Relieved, he walked up to the bed and leaned over to kiss her on the forehead. But as soon as he touched her skin, he knew Catherine was gone. She felt unusually cold. When he put his ear to her chest, it didn't rise and fall. The breath of life had left her.

Noelle walked calmly out of the room to find Sister Theresa. A male night attendant appeared, and on his heels was Sister Theresa. A grave expression shadowed Noelle's face. Without him saying a word, the nun knew. She was at Catherine's side in a flash, pressing her finger to Catherine's neck to check her pulse. Sister Theresa turned to Noelle with tears in her eyes. "Oh, Nick! I'm so very sorry," she said, her voice wavering. "It appears that our dear Catherine has left us." Sister Theresa paused to regain her composure. "By the look on her face, I can assure you that your mother had a peaceful death."

Nick stuttered, "I had a dream last night. She was beautiful…young…happy. You know, I think maybe, she *is* at peace."

Sister Theresa spoke softly. "Even if you don't believe in life after death, you can take solace in knowing that at last, your mother is in a better place." Silent tears ran down Noelle's face but Sister Theresa didn't mention them. "Nick, would you like to be alone with her for a few moments? To say goodbye?"

Noelle nodded.

After the nun and the attendant left the room, Noelle pulled up a chair. He sat beside his mother, looking at her sadly. He bent over her face and kissed her gently on the lips. From somewhere deep inside, Noelle found the words he could never say to her when she was alive. He took a deep breath and began.

"Mom, I'm so sorry I wasn't the son you had hoped for. I know you were probably proud of me for my accomplishments but that doesn't make up for the men in your life that broke your heart. Even me."

Noelle paused and wiped his eyes with the back of his fist.

"Although it's been hard to read, I'm glad I finally learned the whole truth about your life. I'm sorry for what you went through. I'm so sorry I couldn't have eased your pain when you were alive but I promise you one thing: I will do my best to find your son—my brother—Brandon. And when I do, I will treat him like a brother. Mama, I will also arrange to have you buried near me in Houston so I can look after your grave. If there is an afterlife, I hope you're looking down on me now and really know how much I love you. And if you do find that God, you know the One you wrote your diary to, please ask Him to help me. I need to be a better man."

By now, Noelle was crying hard again. "I'm also sorry you never met my wife, Sally. She wanted to come and meet you but I stopped her. I know you would have loved each other. Please, forgive me for being such a foolish man. I promise you I'll try to do better." Noelle kissed his mother one last time. He pulled the sheet up and tucked it around her body, as one might do to a sleeping child.

As he left the room, Noelle called out for Sister Theresa.

The nun joined him in the hallway. She told him that she would give orders for the attendants to prepare Catherine's body for the funeral.

"Nick, are you up to talking about your mother's funeral arrangements? If not, I understand completely, but I'm here to help you in any way I can."

Noelle smiled gently, "Sister, you have done so much for my mom—and me—already. Yes, of course we can talk now. Maybe you can suggest what you think she would have liked."

Sister Theresa nodded. "Let's go to my office."

She led Noelle down the hall to a small, pleasant room. She offered him a seat. Noelle didn't know where to begin.

"Sister," he sighed, "I started to tell you how my mother came to me in a dream early this morning. I tried to convince myself it was a dream, but honestly, I think it was real. She looked like her younger self. She was dressed in white, like a bride. She was so beautiful."

Sister Theresa replied, "It's not uncommon for the spirits of our loved ones to show themselves on their way out to the other side. They visit to say a final farewell in the hopes of comforting the one they're leaving behind. Catherine obviously felt very close to you. I'm sure all this time you've spent at her bedside trying to get to know and understand her life brought you two closer than ever. She felt your love."

Noelle nodded, comforted by the thought. "I sure hope so, Sister. It's hard to know how much she suffered. But like you said, maybe she's in a better place now. I think I believe that. I *want* to believe that."

"That's the best way to look at it," Sister Theresa said.

Noelle was silent, trying to take it all in.

"So, what do you think we should do for her service? I don't know any of my mom's friends down here or if she even had any still alive. I haven't made too many of my own either. I do know that Father John from Saint Catherine's Cathedral would facilitate the service if I asked him."

"Yes, Father John. I know him well. He's a good man. Also, if I have your permission, I'll write up a notice for the local paper's obituary column. If someone out there knew your mother, we can let them know that way. I hope you'll contact your wife now and invite her. I'm sure she'll want to comfort you at this difficult time."

Noelle shrugged. "Well, I'm not so sure. She's been avoiding contact with me lately but I can't say I don't deserve it. I'm going to send word to my buddy, Juan. His wife is Sally's best friend."

Sister Theresa patted Noelle's hand. "I'm sure she'll come when she learns you've lost your mother. In the meantime, it might be best to have a brief viewing in a day or two, followed by a service in our own little chapel here at Saint Mary's. I know your mother liked it there. From what I recall, she used to go there to talk with God before she became bedridden."

Noelle laughed softly. "So, she still liked talking to God? You know, Sister, her notebooks were filled with her letters to God. They were like prayers. It was only when she got older that she started to lose faith."

The nun shook her head in acknowledgment. "Nick, I knew all about that. Catherine knew I understood her. That's why she confided much of her history with me when she was still able to do so. Like I've told you, I haven't always been a nun…"

Sister Theresa bit her lip then continued. "As a matter of fact, I, too, was abused as a very young girl and fell into a life of prostitution. Like your mother, I felt I had no alternative. Before your mom started falling in and out of consciousness, we talked a lot. Like Catherine, I returned to the God of my childhood, the God I felt had abandoned me. But He didn't abandon me...quite the contrary. He saved me. He saved me from the horror I was living. When I was saved, I knew that I wanted nothing more than to be a nun. Since that day, my life has been peaceful and I never regretted my decision and the vows I took one bit."

Noelle was shocked. "Sister, don't you ever wish you had a man and a family of your own?"

"I married Jesus," she responded. "He's more real to me than any man I know in the flesh and he gave me a family—all of humanity—the men and women who I help on their journey. From them, I get all the love I could possibly want."

Noelle smiled, "Well, I have to take your word for it, Sister. You let me know what day the service will be and I'll invite some of the folks from my boarding house. I'd love to see my mother have a nice send off. I'll give you whatever you need as far as money goes, for food and flowers and the works."

Noelle left Saint Mary's with mixed feelings that afternoon. He was heavy-hearted, yet somehow relieved that he was free to go back to finishing the job he'd started...solving the serial murders. It seemed to be the one thing he was good at.

As Noelle walked through New Orleans, he thought about the Holy Roller Murders. He knew he had to find the killer, especially since the investigation was being led by a dirty detective. Tucci would probably pin the rap on anybody just to get it off his roster of unsolved cases.

Noelle thought that his mother's spirit might even start guiding him. Divine intervention, so to speak. He knew he had changed drastically after his mother appeared to him in his room.

Noelle's mind traced back to what it did best; obsessing over murders. All that had happened lately flooded through him: the incidents with Rose, Father John and the mobster Rocco. Noelle breathed deeply and stood still. He tried to quiet his thoughts because he realized that his hands were shaking. He couldn't control the tremors. So Noelle headed straight to the liquor store, pushing the bottle down in the bag to hide the evidence.

He thought, 'I can hide the bottle, but I can't hide the truth from myself? Who am I kidding? But how am I going to get through the next few days? When I finally get in touch with Sally, what will she say? And if she agrees to come to New Orleans, with one look at me, she'll know the whole truth.'

Noelle caught a glimpse of himself in a souvenir shop window. He looked ratty, like an alcoholic bum. His nose was gin-blossom red. His body shook unless he indulged. He was getting a gut again. He knew the minute she saw him, she'd leave and never look back.

With reality hitting hard like a sledgehammer, Noelle popped into a greasy spoon diner for some fried eggs and coffee. A fat, slovenly waitress placed a cup of black coffee in front of him. She took his order while he gulped down half of the hot liquid, burning his throat in the process. When the waitress left the table, Noelle looked around to make sure no one else saw him. He refilled his coffee cup from the bottle of Jack Daniel's hidden in the bag.

When the waitress returned with his sunny-side-up eggs and ham, she turned her nose up at him. Noelle knew she could probably smell the booze in his coffee but he didn't care. As she walked away, he repeated the drill.

After breakfast, with a good buzz on, Noelle drove past the fortune teller's storefront. He parked a few car lengths away, past the store across the street. He paused behind the steering wheel, contemplating whether or not to go in.

Before he could make a move, the shop's door opened. Out came Detective Tucci holding Esmeralda's arm. Tucci escorted the fortune teller as if he were taking his own mother out for a Sunday jaunt. Tucci opened the door of his unmarked Dodge. He helped her into the passenger seat, carefully tucking in her dress as he closed the door. Tucci got behind the wheel and drove off.

Noelle was conflicted about going in to see Rose, especially since he had no real excuse. His other option was to follow Tucci and Esmeralda but it seemed too risky in broad daylight. The last thing he needed was to piss off the crusty detective again.

Noelle thought he had the perfect excuse: to ask for a reading, especially now that his mother had died. He hoped it might soften up Rose and make her feel some compassion for him. Noelle could use a little compassion…and so much more.

Just as he made up his mind to go into the shop, he noticed the big, white Cadillac pull up in front. Behind the wheel was Rocco. Noelle thought that he and that dirty cop must have their filthy hands in so many pots that Noelle was losing track.

There was no way he could confront Rocco and risk being recognized as the guy who'd knocked his lights out. At the same time, Noelle was worried about Rose's safety.

It was too late to trail Tucci so he dropped down behind his steering wheel to wait it out. Not long afterward, Noelle heard two car doors open and close then the Cadillac started up. He caught a glimpse of Rose and Rocco in the front seat. It would be too obvious if Noelle followed the Caddy.

Unsure what to do next, Noelle felt worn to the bone. He had to get some shut-eye to make up for his sleepless night. He headed in the opposite direction back to the boarding house.

The first thing Noelle did was to call Sally. For the millionth time, there was no answer. Noelle dialed Lopez. He didn't answer either.

Then Noelle remembered that he needed to call Billy Bob Barton in Mayfield, Mississippi about his brother Brandon. He dialed the good old boy and held his breath.

Chapter Twenty-Six

Esmeralda Schools Tucci

Esmeralda was pleasantly surprised when Tucci rolled up in front of Gene's Po-Boys. She loved the down-home, no-frills sandwich shop known for their hot sausage po'boys and the best desserts in town.

Tucci parked his unmarked car and winked at her. "Come on, Mama," he cooed. "Let's have some lunch before you roll up your psychic sleeves and get to work. This one's on me."

He escorted Esmeralda into a private booth in the back and asked what she wanted. Then he walked up to the counter to place their order.

The gypsy queen mother and the hard-nosed cop made small talk, catching up like close friends until the waiter dropped off their food at the table. Esmeralda tucked her napkin into her collar like a bib to cover her ample bosom just before she went for her po'boy.

"You know how my shelf catches every drop that doesn't go into my mouth," she said in a gay tone.

Tucci chuckled as Esmeralda wrapped her scarlet lips around the hot sausage sandwich just like a working girl, doing her best job to take it all in at once.

"That-a-girl," he encouraged. "You can save the crumbs for your dog."

This wasn't the first time Tucci had spent his lunch hour with Esmeralda, both personally and professionally. He had hired the psychic for her services on several past cases. This afternoon, he sought information about the murdered Bizango. It took real talent to do this while not letting on that Esmeralda herself was a person of interest in the Voodoo Murders. But then again, Tucci was a seasoned detective, one of the best.

Underneath it all, Tucci actually had a dual purpose for this outing. His buddy Rocco had asked him to detain Esmeralda for as long as possible since Rocco needed time alone with her daughter, Rose, for different reasons. Tucci suspected that Rose was hiding something but couldn't say what.

What Tucci didn't know was that on many a drunken night, Rocco had blabbed one too many secrets to Rose about their involvement with the Marcello and Carlucci families. Rocco kept the details of his future business with Rose a secret. He was hoping to put the fear of God into her. He wanted to make sure she kept her mouth shut about the things she had no business knowing in the first place.

Tucci casually asked Esmeralda, "So, tell me about your daughter. I heard Rose gave up her occupation for religion. That true? "

Esmeralda swallowed her mouthful of sausage and snapped back, "You'd get religion too if the last dick you sucked was hacked to bits by a freak killer,"

Tucci continued, "We have reason to suspect her friend Father John of a cover-up, most likely following orders from the very top of the Church. You wouldn't want Rose getting in the middle of that."

"Detective, before you talk dirt about my daughter or any religion, you should know that Creoles, particularly in New Orleans, are strongly influenced by the French Catholic culture," Esmeralda warned him.

Tucci scratched his kinky hair, perplexed. "But I thought you told me that you were no friend of the Catholic Church," he pressed. "You said that your grudge went way back. That's why you went voodoo."

"Did you know I can trace my oldest ancestor back to one of the many women the French authorities deported to New Orleans from their prisons to help populate this colony? Most likely a prostitute or a felon. Along the way, our blood got mixed with the Africans and the Native Americans. My people got more religions to flavor us than the spices we use in our jambalayas. We're a lot like you Italians, especially the ones from Sicily, who are only passing for white."

Tucci visibly bristled at her remark. He looked at Esmeralda oddly. "I've never been to Italy, so I wouldn't know."

Esmeralda opened a Wet-Nap package with her teeth and wiped her hands clean. "Come on, Tucci, even you know that blood is thicker than water. I'm ready for dessert now."

"Get whatever you like. The New Orleans Police Department can afford it."

"My daughter and I are close but she's got her own mind. Rose has been on a mission to help abused young girls find suitable work. She thinks she can do this without hurting our mutual friends in the mob families."

Tucci's expression changed. He was clearly pissed off. His raised voice had an edge when he barked, "I thought Rose was smart. Doesn't she realize the very girls she's trying to get off the streets cut into the families' bottom line? Drugs and prostitution. Rose is playing with fire, messing with the families' revenue. If I were you, I'd get your girl under control before something happens to her. You know, I can only offer her so much protection. She has to play by the rules...or else!"

Esmeralda's pulpy, generous body stiffened. She tried to appease Tucci. "Detective, my Rosie has always been faithful to Rocco—and you. There's no reason to think this is going to change. She'll get bored with her new mission soon."

As Esmeralda got up to use the restroom, Tucci waved to the waiter so they could order dessert.

"Just get me the house special," she told him as she stood. "You know that delicious beignet sundae with the vanilla ice cream, fresh strawberries and whipped cream...and black coffee."

"You got it, mama," Tucci said, his voice cutting like a knife.

When the waiter came with the coffee, Tucci took a packet out of his suit jacket and poured its powdery contents into Esmeralda's cup. He stirred it quickly with a spoon then wiped it clean.

Esmeralda and her dessert arrived at the table at the same time. She devoured it, smacking her lips then gulped down her coffee. Once satisfied, she announced, "Okay, I'm ready now for the business part of our lunch."

"Good. But I want to do the reading at the station so I can record it. I left my gear there."

Tucci threw cash on the table to cover the bill and the tip. Smiling like the gentleman he wasn't, he grabbed Esmeralda's arm and marched her back to his Dodge. The moment they reached the car door, the old woman collapsed in his arms. To passers-by, it looked like they were hugging. Tucci opened the car's rear door and sprawled Esmeralda across the back seat. He locked the door and sat behind the wheel.

'It's all going according to plan,' Tucci thought as he drove away.

Chapter Twenty-Seven

A Special Meal

After picking Rose up at her mother's store, Rocco escorted her to his apartment in the Garden District. With bravado, he ushered her through the front door. Rose grinned like a simpleton, hiding her fear behind her phony smile.

"Smells good in here," she stammered. "Like you've been cooking all day."

Rocco seemed different, as he spoke in an odd, stiff tone. "I got oysters on ice for starters. That's my insurance policy to get you in the right mood."

Rocco planted a harsh kiss on Rose's mouth, bringing his teeth down onto her lower lip. He wedged his tongue far down her throat. She thanked God she knew how to avoid the gag reflex. Whenever Rose had to perform a disgusting act with a man, she calmed herself by thinking about another man...a man she secretly desired but knew she could never have.

Rose's suspicions about Rocco flared up full-force. Something had changed in his attitude lately. Rocco was more than just rough with her but he seemed more aloof too. What started out as a sex game seemed to be escalating and it made her anxious. Rocco shoved Rose into the living room.

To ease her nerves, Rose admired all the new beautiful things Rocco had collected since she'd last been to his apartment. Rose could never understand how such a brute could have such love for art and music. He was unlike any of her other crass clients.

Before she met Rocco, Rose worked for a high-class escort service. For the most part, her johns had treated her like a lady. They taught her about the finer arts and talked to her about classical music. She could distinguish Debussy from Mozart, a Ming vase from a made-in-Japan fake. Despite the fact that Rocco took her to an opera once, he lacked real class. Rose chalked up his brutish nature to his low birth. Being Creole, she thought very highly of her own culture regardless of her current circumstances. She thought Rocco fit the disparaging term for Italian immigrants, WOP, perfectly. It stood for "without papers," and referred to the way some Italians snuck into the country illegally. Yes, Rocco was a WOP, no doubt about it.

Rose knew that his apartment and all its contents were paid for by the hits he'd done for mob families. Rocco took sick delight in the horrible, twisted ways he punished people who didn't pay their debts to his bosses. Rocco only occasionally got tight, but when he did he had loose lips, especially after their sordid, alcohol-laced sex games.

Without warning, Rocco pushed Rose against the wall, pawing her breasts. After a tortuous few minutes, he let them go. Rose had to remind herself to breathe. Somehow she would get through this night in one piece, she told herself.

Totally switching gears, Rocco casually threw open the kitchen door. Like a demented Julia Child, he smiled, "Sit down, Rose. I'm going to finish up dinner. I want to gaze at your beautiful eyes while I cook."

Rose thought to herself that Rocco seemed to be losing it like some schizophrenic switching gears with every sentence. Rocco busied himself around the kitchen and put a large pot of water on to boil. He poured them each a glass of wine and growled, "Don't make me regret wasting this vintage on you."

Next, he set a platter of iced oysters in front of Rose. "Now dig in while I finish up the sauce!" It wasn't a suggestion; it was an order.

Rocco lifted his glass to touch Rose's. With an air of superiority, he stated, "To our night together. It better be worth all the trouble I went through. Before I'm done seducing you, you will love me like you used to."

Rose hid her fear behind a girly giggle but was thinking of how twisted Rocco was to believe that she had actually ever loved him. Once the water was boiling, Rocco threw a pound of linguini in the pot and stirred.

He stared hard at Rose and told her, "It won't be long now. Go on, have a few more oysters. No bird-like eating tonight." He gave the sauce another stir. "I can't wait to watch you slurp up my Bolognaise. I made it extra rich." With eyes dark as midnight, he looked at Rose, trying to gauge her reaction. He turned back to the pot and threw a handful of fresh, chopped parsley into the sauce.

Rose was growing more and more nauseous as he continued to shove raw seafood down his gullet. Rocco cleaned his fingers on a linen napkin and washed down the oysters with more fine wine. Rose thought about what her mother had once told her, "For a WOP, that Rocco's got some champagne taste." It was true.

Rose had a hard time forgiving her mother for getting them into this mess in the first place. Rose had been doing just fine with her high-class escort job before Rocco was forced upon her. Esmeralda had played the numbers one too many times. A losing streak caused her debt to the mobsters to mount. The only way she could get out of not having her legs broken was to give her daughter over to Rocco. In exchange, he paid her debt to the mob and let the gypsy keep her legs and fingers intact.

However, once Rose got into bed with Rocco, she learned the truth. He was one twisted fuck, for sure.

After cooking it to a perfect *al dente*, Rocco drained the pasta in an enamel colander. He transferred it onto an antique Chinese platter and poured the rich meat sauce over the top.

Lifting the platter, Rocco smiled maniacally at Rose. Forcefully, he said, "Come on, Rose, drink that wine already!"

She took a big gulp, afraid to incite his wrath. "This food is too special to eat in the kitchen," he barked. "Let's go into my dining room."

Carrying the platter, Rocco called out to Rose, "Grab the wine."

Rose took the bottle by the neck with one hand and both glasses in the other. It was going to be a long night.

With dread, she followed Rocco into the dining room. His twelve-foot long mahogany table was covered with the best linen tablecloth money could buy. Two places were already set with his fine china and polished sterling silver cutlery. Rocco put the platter down and sat at the head of the table. With one of his fat, sausage-like fingers, he gestured to the place setting at the other end of the table.

"Sit!" he commanded.

Rose sat.

In the center of the table was an elaborate floral display with graceful, silver candlestick holders on either side. Rocco leaned over and lit both candles with a long matchstick.

"Well, isn't this special!" Rose remarked cautiously. It had the makings for a perfect romantic evening, except it was anything but. 'Only an asshole like Rocco could have such delusions of grandeur,' she told herself.

Rocco grinned maliciously, showing his set of too-perfect gleaming, white teeth. His tongue slid out like a lizard's as he said softly, "On second thought...I want you closer."

Without waiting for Rose to move of her own accord, he stood and roughly pulled her up out of her seat. With his free hand, Rocco slid Rose's place setting down the table until it was beside his chair. All the while, he never let go of her arm. Instead, he squeezed it tighter. When he finally released Rose, she sat down. Her arm ached where he had grabbed it.

"It all looks so wonderful," she said carefully. "This will definitely fill me up."

Rocco snickered, "You better eat! And don't you worry; I have an extra special treat in store for dessert." Rose could only imagine.

Rocco served her a healthy portion of the pasta. Out of the corner of his mouth, he remarked, "I just love pork. Growing up in Sicily, this was something we only got on holidays. I loved watching my father slaughter pigs. Little did pop know he was training me for my future career."

Rose gave him a weak smile. "I'm full from all those oysters you made me eat. You know I can't perform well if my belly's stuffed, honey."

Rocco polished off all the food on his plate.

Suddenly, without a word, Rocco stood and pulled Rose to her feet. Grabbing her tightly by the wrists, he pushed her up against the wall. With one hand, he pinned her wrists up over her head. In a New York second, a long, silver knife flashed in front of her eyes. Rocco slid it down to Rose's throat. He tightened his grip on her, pushing the dagger into her jugular vein. The pressure was slight but his motive was clear—he intended to terrify her.

Whispering maliciously in her ear, Rocco hissed, "Come on, you whore, let's go upstairs."

When she tried to obey his command, he yanked her wrist. "On second thought, you go up ahead," he told her. "I'm going to open another bottle of wine. You know where my dressing room is and you know where the mask and clothes are. Go get everything ready!"

Rose trotted up the steps, knowing she was going to have to fake it to make it work. She had to convince Rocco that she cared about him by playing his favorite game. At this point, it was her only protection.

In Rocco's secret closet, Rose found the black leather pants and vest he liked to wear. She pulled her costume out from the back of the closet. He kept Rose's nun outfit in a special place. In every respect, Rose's outfit looked like an authentic nun's habit from the Salient Order of Sisters that Rocco had grown up with back in Sicily. However, the nun's garment had been slightly altered; there were holes cut out to expose the breasts. There were also slits in the floor-length, black frock that were meant to expose the vagina. The outfit came complete with black "granny panties" with one slight alteration—they too were crotchless.

Rose put on the perverse costume pieces one by one. She tied back her long, dark hair, covering it with the wimple. As soon as she was fully dressed, she trembled as she heard Rocco marching up the stairs. With every step, Rose could feel the inner rage of a harshly punished child, and the angry man who never got over it. Rose wanted to cry, pray and scream all at the same time.

Rocco snatched the black leather pants and vest out of Rose's hands. He slipped into the bathroom to change. When he was finished, he slithered back into the room like a king cobra ready for the kill. He grunted, pinching her nipples. "I want *you* to undress me now...one piece at a time," he commanded in a raspy whisper.

Rose spoke in a deliberately sexy tone, "Shouldn't we have some music?"

"Good idea," Rocco agreed. Still snakelike, he seemed to glide over to the stereo. He selected his favorite opera, Carmen, then joined Rose back in front of his vanity mirror. It reflected Rose's shame.

Rocco watched Rose unwrap him. When she got down to his undershorts, she paused.

"Let's have another glass of wine...in remembrance of our Lord's blood—the blood that was shed for our sins."

She was hoping that if Rocco drank enough, he might just pass out. She knew that if he didn't pass out, *she* would need the whole bottle of wine for what she knew was coming next.

Rocco poured them each a glass and downed his in a flash. He pressed close to Rose's face.

Suddenly Rocco was all over her, all at once. He pulled Rose into his beefy hairy arms, but not to caress her. Instead, he shoved her down onto the floor as he jabbed himself into her. She shrieked. Rose's pain fueled him. He pushed himself harder and harder inside her, slamming against her hipbones.

He grabbed Rose by the waist and tore off what was left of her dress. He finished himself off on her as though she were garbage, a rag that existed only to soak up his refuse. Like a dog pissing on a tree to mark its territory, Rocco rubbed his semen all over Rose's thighs, soiling her. Cackling hysterically, Rocco grabbed the wine bottle, draining every last drop in one long, continuous swallow.

Rolling over on his stomach, he grunted, "You can let yourself out. I don't want to see you here when I wake up." He drifted off to sleep almost immediately and was soon snoring like a hog wallowing in its own filth.

Shot through with stabbing pain, Rose wiped herself off and dressed. Her every move made the ache inside her throb. She was bleeding and could feel bruises growing where Rocco had struck her. She was a mass of hurt, both inside and out. After this brutal attack, she grew even more worried about her safety and especially Father John's. If Rocco had suspected her true feelings for the man she loved, the priest would be a goner.

Rose listened as Rocco snored loudly in the adjoining bedroom. She thought about killing him but she was clearly aware the repercussions from Tucci and worse yet, the mob. She was trapped. She would be the one to pay the ultimate price and who knows what they would do to her mother, Esmeralda.

After she dressed, Rose took each step very slowly, holding onto the polished mahogany bannister. As she let herself out, Rose wondered where she could go. Her bruises and bleeding brought Christ to mind and then Rose thought of him again, her comforter, her priest, the man whose arms she longed for. Rose pushed away her fear and headed to the cathedral. She didn't care. She *had* to see him. In the fierce city night, Rose rushed toward the only man she had ever loved.

Chapter Twenty-Eight

Baby Shower, No Surprise

Sally cut the crusts off slices of Sunbeam bread. She was in the middle of making mini tea sandwiches for the fancy mother-to-be get together she'd planned for Maria's baby shower. Her stomach rolled slightly as Sally lightly buttered the white bread and arranged thinly-sliced circles of cucumber on them.

As she put her hand over the tiny bump she'd been concealing from the world, Sally felt a twinge of guilt for not confiding in Maria about her pregnancy. After all, Maria was her best friend. Sally's rationalization for not sharing the news with Maria was that she didn't want to upstage her friend's own blessed event. Sally prayed she still had plenty of time to keep the secret, before her own belly became obvious.

Lost in thought, Sally began to worry about the life inside her. 'How will my child survive without a father? Will I be able to do it alone? Will I be a good mother?'

As if awakening from a trance, Sally heard someone calling her name. Maria was standing on a stool, holding ribbons and scissors in her hand, grinning at her.

"Earth to Sally…where are you?"

When Sally snapped to attention, Maria asked, "How do you think this looks, *chica*?"

"Maria, get down from there! I said I would put up those ribbons. You shouldn't be standing on a chair! With scissors, no less! What if that stool turned over?"

Maria stepped down and spoke softly, "And you think *you* should?"

Sally shook her head, "I'm not the one who's pregnant," she said.

Maria walked over to Sally and gently touched her tummy. She looked into Sally's eyes. Maria's voice was firm but her lips turned up into a smile and her dark eyes danced with pleasure.

"Sally, do you really think I don't know?"

Sally's face flushed as Maria continued.

"You have that glow."

"I...uh..." Sally stammered.

"Don't feel bad," Maria told her. "I understand why you didn't tell me."

Sally smiled, relieved, "So, am I showing?"
Maria put her arms around Sally's waist. "No, but you've gone from looking like a half-starved deer to a babe filled out in all the right places...a voluptuous woman in a matter of weeks."

Tears dribbled down Sally's cheeks. She brushed them away. "I just didn't want Juan to know before I was ready to tell Nick," she cried.

"I get that," Maria said. "But Nick's got a right to know"

"He's been gone over six weeks! I miss him but I have to admit my life has been more peaceful without him."

"I trust you will do the right thing. This is a secret that won't keep long," Maria added, as she gently rubbed Sally tummy.

Sally sat down on the step stool. She wrapped the ribbons around her neck and sighed, "How about I just decorate myself and make the announcement at your party?"

Lately Sally's mood changed erratically from the surging hormones. She went from pleased to pissed in a matter of seconds. Frustrated, she hurled the Scotch tape against the wall.

"Shit! I still love that asshole!"

Although Maria laughed, the look in her eyes was serious. She gave Sally a hug. "I know you do. So, what are you going to do?"

Before Sally could answer, Juan barged in through the front door. Juan caught his wife and Sally locked in a sisterly embrace. They moved apart and started fussing with the decorations again.

"Well, I see you two are busy," he told them. "I promise I'll be out of here before the guests arrive but I have something important to give Sally."

Juan slipped an envelope out of his jacket pocket then took Sally gently by the arm.

"Nick just called. His mother died during the night. He sent you a plane ticket to come to the funeral service. He said he doesn't blame you for keeping your distance but he could really use your support right now, even if it's just for a day or two."

Maria just shook her head and neither woman said a word. Juan continued.

"Sally, I know Nick is a lot of things but he loves you. True, he has problems but deep down, he wants to do the right thing by you."

On the verge of tears, Sally said, "Well, he has some crazy ways of showing it."

"Not that you asked my opinion, but I think you should go to him," Juan told her. "If anyone could be a positive influence on him, it's you."

Sally breathed deeply. She looked to Maria for support.

Her friend clucked gently, "*Chica*, it's the Christian thing to do…taking the high road. You love him, no matter what you hate about him." She put her arm around Sally's shoulder. "In the end, love is always the way."

At this, both women teared up. Juan looked at them and laughed, "*Dios*, Maria! I can't handle two women in tears. I'm going back to work."

Before he left, Juan handed Sally the envelope.

"Your mother-in-law's funeral is in two days. They're having a small, private service at Saint Mary's Home."

Chapter Twenty-Nine

A Meeting of Importance

Although his mother's death had brought Noelle some relief, it was the two fifths of Jack that helped him sleep uninterrupted for several hours. The vision of his mother had altered his life but unfortunately, not his drinking habits.

Noelle was jolted awake, not knowing whether it was day or night. Once his focus sharpened, he saw the clock on the nightstand read 9:45 pm. He tried to get out of bed but his knees buckled and he fell back onto the mattress. This was a sure sign he had to cut back. But not right now. Noelle knew that Jack Daniel's was the only reason for getting out of bed at that moment.

He stumbled to the table where he found a few shots left at the bottom of his last bottle. Popping four aspirin, he washed them down with booze. Slowly, his motivation returned. Noelle took a quick shower and headed out. Although it was late, he thought he might be able to catch Father John before his nightly prowl to save hooker's souls.

Even though he knew that if he didn't get sober it would be the death of him, Noelle dropped into the neighborhood liquor store, then drove the Ford over to Saint Catherine's Cathedral. He knew he was risking the wrath of Mrs. Murphy but he also knew that he had a good enough reason to disturb the old hag; his mother was dead and he needed Father John.

This time when the door swung open, Mrs. Murphy, in her fetching curlers and flannel robe, flashed Noelle a big, wide grin. The normally gruff Irish housekeeper was so friendly it startled him. In her rippling brogue, she said, "Oh, I see you're here for the party, too!"

Noelle nodded.

"You might as well go in then. You'll feel right at home. He's entertaining all kinds of riffraff tonight." Noelle had judged her attitude too soon. Mrs. Murphy left him in the door way and hightailed back to her room in a huff.

Down the hallway, Noelle saw the light on in the priest's office. The door was cracked open slightly. Smelling like an old, musty bar, Noelle barreled down the hall toward the office. To be polite, he knocked on the partially open door. There was no response. When Noelle popped his head in, low and behold, there was Rose curled up asleep on Father John's little couch.

"Well, what do we have here? A poor soul looking for a priest or a detective looking for clues," Father John said, catching Noelle off guard as he came behind him from the hallway.

Noelle smiled, "A bit of both, you might say. But first, I'd like to know how you managed to sneak a pretty woman past Mrs. Murphy."

Father John laughed, "Nothing gets past Mrs. Murphy." A little too loudly, he added, "The poor girl was in need of a confession."

Noelle smirked, "Yeah, I bet!"

When Rose heard their banter, she rubbed her eyes and sat up. "Who's this?" But before Father John could make the introductions, Rose cut him off. "Wait, don't tell me. You're a tourist and you're lost again." Turning to the priest she pointed, "This is the mysterious stalker I told you about."

Sensing the tension, Father John defused the situation by offering them both some brandy. He poured a glass for himself as well.

"It's a good thing that Detective Noelle is here. He might be the only clean cop within a fifty-mile radius. I think it's a good idea to tell him what you told me tonight, Rose."

Her onyx eyes flashed with anger. "What can he do about it? His last attempt to save me from Rocco only made things worse."

Father John sat down next to Rose and took her hand. "Look, I know how you're hurting after what that pig did to you, but the detective here might find Rocco's behavior enough to link him to the murders."

For a moment, Noelle forgot why he'd come to Father John's in the first place. He immediately shifted into cop mode.

"What behavior?"

"Oh, you know, Detective, your everyday garden variety sexual assault."

Noelle was drawn to Rose's dual personality: a sad bad girl. "I'm sorry you had to go through that," Noelle said, attempting to comfort her.

Rose's vulnerability made Noelle think about Sally and about how pathetic she had been when she still worked the streets, taking all kinds of abuse from men like Rocco. Rose's raw beauty only made Noelle miss Sally more.

His police instinct overtook his sentimentality. Noelle switched gears as he wondered how to get more information out of Rose. He wasn't a hundred percent sure Rose was on the level about everything. For that matter, he still had doubts about Father John. Noelle had the strong suspicion both of them were hiding something from him but he couldn't put his finger on it. Not yet.

Father John poured more brandy into Rose and Noelle's snifters, and added to his own. The priest asked, "What do you think, Detective? Is Rocco the killer?"

"It's possible."

Rose threw back the contents of the snifter, mumbling, "I know for a fact that Rocco is a hit man for the mob families. He's told me so."

"Which families?" Noelle asked.

"The Marcello's for sure and maybe others too. He likes

living on the edge. If he could murder for money, don't you think it's even easier to kill for personal payback, right?" Rose asked.

Noelle nodded in response.

"I know that Rocco has resentments toward the priests and nuns who abused him in his childhood. He likes to 'roleplay'... if you know what I mean. I have never known a perve as twisted as Rocco."

Noelle sat in the armchair across from Rose and Father John.

"We can't trust Tucci," he told them. "I'm pretty sure he's covering for Rocco, too."

Rose rolled her eyes and snapped sarcastically, "You think, Detective?"

Noelle ignored her snarky comment then continued, "Rose, is there any way you can get back into Rocco's apartment without putting yourself in harm's way?"

Father John frowned. "I won't let Rose do that. She's not going back into the mouth of that monster." The priest glowered at Noelle. "You have no idea what he's done to Rose and her mother."

"I think I might know," Noelle told him. Father John shook his head. "Detective Noelle, as long as Rose let Rocco pimp her out and have his way with her, he spared Esmeralda from her bad gambling debts."

Rose lowered her eyes as the priest continued.

"I just know that he will never, ever let Rose go—no matter how much money is paid back to the mob."

Noelle tried to stop the priest's sermon but Father John wasn't having it.

"And here's another thing," he added, his voice trembling. "I've been trying to find a way to get Rose and her mom away from him for over a year now."

Noelle scratched his head. "Well, Father, it's possible I can help. Back in Houston, my wife works at a women's shelter. I may be able to keep them safe while I find proof to put him away for life or better yet, put him in the electric chair."

"That is one execution I'd like to witness!" Rose exclaimed.

"Nick, I'm not sure you can fully comprehend how corrupt and far-reaching these mobsters are. I'm pretty sure they could easily find the women, even in Houston," Father John insisted.

"If I can get enough evidence on Rocco, I can bring the Feds into this. If Rose and her mother testify, we can bring down the *whole* crime family. The FBI will secure Rose and her mother in the witness protection program."

Instead of being relieved, Father John looked worried and Rose laughed out loud.

"I can just see me and Esmeralda setting up a shop in Yuma, Arizona. The only way my mother will ever leave New Orleans is in her coffin. It goes against her Creole code."

Noelle smiled. "Rose, I can be very persuasive. Besides, there are Creoles all over the country—East Texas, the Gulf Plains, even Alaska."

"You don't know my mother. Good luck."

Noelle changed the subject. "Speaking of mothers, that's why I'm here. Father John, my mother passed very early this morning. I came to ask you if you might be free to officiate at her service the day after tomorrow."

Father John looked at Noelle with compassion. "I'm sorry to hear about your mom, Nick. But it must be a relief to know that she is in a better place."

Noelle shrugged. "Yeah, you Catholics seem to all agree on that point. I wonder how you can be so sure."

"I'll be happy to argue with you on theology some other time. But I'd be honored to do your mother's service. And it's on the house. It's the least I can do. I'll clear my calendar. Just let me know the time and where."

"How's Saint Mary's little chapel at three pm?"

"Perfect. It will be lovely to see Sister Theresa again. Will I finally get to meet your wife?"

"I sure hope so. I sent her a ticket but we haven't spoken yet."

Noelle turned to Rose.

"I saw Detective Tucci taking your mother out for a ride earlier today. Do you know anything about that?"

"Tucci invited her down to the station to look at mug shots of suspects in the Voodoo Murders. When I closed up her shop at six, she still hadn't come back yet, though."

"Weren't you worried about her?"

"My mom's a tough, old broad and I know that Tucci and Rocco are a little afraid of her. They think she can cast spells on them, especially if any real harm ever came to me."

Noelle promised to look into her mother's whereabouts.

"In the meantime, I think Father John is right. It's too risky to put you back in Rocco's apartment. I can probably get Sister Theresa to hide you at Saint Mary's while I make arrangements for a temporary safe house for you both."

Rose shook her head in disagreement. The two men exchanged weighty glances.

"Rose, I agree with the detective," Father John said. "Let him look for your mother. You need to let him keep you hidden from Rocco right now... and forever hopefully."

Rose pushed herself up from the couch and raked her hands through her hair.

"Okay," she sighed. "But first, I need to go powder my nose."

"You know the way," Father John told her.

Rose hurried to get to the bathroom.

Once Rose left, the priest asked, "Nick, how are you holding up?"

"I'm sad, but I'm also glad I learned a lot about my mother in her final days. I didn't know much until Sister Theresa gave me her diaries. My mom's life was much worse than I had ever imagined."

Father John shook his head in sympathy.

"Now I know why I've always been drawn to helpless women," Noelle continued. "Speaking of which, I wonder if my wife will come, Father. My non-stop drinking and gambling has really taken its toll on Sally."

"Do you love her?"

"Yes, I love her, Father, and don't want her to leave me."

Father John took away the snifter of brandy from Noelle. "Let's start with this," the priest said. He put down his own glass as well. "Yeah, helpless women," Father John told Noelle. "Brother, you're not the only one."

Noelle shot the priest an odd look. "Father, is this a confession?"

The priest smiled sadly and changed the subject. "Nick, what would you like me to share about your mother's life for her eulogy?"

"I'll jot down some of my good memories but I think Sister Theresa can contribute more than I can. Let's try and keep it short and sweet, shall we?"

At the same moment, it dawned on them that Rose had been gone for quite a while.

"Rose!" Father John shouted. He jumped up and ran down the hall to the bathroom. Noelle followed him.

Like a bat out of hell, Mrs. Murphy shot out of her room.

"If you're looking for that floozy, she ran out of here like the building was on fire."

"When?!" Noelle demanded.

"A few minutes ago, I guess," Mrs. Murphy huffed, annoyed. "I'm not a warden, you know. I'm just trying to get some sleep." She went back in her room and slammed the door.

Father John turned to Noelle, "Nick, I'm really worried about Rose. Even if Rocco doesn't hurt her, there's a good chance she might hurt herself. Since I've known her, Rose has had a couple of failed suicide attempts." Father John lowered his voice and admitted, "I'm ashamed to say that I let myself get intimate with her. I regret it now, not so much because of the sin against my vows of chastity but mostly because ever since it happened, Rose has been tortured by her love for me. It's only made her bondage to this monster more intolerable for her. She puts on a good act but she's more vulnerable than you can imagine. Rose is less worried about her own safety and more for what could happen to me if Rocco knew the nature of our relationship. Neither of us really knows what to do."

Noelle was shocked but not surprised. "Father, my gut told me that you two were hiding something. I'm glad it's this and not what I was thinking. In my line of work, I've seen that anything is possible. I'll try to find Rose…and Esmeralda."

Father John put his hand on Noelle's arm.

"Thanks, Nick. It feels good to give my confession to a man who understands these complicated matters. Someone who won't judge. You're the only friend I have who could help us."

"Father, I'm no saint and I'm no judge," Noelle told him. "You stay here, in case Rose comes back. I'll hit the streets. I'll let you know as soon as I find her. I need to focus on this right now. Crime work keeps me from wallowing in my own sorrows."

Noelle combed the streets of New Orleans searching high and low for Rose, going from the French Quarter to Tremé, all the way out to Marigny on the banks of the Mississippi. But he had no luck anywhere. Along the way, he hit up every gin joint he knew. Of course, at each bar, Noelle had a drink or two, asking questions, but getting no answers.

As the night wore on, Noelle got more and more inebriated. Although he was ashamed of himself, it didn't stop him from drinking. By three am, he headed home. The first thing he did was check the house's mailbox to see if there were any notes or messages for him. He was especially anxious to hear from Sally about her plans, if any, to fly down the next day.

Noelle was also hoping to get word from Billy Bob Barton, the cop from Mayfield, Mississippi. Noelle was disappointed to find nothing—nothing at all waiting for him.

Frustrated by a night of failures, Noelle called Father John to see if he had any good news. The priest told him he'd heard from Rose. She assured Father John that her mother was fine and they were both hiding out with a friend. Rose also promised Father John that she and Esmeralda would come to meet Sister Theresa at Saint Mary's the next day.

The good news about Rose and Esmeralda brought Noelle some relief. With that, he took his last drink and tried to get some sleep.

Chapter Thirty

The Funeral

Noelle entered the intimate chapel. He was glad it was empty and he could sit down before anyone else came in. The chapel held no more than twenty people but it was perfect because it wouldn't take much to make it look full. Noelle's eyes drifted to a fresco of the Virgin Mary holding the baby Jesus that was painted above the small, simple, mahogany altar. It was pretty and peaceful.

Noelle was feeling rough around the edges and needed liquor badly. At first, he tried to avoid looking at his mother's coffin but he had no choice. His eyes fell on the polished wooden box. The lid was up. 'Don't you dare look,' he told himself. He was afraid that seeing his mother's corpse would make him fall to pieces. Noelle took a deep breath and sat back down. He absolutely *had* to keep his composure when the guests, if any, started to arrive. Especially Sally.

Noelle sat in the front pew and bowed his head, watching his hands shake. He'd brought a small flask to remedy his affliction and looked around before he took a swig. Just as he put the bottle to his lips, he heard Sister Theresa say softly behind him, "Nick, is that what it takes to give you the courage to say farewell to your mother?"

Noelle jumped, startled. He stood up to greet Sister Theresa as she approached him, holding two gorgeous bouquets of flowers beautifully arranged in white ceramic vases. He took one from her and followed her to the altar. She made the sign of the cross with her free hand. She placed the vase on one side of the altar. Noelle did the same with the other on the opposite side.

Feeling like a child, Noelle spoke, "I'm sorry, I meant no disrespect, Sister, but this is a hard time to get clean. If I go too long without a drink, I'll be so shaky I'll look like I have Parkinson's."

Sister Theresa took Noelle's trembling hand and gently guiding him to Catherine's casket. "Nick," she began, "You know your mother is no longer in her earthly body but just in case she's looking down, you want her to see you being a gentleman."

Noelle had viewed more than his fair share of corpses over the span of his long police career but this was one he wasn't quite ready to see. To him, a casket was a glorified wooden box but he'd made sure to give Sister Theresa enough money to buy a good one. It was nice, simple and elegant, with a billowy, white silk lining and warm, polished cherry wood.

Side by side, Sister Theresa and Noelle knelt on the red velvet step that was set in front of the casket. He slowly opened his eyes. The moment he saw his mother, he felt a calm come over him. Sister Theresa had dressed her in fine, white lace. Her face looked lovely and at peace. All of her wrinkles had been smoothed over in death and her silvery head of hair looked full and lush as it fell on the snowy silk pillow beneath her head. As if in prayer, her hands were crossed just below her chest with a mother of pearl rosary in them. Noelle reached out and touched them. They felt cold, like wax.

He placed his large, unsteady hand over hers and wondered, 'Could I warm her with the vibration of the human touch?' Tears filled Noelle's eyes.

Sister Theresa placed her steady hand over his.

"Nick, it's okay to feel your feelings," she whispered. "The best way to get through grief it is to allow it. You don't always have to be a tough guy."

The tears welled up again, but this time, Noelle let them flow. As he kissed his mother's cold lips for the last time, he knew in his heart that his mother would have loved being in that sweet chapel, surrounded by serene beauty.

Father John joined them at the casket, carrying a prayer book in his hand. He tapped Noelle on the shoulder and bowed his head in greeting to the nun.

At the back of the chapel, Velda made a racket, her high heels clacking on the tile floor. She bustled in wearing a tight-fitting black evening dress. She even had a black lace veil on her head, covering her eyes. By the looks of her, Velda could have been a gay widow ready to cash in on her third husband's life insurance policy.

When she saw Noelle, Velda's loud voice reverberated in the tiny space as she shouted, "Oh, Detective, Detective Noelle! I'm here for ya baby!"

She ran up to him and threw her arms around Noelle like a long-lost lover.

"I just had to be here to offer you my condolences and pay my respects to your poor, dead mother. If there's anything I can do to bring you comfort, just ask. Am I the first guest?"

"Besides Father John and Sister Theresa, yes."

He and the nun made their way toward the front pew as Father John said a short, silent prayer at Catherine's coffin.

"Well, Mr. Fletcher left before me," Velda huffed. "I thought he'd be here by now. I hate to be too early but it's probably God's will so I can look after you... if you need me."

Velda nodded "hello" to Sister Theresa. She almost tripped over the nun, jockeying for position to sit on the opposite side of Noelle. Wedged between the black nun wearing all black and the wacky black widow, Noelle felt like the white meat in a strange sandwich.

With that thought, he turned his head just in time to see Fletcher saunter in. He was dressed to the nines in a charcoal gray sharkskin Italian suit with a red rose in his lapel. Fletcher tipped his fedora toward Noelle, Velda and the nun. He removed his hat as he took the pew on the opposite side of the aisle.

Sister Theresa whispered to Noelle, "Now's a good time for you to stand beside the coffin so the guests can offer you their condolences if they wish to view your mother's body."

Sister Theresa ushered him to the casket. Noelle saw Eric enter from the back of the chapel. Noelle felt a twinge of sadness at the paltry gathering for his mother's sendoff, especially with Sally being a 'no show'. He was left with only a floozy, a fag and a nursing home's receptionist.

He started to tear up but his 'pull yourself up by your bootstraps mentality' held him back from showing any emotion.

Eric approached and offered his condolences. He handed Noelle a note and said, "Detective Nick, some big dude left this letter for you at reception a few minutes ago. He said to give it to you after the service but I don't want to forget."

Noelle thanked Eric and as he reached for the note, Sister Theresa intercepted it and said, "Here, let me hold it for you now. I have big pockets."

Trembling slightly, Noelle sunk to the kneeler in front of his mother's casket. As he did, he noticed Detective Tucci and his sidekick Melville peeking their heads through the chapel's door before they entered.

'They have some nerve,' he thought, watching as they took seats in the very last row. Ever the social butterfly, Velda, jumped up and starting waving wildly to Tucci. She motioned for them to come up front and join her in the first pew. Although Tucci acknowledged her, he remained in the back.

Noelle was miffed that the detectives had the balls to come to his mother's service, especially after the last harsh warning Tucci had given Noelle.

Seeing Tucci and Melville reminded Noelle of the many times he attended the funerals of murder victims. As a detective on the case, he often used it as a ploy to see if he could cull information from the friends and relatives of the deceased—but his mother was no murder victim.

Noelle stood up. Sister Theresa was beside him at the coffin as they waited for more mourners to arrive. In an odd way, Noelle wished some ex-hookers who knew him and his mother back in the day would show up. They were most likely all dead and gone, too. It was a rough life on the streets and few made it to old age. His mother was one of the lucky ones, whose husband took her off the streets, but in the end not so lucky. He only prolonged her life for more abuse.

This train of thinking only made him think of Sally and how she traded the streets to be his wife. After all they had been through together, he didn't blame her for not showing up for him.

Tucci, Melville, Velda, and Fletcher left the pews to form an orderly line to pay their respects to the bereaved. As they approached, Noelle mused that this was one weird ritual and a good reason he never wanted to join a religion, particularly the Catholic religion.

The whole event felt like a scene in a bad movie, especially when one random little old lady with advanced Alzheimer's accidentally entered the chapel. She kept hitting the back pews with her wheelchair until Eric jumped up and rolled her out.

He wondered what any of these characters wanted with him or his mother. Yet he was glad someone was there to fill the empty space, even if none of them had known Catherine or could fill the emptiness in his heart.

Father John made his way over to Noelle and asked how much longer he wanted him to wait before starting the eulogy. Looking pathetic, Noelle said, "The one person I was hoping would come isn't here, so I guess you can start as soon as everyone gets back to their seats."

Noelle knew Sally was angry but he really expected her to show up—or at least send flowers and a note. Her absence made him lonelier than ever. Noelle was also concerned about Rose and her mother. They hadn't come as Rose had told Father John they would. It was pretty obvious Father John was worried too. The usual twinkle in his eyes was absent when the priest took the pulpit. Noelle thought Rose and her mother might have spotted Tucci on their way in and did an about-face and left.

Noelle's mind fluttered from one thought to the next. This all felt so bizarre, like an out-of-body experience or a surreal dream.

For a split-second, Noelle thought about the note Eric tried to give him. He was itching to know what was in that note deep down in Sister Teresa's pocket. He wished he could read it now. Maybe it had been from Sally, telling him why she didn't come. Until Noelle remembered that Eric had told him a big guy had given it to him. Possibly Rocco or some other thug.

Father John cleared his throat and invited the small congregation to join him in the Lord's Prayer. Everyone prayed out loud, particularly Velda, whose volume rose above the others. She certainly made up for Fletcher's silence. The incantation was disjointed, out of sync with voices rising and falling throughout the prayer.

Noelle thought Father John was going to recite something out of the prayer book he was holding but the priest set it aside and began to speak from his heart.

"Welcome everyone, to Catherine Noelle's farewell service. I know only two people in this room have had the pleasure of knowing Catherine well. Her son, Nick and her caregiver, Sister Theresa. They have shared much about her with me."

"According to Sister Theresa, Catherine found comfort in the Church later in life. And according to her son, who spent several weeks at her bedside reading the journals she wrote as a child and a young woman, his mother had a passion for talking to God. In her diaries, she wrote volumes to our Lord whenever she had free time from school and her hard life working on her parents' farm."

"Catherine was a child with responsibilities far beyond her years particularly because she lost her mother at only fourteen years of age."

"Nick also shared that his mother had suffered at the hands of an abusive father. Nick, who grew closer to his mother at the end of her life, brought a new revelation when he learned that he had an older brother named Brandon, a secret Catherine was determined not to take to her grave."

"To escape the wrath of one of her abusers, the poor woman was forced to abandon this child against her wishes. It was this injustice, which took her on a path of sin and degradation. This led her away from her faith. But in my humble opinion, God doesn't care how long one of His children strays. His arms are always open to welcome them back home to Him."

"Sister Theresa shared her first-hand knowledge with me that Catherine had indeed renewed her deep connection to God before she passed. I'd like to quote Theodore Parker, a Unitarian minister I discovered in my studies. Minister Parker was the first to rise up against the cruelties of slavery in eighteen fifty-three."

Father John opened his little notebook and read the passage from Minister Parker, "The arc of the moral universe is long, but it bends toward justice."

"For Catherine and her sons, I believe this is true and applies to her life. With Nick's loss, he has now found a new purpose—a mission to find justice along with finding his long-lost brother. Finding his brother was his mother's dying wish. From the little I've learned of Nick's character, I know he will honor his mother's wish as she now rests in the peace and comfort with our Lord in heaven.

"Now we will have a few words from Sister Theresa."

The nun stood and made her way to the pulpit.

"I will make this very brief since it is not my habit of speaking in public," she smiled warmly. "But I had the great pleasure of knowing Catherine Noelle and I only wish that all of you assembled here could have known her lively spirit and great sense of humor. Despite Catherine's physical and emotional pain, she always found a way to shine that light within her. She was truly a beautiful soul. Before she took a turn for the worse, while she was still able, she entertained me for hours with her stories. Catherine was the kind of patient who makes my calling to serve the sick and dying sheer joy."

"It didn't take me long to realize that God sent me Catherine so I could help guide her back to Him. Knowing that she died in perfect peace with a smile on her sweet face has strengthened my own faith and dedication to my calling."

Sister Theresa became emotional as she looked toward the open casket. She paused and bowed her head for a moment to pray and compose herself. "Thank you, Catherine Noelle, for being the precious child of God that you are."

With that, the nun made her way back to her pew.

Father John stepped back to the pulpit. "Nick has requested that his mother's final resting place be close to his home and arrangements have been made to send her body to Houston. So this concludes our service. But I invite you to please stay for the repast. There are lovely refreshments: tea, coffee, savory and sweet treats being served in Saint Mary's dining room. Please join Nick, Sister Theresa and myself there. All are welcome."

During Father John's closing prayer, Noelle heard footsteps at the back of the chapel. When he turned around, he was delighted to see Sally standing there, looking radiant in a simple black linen A-line dress. She came forward and bowed her head to kiss him. Noelle knew he reeked of alcohol and prayed she would forgive him.

When Sally looked lovingly into Noelle's eyes, he was surprised to see her love for him was still there. She took his hand and whispered, "I'm so sorry I'm late. My flight was delayed."

Noelle smiled. "I'm just glad you're here now."

The sound of Father John's prayer and everyone surrounding Noelle faded as his eyes remained fixed on Sally. Noelle waited until all the guests moved out of the chapel before he escorted his wife up to the casket to meet his mother. "I'm really sorry it had to be like this," he told Sally. "She would have loved you as much as I do."

Sally looked down at Catherine's peaceful face as she pressed one of her hands to her heart in prayer. She slipped her other hand into Noelle's then turned to face her husband. "I'm learning to accept God's will," Sally told him. "So I know that whatever happens, it will all be fine." She gave him a tiny smile. "Come on, let's join your guests, I'm starving and haven't eaten in hours."

When Noelle and Sally entered the reception room, he pointed Sally toward the wonderful buffet Sister Theresa had set up for the repast. "I need to use the gents," he whispered to his wife. Noelle assured her he'd be right back to introduce her to his few friends.

The moment Velda saw Sally alone near the buffet, she made a beeline to the table, determined to be the first one to introduce herself to Noelle's wife. After piling as much food as she could possibly fit onto the tiny plate, Velda squawked, "Oh, you must be the beautiful Mrs. Noelle. Nicky has told me so much about you."

Without taking a breath or allowing Sally a response, Velda babbled on.

"I've just been dying to meet the woman behind the man. I'm more than honored to be hosting your dear husband at my boarding house. He's been nothing but a true gentleman. It gives me great comfort knowing I've got a lawman on the premises. Your husband helps me sleep at night."

Sally looked at Velda in wonder as she took a gulp of air and plowed on.

"I'm sure Nicky has told you all about how he's been lending his expertise to our own best of the best, Detective Tucci. Helping solve our horrific serial killings. It's been just awful down here, so terrifying, but I suppose you must be used to your husband being the hero like he was back there in Houston."

Sally opened her mouth to speak but couldn't get a word in. Velda gestured in Detective Tucci's direction and continued.

"Do you see him? Over there? That's the illustrious Detective Tucci. It's so kind of him to take time out from his busy work to come pay his respects to your husband's mother. That's how highly he thinks of your husband. I know it's an honor code among law officers to respect the fallen but it shows great character in Detective Tucci, don't you think?"

Velda finally shut up long enough to load her trap with a bite of a cream puff from her plate.

Sally took the opportunity to jump in. "Who did you say you were?" she wondered.

With a full mouth of whipped cream, Velda spoke.

"Oh! Please! Do excuse my manners, I'm Miss Velda, the proud owner of one of New Orleans finest boarding homes." She paused to wipe the dollop of cream that was dripping down her chin. "I do hope you'll be staying with us. I can make room for you by moving your husband to a larger suite of rooms with a king size bed in it. It just became available on the main floor. It will be much more comfortable for you both than trying to cram into that tiny musty basement apartment. I'm sure it would be more to the liking of a fine lady as you. Just say the word and I'll have my maid ready the apartment suites for y'all."

"That's very kind of you," Sally told Velda, "but that may not be necessary. I'm not sure if I'll stay the night."

"Oh, I know Mr. Noelle won't want to leave town until he finishes up his business with Detective Tucci. They are putting their talented heads together to solve our Holly Roller Murders," Velda said knowingly. "I'm sure he's told you about them."

While Sally was pinned to the buffet table by Velda, Noelle asked Sister Theresa for the letter she'd been holding for him. He walked briskly to the men's room so he could read it in privacy. He closed himself into a stall and opened it. The note was from Rose.

Noelle wasn't surprised by its contents. Rose's handwriting looked shaky, as if she'd been told what to write at gunpoint. It said that she and her mother were being held hostage by Rocco and wouldn't be released until Noelle met him at midnight in a secret location to be revealed in another note that would be delivered later that day. Rose also added a warning not to tell Father John or Sister Theresa about this meeting—or they might become the next Holy Roller victims.

Visibly shaken, Noelle came out of the bathroom. He immediately looked for Sally and found her at the buffet nibbling at a plate of food. His heart raced when he noticed that the shift in Sally's demeanor that only moments ago was loving now seemed cold.

"Look, Nick, we need to talk," Sally said sternly.

Noelle braced himself for what he knew was his deserved condemnation.

"Nick, I know you've been drinking, gambling and God knows what else while you've been here in New Orleans. And I was seriously thinking of leaving you for good. But recently God has given me the courage to take the high road in all my affairs." She paused, her eyes glowing. "I do love you with all my heart, Nick Noelle. And I probably always will. But I don't know if I can live with you ever again unless you get sober and quit gambling. I need the kind of man who can face up to the responsibilities of being a husband and father."

"A father?" Noelle stammered.

Sally looked down at her shoes then at Noelle. "Yes, Nick," she cried. "You're going to be a father. I'm about six weeks pregnant."

Noelle's heart started beating so fast he feared it might burst through his chest. His hands began to shake and he needed a drink badly. Fumbling for words, he stammered, "I knew there was something different about you. But I was afraid it was that you were just happier being away from me. Are you really pregnant?"

Sally nodded. "I know we've never even talked about having kids but I've wanted to have a baby with you ever since I got clean and sober. Only I knew you weren't interested so I kept my mouth shut."

Sally waited for her husband's response but he was silent, still in shock.

"I want you to know that I'm going to have this baby, with or without you. A child is coming and your actions will determine if our child and I will be in your life."

Noelle pulled Sally toward him. He wrapped his arms around her and whispered in her ear.

"Sally, I want you so badly that I want whatever you want. I don't know if I can fight this demon alcohol." He added hesitantly," But I will try!"

"You're going to have to do better than try," Sally told him. "You'll have to prove yourself before I let you anywhere near us, even if it means being a single mom. I don't want that but God's given me the strength to do it if I have to."

Noelle held Sally tighter. "I don't want you to have to."

"Nick, if I could get clean and sober, you can too,"
she said.

Noelle pulled slightly apart from Sally and stared into her eyes; they were as blue and true as sapphires.

"Look, we can talk more about it once everyone has gone. This isn't the right place," he told her.

Sally agreed.

"So, let me introduce you to Father John and Sister Theresa."

Noelle took his wife by the hand and began moving toward Sister Theresa, who was checking on the buffet.

"I know you'll have a lot in common with her," he said.

Before Noelle could reach the nun, Velda and Fletcher stopped Noelle and Sally in their tracks. Velda bubbled excitedly, "Oh, Mrs. Noelle, please let me do the honor of introducing you to my fine boarder, Mr. Fletcher. He and your husband have become good pals during Nicky's short stay with us."

This was the last thing Noelle had the patience to deal with. His tremors were getting worse and he needed to get out of there as fast as he could. After learning that he was going to be a father, now the weight of his problems pressed down even harder, like a six-ton elephant. Noelle hoped to put Sally into the safe hands of Sister Theresa so he could slip off to get a drink. Now he knew that wasn't possible.

Fletcher gave Sally a slight bow and took her hands in his. In a dramatic gesture, he placed a kiss upon each hand in a royal greeting.

"Oh, Mrs. Noelle, you have no idea how happy I am to meet you! For a while there, I was starting to think you were a figment of Nick's imagination. But low and behold, you're really here and you're stunning just like he said you would be! Miss Velda has told me you'll be staying with us. I do hope we can become friends."

Velda interjected, "Oh, yes, Nicky dear, I told your wife that I have a comfortable, larger suite available for you both to move into for the remainder of your stay and for however long you need it."

"Yes, *Nicky dear*," Sally gushed, mimicking Velda and nudging Noelle. "Velda also said she was sure you wouldn't want to leave town until you helped Detective..."

"Detective Tucci," Velda offered, giving her big, scary jack-o-lantern grin.

"…helped Detective Tucci crack his case," Sally continued. "Isn't that right, honey?"

Noelle had a hard time keeping his poker face. He grumbled, "Miss Velda seems to know way more about it than I do. I'm not even sure if my wife is spending the night," he said to Velda.

Fletcher took the opportunity to jump back in. "Oh, Sally, you must let me show you the Big Easy. I know all the best restaurants in town and Nick has told me that you love antiques. I can introduce you to some of our finest vendors and even get you a good price on anything special that might catch your pretty eye. I can see you are a woman of good breeding just by your wardrobe. Antiques and design are my areas of expertise."

Despite Noelle wanting Sally nowhere near these two characters, he knew that antique shopping would be the perfect diversion to keep Sally busy while he went off to take care of business. So he bit his lip and smiled at Fletcher.

"Why, Christian, that's a great idea. I know my wife loves to shop. I've wanted to get her something special before we return to Houston and you'd be much better at helping her find it than me."

Sally spoke quietly, slightly overwhelmed by the New Orleans eccentrics engulfing her.

"Well, I haven't reserved my return flight yet and don't need to be back at work until Monday," she conceded. "So perhaps a little shopping spree might be in order."

Fletcher clapped his hands together like a gleeful child.

"That's my girl! Always looking to make our home more beautiful," Noelle said and gave her an affectionate squeeze. Noelle knew that Sally was charmed by flamboyant gay men like Fletcher; he figured Sally would enjoy Fletcher's company more than he ever could.

Noelle was relieved when Sister Theresa and Father John joined them.

"I hate to interrupt the party," Sister Theresa said, "but the Sisters are getting ready to clear the room for the patients' dinner hour. Plus, I couldn't wait another minute to meet your wife, Nick." She turned to Sally. "We're so happy you made it down here. Your husband needs your love and support now more than ever."

Father John nodded in agreement. "Yes, ditto to that. According to Nick, you're the best part of his life. It's such a pleasure to meet you, Mrs. Noelle."

Sally blushed, humbled.

"Oh, please, call me Sally, Father..."

"I'm Father John. And this is Sister Theresa." They both shook hands with Sally as Father John continued. "I'm so glad Nick has a good Catholic woman in his life to get him on the right track. Sister Theresa and I have done all we could to get a new convert to our faith but there's no better person than you to give this man the nudge he needs."

"Yes, human love is the first step to understanding God's love," Sister Theresa confirmed.

Noelle smiled uncomfortably. "Jesus, you guys, the next thing I know you'll be calling the Pope on my behalf. Sally and I need a little time alone to catch up. We haven't even discussed our plans for the next day or two, let alone my conversion to Catholicism. You two are worse than Jehovah'sWitnesses."

The nun and the priest laughed at Noelle's joke but Sally said nothing. Velda filled in the awkward pause.

"Oh, excuse me," she announced. "I see they're clearing the table and I just *have* to have another one of those delicious cream puffs."

Velda tottered off to the buffet, grabbed another plate and quickly filled it with a mountain of pastries. A stern older nun swept away the almost empty tray from beneath her.

Fletcher offered his goodbyes with a graceful tip of his hat to all. He spoke directly to Sally.

"My dear, I trust I'll see you back at our home a little later. I'll get busy planning an itinerary for your Big Easy tour. I look forward to being in your presence again and at your service." With that, Fletcher left with a delicate swagger.

Father John pulled Noelle aside, leaving Sally and the nun to converse. Father John asked in a whisper, "Any word you need to share with me?"

Noelle nodded. "Yes, but not now. I'll call you in a bit." He thanked Sister Theresa for all she'd done and promised to visit the next day with Sally.

"I'd like that," both women agreed. Everyone went their separate ways.

Outside Saint Mary's, Nick opened the Ford's passenger door for Sally. As he put her small overnight bag in the back, he regretted not getting the truck washed even once since he took off for his road trip to New Orleans. The outward appearance of his Ford reflected the way he felt inside: dirty and in much need of repair.

"So where to, my lady? A hotel, or my place or do you want me to drive you back to the airport?"

Sally smiled. "Well, there's no use in wasting a perfectly good, opened-ended ticket. And since it's my first time here, I'd love to see a little of New Orleans. But from what Velda told me you might be too busy solving murders to show me a good time."

"Velda likes to exaggerate," he admitted. "But I won't lie to you. I've had a tough time keeping myself in retirement. Before you make any more assumptions, though, I'd like to talk more before you run back to Houston."

"Yes, we need to have that conversation," Sally agreed. "So, I guess I'll start my tour of the Big Easy at Velda's charming boarding house. I assume I already got a good preview just meeting the landlady and Fletcher. An overnight stay there might be more entertaining than dinner and a show."

"You assumed right, my lady," Noelle laughed and started the truck.

Chapter Thirty-One

Love and Sympathy

Noelle and Sally entered the lobby and were confronted head-on by Velda. She literally blocked their path, huffing and puffing.

"Detective Nick, I've taken the liberty to have all of your belongings moved up here so you and your lovely wife can have my best suite," she piped. "Don't thank me yet. Just wait until you see my finest room. It's well appointed with a large walk-in closet and a luxurious bath. Miss Sally, I swear, you'll feel like you're on your second honeymoon in this suite!"

With a scowl on Noelle's face it took all his strength not to snap at Velda for making that call without his permission. Before Noelle could say a word, Velda added, "And I want you to know, I'm not charging you one cent more for double occupancy. It's my gift to you." Velda handed Noelle a set of keys. "Please, let me show you the way."

Sally and Noelle followed Velda down the hall. They were both pleasantly surprised when Velda threw open the large set of double doors to reveal an elegant luxury suite, which resembled a period room in a Confederate war museum. With glee she announced, 'Now isn't this an upgrade from the cramped musty basement studio?"

The wide windows cast a flattering light on the greenish-gold wallpaper. A forest green damask couch with two large chairs and a matching sofa sat on either side of the windows, complimented by a low cocktail table. Off to the right, stood a four-poster king bed, sporting the same verdant pattern on its curtains, which were tied back to the posts. The bedspread was of the same lush green fabric as well, and had a sumptuous, gold silk comforter folded down on top of it.

"I helped the colored girl with the packing so it would be just right and ready for you." Velda piped. "And if not, you just come a knockin.' I'm right next door."

Noelle gulped when at the left side of the sitting area he saw a mini-fridge and an ice bucket. In it, a bottle of Dom Perignon sat chilling. Noelle stiffened when he also noticed a fifth of Jack Daniel's beside the cocktail glasses. He imagined Velda rifling through his trash to discover his drink of choice, and worse yet, her choppy hands going through his personal items to pack them. But he worried most about the box of his mother's fragile journals. Noelle looked over at the dresser to make sure they were still intact. They were piled neatly in the box Sister Theresa had given him, safe and sound.

"I trust you'll find everything to your liking," said Velda as she left like the tail end of a hurricane.

Before Noelle blew up with anger, he saw that Sally was delighted with the accommodations. This was her first vacation since their actual second honeymoon. She was giddy at the idea of being in New Orleans. Although she wished it was under different circumstances, she was determined to make the best of her time there.

Noelle was almost shy with his wife. He asked, "Well, my bride, would you like to share this king-sized bed with me or would you prefer I sleep on the silk sofa?"

Sally laughed, "Don't be silly. You know I'm going to give you some, even if it's just for old times' sake. We can call it your farewell fuck. Or who knows, it could be the beginning of a new life. That's your call."

Sally lay seductively on the sprawling bed. She summoned Noelle to join her with the curl of an index finger.

When he lay beside her, she put her arms around him and he pressed his lips to hers. Sally practically tore off the buttons of Noelle's shirt as she struggled to strip it from his body. With great relish, she slipped down his trousers. The moment Sally tugged off Noelle's undershorts, her lips wrapped around him. He almost climaxed immediately but forced himself to wait. Gently, he pushed Sally onto her back. "You first," he whispered.

Noelle looked deeply in Sally's eyes. He undressed her slowly, nibbling at every part of her beautiful, full body until his mouth slipped below her waist. He licked and teased her with the tip of his tongue as she moaned. Then Noelle slipped inside her. He almost climaxed, but he held back to rock her slowly as she melted beneath him, shuddering and moaning his name. Noelle came a beat behind her, tremoring in unison.

Afterward, they lay there quietly. Noelle's head rested on Sally's breasts.

"That's my idea of heaven," he told her. "I've been missing you something awful."

"I can tell," she said, stroking Noelle's hair. "I've missed you, too, but I don't want you to get too comfortable. I meant what I said. No matter how great we are in bed, I'm going to have to see some real changes in you before I let you back into our home. Do you think you can be man enough to change for me? Noelle's bliss quickly evaporated; it was replaced by stark, honest reality.

"Sally, I'm not sure," he told her. "I'll need some help. Some kind of treatment, I think. But I'm not quite ready just yet. I have to finish up my business here. There are some people who are counting on my help and I don't know how I can manage getting sober while doing what I have to do right now."

"Some people? What about me?" she asked. Sally jumped up and started going through her suitcase. Angry, she fished out her robe and put it on. "Why are *some people* your responsibility?"

"I'm talking about Father John and others involved with him, he pleaded. It's more complicated than I can explain to you in a few minutes."

Sally snapped, "Don't they have a police force in New Orleans?"

Noelle continued to explain. "The corruption at the top is even worse than it is in Houston. But I need at least a few days to try. Sally, if you give me that, I promise you, I'll check myself into wherever you think I should go to get help."

Sally sulked, "So I guess I'll be spending most of my time with Mr. Fletcher. You'll obviously be too busy!"

As Sally gathered her toiletries for a bath, she told him, "Well, I'm not going to leave until late Sunday."

"Sally, try to understand. People's lives are at stake!"
"What about *the life of our baby growing inside me*?" Sally piped.

Noelle said quietly, "Look, I'm sorry about this. But I need to run out right now. You relax, take a nice bath and get settled in. I'll be back in time to take us out for a nice dinner tonight. There is a time-sensitive meeting I have with Father John. I promise it won't take long. I'll check and see if Fletcher is free to entertain you for a couple of hours. That should give me enough time to do my business and get back in time for a late supper."

On the way to the bathroom, Sally told him, "You do that. If Mr. Fletcher isn't available, I'm a big girl. I can find my way around without an escort. Just go ahead and leave."

Although Noelle felt like a heel, he needed to check if a second note from Rocco had arrived. Noelle knew that the longer he took to find Rose and her mother, the more danger they faced. As he heard Sally getting into the bathtub, Noelle dressed in casual slacks and a light shirt and filled his flask back up from the complementary bottle of Jack Velda had left for him. Without a goodbye, Noelle slipped away.

In the lobby, he ran into Fletcher and told him that Sally would be free for a couple of hours to shop that afternoon if he was available. Fletcher was delighted. Noelle instructed him to knock on their door in about thirty minutes since Sally was in the bath getting ready. Fletcher assured Noelle that he'd take good care of his wife and went upstairs to change.

When Noelle checked his mailbox, there it was: a note

with his name on the front of a sealed envelope. He tore it open,
read the instructions then dashed out the front door.

Chapter Thirty-Two

A Date with Destiny

Within the pit of his gut, Noelle sensed danger as he reflected on how the average citizen couldn't even imagine the criminals who lurked in the moldy bars, clubs and shops of the Big Easy.

Determined to prevent a catastrophe without having the slightest clue, Noelle had to rely on his broken intuition. He hadn't had a drop of whiskey since he emptied the flask at his mother's service. Noelle was exhausted from fighting the tremors and downed the entire contents of his flask. He popped into the corner store and picked up another bottle, then climbed in his truck.

Although Noelle wasn't thrilled about Sally going out with Fletcher, it was the perfect distraction to keep her occupied. Before Noelle left, he put a wad of cash on the dresser to fund her shopping spree. It suddenly occurred to him how Sally might take it as an insult, especially since they'd just had sex. Noelle regretted the act, thinking she could easily interpret the money as his way of reminding her of her hooker days. He hoped like hell she didn't.

There was a good chance Sally would decide to never see Noelle again—or wouldn't let him see his child. His remorse about everything in his life loomed over him like a specter but he took consolation in knowing that at least Sally would be safe with Fletcher while wandering the dangerous city streets. Although he might be old, Fletcher was as strong as an ox.

Noelle needed his mind free to focus on the task at hand—finding Rocco's potential hangouts. Without realizing it Noelle saw that he was halfway to Jackson Square and Saint Catherine's Cathedral. He parked his truck and got out in front of the rectory. The fall feeling in the air had gone away and once again the humidity hit him head-on like a sucker punch. It felt like one hundred and fifty degrees and the stale New Orleans air mixed with the scent of incense wafting out from the cathedral and it made the air smell like dead fish.

Noelle tried to erase all of the bad scenarios playing in his head. He tried not to think of what Rose and Esmeralda might be going through as he rang the rectory's doorbell. The last thing he wanted to do was bring more torment to Father John.

Noelle leaned on the buzzer until the priest opened the door. When he saw the look on Noelle's face, Father John panicked. So much for Noelle's poker face. He obviously could no longer rely on that old trick.

"I've been a wreck waiting for your call. What happened?"

"Can we go inside?"

The priest showed Noelle to his office. Once there, Noelle told him, "I'm sorry I took so long but I had to get my wife settled."

He waited for Father John to sit down.

"According to a note that was delivered to me before my mother's service, Rose and Esmeralda have been kidnapped. I just got a second note instructing me to wait at the Bourbon Street Bazaar tonight at eight o'clock. That's where I will be given my next instructions by one of Rocco's men."

Father John gasped, "Nick, are you crazy? That's a suicide mission. You can't go there alone."

Noelle knew he must be insane to be doing this at all, especially after learning about Sally's pregnancy. But he couldn't just quit his obsession to find the killer or to save Rose and her mother. Noelle told him, "I'm not going to say goodbye, Father," he grimaced. "But please pray that I find your girlfriend and her mother in one piece."

"Let me go with you as backup!" Father John cried.

Noelle shook his head. "Seriously, do you think that's a good idea? There's enough crazy right here for the both of us. If something happens to me, you're my designated survivor. I trust you to take care of Sally."

The priest was dumbfounded. "Of course, but…"

Noelle stopped without letting Father John finish. His first stop was Esmeralda's storefront. He parked the truck and searched the street to make sure no one was lurking about, especially Tucci.

When Noelle was confident the coast was clear, he approached the front door, only to find that the lock had been broken. He stepped inside, holding his breath as the small hairs on his arms stood at attention. The place had been torn apart. The glass cases were smashed and all their contents were broken to bits on the floor. Whoever did this was obviously not looking to rob the shop since, as far as Noelle could tell, even the most costly items of jewelry and crystals were crushed on the tile floor.

Noelle stepped gingerly through the space, looking for signs of life, slightly relieved he found no blood or fingerprints. Next, Noelle ran upstairs to Esmeralda's bedroom where he found a neatly made bed and well-appointed bric-a-brac on her dresser and end tables. He even searched through her closet and bathroom but found no signs of a struggle, a speedy departure or anything else out of the ordinary.

Frustrated that he had no clues to lead him, Noelle was stumped. He assumed that whoever had vandalized the shop was trying to send a message. But what the hell was it? He was at a loss of where to go or what to do.

Out of habit, Noelle decided to stop in at Saint Mary's Home. For lack of a better plan, he knew at least Sister Theresa would be happy to see him.

At the receptionist booth, Noelle greeted Eric with a bright, phony smile. "It meant a lot to me that you showed up for my mother's service," he told Eric.

"It's the least I could do," Eric told him. "She was a sweet lady."

Noelle nodded. "Still, it was nice of you. Hey, can you tell me where I might find Sister Theresa?"

A voice directly behind him caught Noelle off guard.

"Ask and you shall receive."

Although Noelle laughed, his eyes were filled with fear.

Sister Theresa was all business and asked abruptly, "What is it, Nick?"

"I'm sorry to bother you but I need to ask one last favor," Noelle told her. "If anything happens to me, will you take care of my Sally? She's going to have our baby and could use a friend like you. She has a past similar to yours and my mother's."

Instead of her usual kindly tone, Sister Theresa yelled at Noelle.

"Father John just called. He told me that you were on a suicide mission. And now you're telling me that you have a child on the way. What's wrong with you besides being a pathetic drunk and a coward?"

Noelle did his best to plead his case.
"Just like you, this is my calling, Sister. I can't ignore it when lives are in danger."

Sister Theresa spoke firmly. "And what about you and the lives of your wife and unborn child? Don't they count? Do you really think it best to bring a baby into this world without a father?"

"Sally and any child of mine would be better off without me. I'm beyond redemption, Sister."

"Suicide is selfish," the nun scolded him. "It's the coward's way out. Even if Sally is the best mother in the world, all the photos and clippings of a big shot hero dad will never make up for the love the child will miss without you. Nick, it's time to be a man."

Noelle could no longer face the nun's incriminations—or her wrath. He flew out the door.

Outside, Noelle looked at his watch only to find that he had two hours to kill before his rendezvous with Rocco's henchman. He decided to go back to the boarding house to see if Sally and Fletcher had returned. If he was going to die, he wanted to hold his sweet Sally in his arms one last time.

Although he found their suite empty, Noelle noticed that Sally had unpacked both his and her bags. Their clothes were neatly arranged in the dresser and in the closet. He supposed that was a good sign, a very good sign.

To celebrate, Noelle poured himself a good, long drink and decided to check the box of his mother's journals. He wanted to be sure nothing was missing. Noelle put the box on the bed, carefully lifting and counting each notebook.

At the very bottom of the box, he found a letter he'd never seen before. The handwriting was very different from his mother's childlike hand. Noelle carefully opened the brittle envelope which had been addressed to Catherine. He gently unfolded it, so as not to further tear the folded page. Noelle began to read it:

Dear Catherine,

You knew me as Mary, the wife of Reverend Garsett. I am very old now and can barely get around. I wanted to write you before I passed in the hopes that I can explain some of my behavior. You might say it is a confession of my sins. I hope you can find it in your heart to forgive me. But I understand completely if you can't. I treated you wretchedly.

Because the Reverend and I couldn't conceive a child—and perhaps to punish me for his own shortcomings— my husband made my life a living hell both in and out of our marriage bed. I cannot apologize enough for the treatment you received from my husband and me. I want you to know that I, too, was his victim.

Unfortunately, not long after you left your precious, Brandon with us, I could not control the Reverend from making your son his prey as well. If you can believe it, the Reverend was even meaner and more ornery after his falling accident. I knew you meant to take the boy with you when you were forced to run away. It wasn't long before you fled that I learned the whole truth.

Once the Reverend finally passed, I had you traced to Madame Trussard's house in New Orleans. I learned that you had become a prostitute. I suppose this was a life you had to endure to survive as a young girl in the world alone. Again, I am sorry you had to go through this.

I thought you might want to know that all of the men who harmed you have now gone to meet their maker. I pray they reap the punishment they deserve, including your mean, old father, your husband and that polecat Justin Morgan, who died in a car racing accident. The best thing about Justin Morgan's death is that your son Brandon became his only heir.

After the Reverend died, Brandon cashed in his inheritance and disappeared from Mayfield. On the Reverend's death certificate, it states that my husband died of a heart attack, but I know the real cause of his death and that is why I never tried to find Brandon. I thought it best to let sleeping dogs lie. Brandon was always sweet to me, no matter how he had been abused by my husband. When he was strong enough to fight back, your son finally avenged the horror the Reverend caused him—and you. I can't say that I blame him.

I don't know if Brandon ever found you but I always prayed that he had. In the name of everything that is holy and true, I am deeply sorry for all of your suffering. And I will pray to my dying day, that the Reverend burns throughout all eternity in the fires of hell.

Yours truly,
Mary Garsett

Noelle folded the letter and put it in his lap. He lay back on the bed to think, his heart beating so fast he feared it would burst. Now Noelle knew that Brandon was wealthy and would have had the means to find his mother if he'd wanted to. He also realized that if Brandon ever made it to New Orleans to look for Catherine he might have found her. He couldn't help but wonder what would have happened if Brandon had found Catherine and rejected her because of the life she was living? Noelle was curious if his brother had ever met him when he was a baby. The possibilities of what might have happened were overwhelming. With his mother dead and gone, there was no way to know the truth unless Noelle could find this brother Brandon.

When Sally returned from her shopping spree with Fletcher, she found Noelle in a heap on the bed staring at the letter in his hands. She sat beside him, took the note from him and read it. When she was done, she put her arms around Noelle.

"I'm sorry for how we left things between us," she whispered. Sally just held Noelle in her arms and for the first time ever, watched him cry like a baby. All she could do was hold him—and that's all she wanted to do.

When Noelle finally dried his eyes, he began to fill Sally in on Catherine's whole story and how he now felt it was his duty to find his missing brother Brandon. Sally had to fight to hold back the tears. To console Noelle, she patted his head as if he were a troubled child. Relaxing slightly, he laid his head against her chest, which swelled with her blossoming pregnancy. Sally began to tenderly stroke his hair and face. One thing led to the next and soon they were making sweet, gentle love to one another again.

Afterwards, as they lay curled against each other's bodies like two spoons in a drawer, Sally told Noelle that she had accepted a dinner invitation from Christian for the two of them that evening. She explained, "I just couldn't say no after how kind he was to me this afternoon. Christian insisted I let him treat us both to a night on the town."

This brought up a whole new dilemma for Noelle. He didn't want to let down Sally again, so he had to find a way to keep the dinner date with her and Fletcher yet still meet up with Rocco's henchman at eight. Noelle smiled at Sally.

"Okay, honey, what time did the gentleman say we were dining?"

"I told him I could be ready by seven."

"That gives us less than thirty minutes to get ready."

Sally sat up. "I'll rinse off and touch up my makeup. I know it doesn't take you long."

While Sally was in shower, Noelle thought he'd ask Fletcher if they could dine over by the Bourbon Street Bazaar since that's where Noelle had to meet the mobster. He figured he could excuse himself to the washroom after they ordered, then slip out to keep his date with destiny. The more Noelle thought about his mission, the more he realized how insane he was and how he might never come back—except in a wooden box.

At seven sharp, Fletcher knocked on their door. Looking radiant, Sally greeted him like her new best girlfriend. Noelle was still zipping up his good dress pants and slipping on his shoes. Fletcher kissed Sally on both cheeks as though she were European royalty.

"Madame, you are magnificent!" he proclaimed. Then he turned to Noelle and commented, "You are one lucky gentleman to have this gorgeous woman at your side. If I weren't a confirmed bachelor, you'd have to fight me for her affections."

Noelle laughed, "Well, thank goodness the days of dueling are over. Otherwise, I'm sure I'd be a dead man by dawn."

Sally jumped in. "Now, boys, as flattering as it is to have two men fighting over you, I'm much more interested in where we're going to dine. I told Christian earlier that ever since I started eating for two, I'm always hungry."

"There are some great restaurants over on Bourbon Street near the Bazaar I haven't had a chance to try," Noelle interjected.

"Oh, I know just the place!" Fletcher chortled. "If you like Italian, that is. Liuzza's a classic!"

Sally was almost giddy. "I just love Italian!"

Noelle agreed, "Our lady has spoken. Lead the way, my good man." Noelle grabbed his dinner jacket and Sally's shawl, and off they went.

Fletcher hailed a taxi outside the rooming house. Ever the gentleman, he opened the back door for Sally and Noelle, and slipped into the front seat with the driver. With dramatic flair, he cried, "Liuzza's Restaurant, please."

Fletcher turned around in the front seat, assuming the role of tour guide. "One of the biggest ethnic groups who contribute to the local cuisine are the Italians," he said. "Despite the fact that we have the French Quarter, the architecture is Spanish, not French, so New Orleans is a true mélange. You're just going to love Liuzza's," Fletcher added, rubbing his hands together. "It's been here since nineteen forty-seven, a true neighborhood gem where the hospitality is warm, the food is scrumptious and there's plenty of it."

"My mouth is watering already," Sally admitted. Then asked, "What are some of their specialties?"

Fletcher put his index finger to his chin in thought. "The stuffed artichokes and lasagna are to die for! They're also famous for Frenchuletta, a robust sandwich filled with Italian meats and seasonings. And if you don't want Italian, they also serve other New Orleans fare like po'boys on excellent French bread. And never you mind their award-winning Cajun and ouille gumbo!"

When they reached the restaurant, Fletcher insisted on paying for the cab. He tipped his hat to Liuzza's maître d' who greeted him like an old friend.

"Oh, Mr. Fletcher, it's been a long time! So wonderful to see you! I'm glad you're here early. I just happen to have your favorite table open."

Noelle could see that the place was packed. He thought Fletcher received special treatment because more than likely these two dandies played for the same team. He noticed Fletcher slipping the maître d' a big bill as their threesome was led to a roomy, round table that fit four.

The maître d' pulled out Sally's chair as he announced, "Mr. Fletcher, I'll send your waiter over to get your drink orders immediately." He bowed neatly to Fletcher before he left, proclaiming, "Enjoy!"

After the waiter took their drink orders, Noelle checked his watch. He saw that he had only fifteen minutes before he was expected at the meeting place. When Fletcher engaged Noelle in conversation about the murder investigations, Noelle tried to be polite but answered with as little detail as possible. He indicated that there were a few loose ends regarding two suspects being considered and added that he believed they were innocent women he suspected of being framed.

For Sally's sake, Noelle offered, "These women are friends of Father John, who is very concerned for their safety. I promised him I'd do my best to clear them before I leave for Houston. It's the least I can do for him. That priest has been a good friend and confidant, even though he knows I'm not religious."

Sally gave Noelle an odd look, trying to take in that her atheist husband's best friend in decadent New Orleans happened to be a man of the cloth. "And what about your brother?" she added. "I thought you were hoping to search for him as well."

Noelle was spared having to answer his wife's inquiry when the waiter came to the table with their drinks. As soon as they finished ordering their appetizers and dinner, Noelle stood. "I'll be right back," he said, excusing himself. "I need to use the little boys' room."

Like the good detective he was, Noelle had noticed when they'd first came in that the bathrooms were at the front of the restaurant. He knew he'd have no problem sneaking out, and hoped he'd be able to slip back in a timely manner.

With Noelle gone from the table, Sally and Fletcher filled the air with conversation about Noelle. Before she knew it, Sally was confiding in Fletcher like he was her best girlfriend.

"The chemistry between us has always been off the charts," Sally blushed.

Fletcher leaned forward with interest.

"It's even hotter now that I'm pregnant. Unfortunately, I can't count on him to be a good father or husband since he's an alcoholic and getting worse every day. On top of that, he's a gambler. I thought Nick connecting with his mom would help him fight his demons, but I think it's made him worse."

Fletcher tutted and sighed at all the right places as Sally went on to share more details about Noelle's past. She confided in Fletcher about Noelle's long-lost brother whom Noelle recently discovered had been abandoned by their mother in Mayfield, Mississippi. Sally also told Fletcher that Noelle suspected he might find this brother right here in New Orleans, after reading a letter to his mother from a woman named Mary Garsett who had been the boy's stepmother.

Fletcher listened intently but said nothing. An awkward pause in their conversation was filled when the waiter brought their appetizers to the table. Sally realized that Nick had not yet returned from the restroom.

"Christian, would you be a dear and go into the men's room to see what's detaining my husband? I've been really worried about his emotional stability lately."

Fletcher was happy to oblige.

Noelle arrived at the Bourbon Street Bazaar a couple of minutes before eight. Like a precision Swiss watch, a black Cadillac with dark windows pulled up. The driver's side window rolled down. A gruff voice commanded, "Get in." The back door opened. As soon as Noelle started to slide into the back seat, a large, meaty fist hit him square in his face. He saw stars, then total blackness.

Back at Liuzza's, Fletcher returned from the bathroom without Noelle. When he joined Sally, he smirked, "Looks like Nick pulled a fast one. I'm sure he must have a hot lead to follow."

Sally frowned and began to get up but Fletcher stopped her, putting his hand on top of hers. "Let's enjoy our meal and worry about him later, shall we?" he suggested.

Sally fumed, "I can't believe Nick would go off and leave me like this after all we talked about today."

"My dear, he left you in good hands," Fletcher told her. Fletcher tried to calm Sally by reminding her of what Noelle had just told them about the promise he'd made to Father John. It had to be something important, perhaps even something about those missing women. "You should be proud of him, not upset," Fletcher added for good measure.

Sally sulked, "My husband has a thing for women in danger and dangerous women, all wrapped into one. The son of a bitch!"

The waiter arrived to clear their appetizer plates and make room for the main course. When he noticed Noelle's starter untouched, he asked, "Should I take the gentleman's plate and hold it in the kitchen?"

Sally looked at the waiter and growled, "Fuck him, he's no gentleman. Just throw his food in the trash."

Unruffled, the waiter took their plates away and another server came with their dinner.

Fletcher was noticeably shocked at Sally's coarse language. He had her pegged all wrong; it was clear that Sally wasn't a cultured lady at all. In fact, she seemed to lack even the simplest of manners. When Fletcher looked at her in shock, she cried, "He knew he was on thin ice with me and now he does this!"

Fletcher took Sally's hands in his and looked directly into her beautiful eyes, which were nearly overflowing with tears of rage. "Look, dear, I can see you're upset but it would be a shame to let that sinful cioppino go to waste. Besides, in your condition you need all your strength. Let's eat. Perhaps your husband will make it back in time for dessert. I doubt he planned on staying away for long."

Sally looked into the large bowl of tomato sauce brimming with crab, clams, shrimp, scallops, squid, and mussels. Lightly seasoned with garlic, onions and fragrant herbs like saffron, the aroma was heavenly. She speared a large chunk of crabmeat with her fork. "Yes, let's eat," she sighed, a bit too loudly. "I'm done waiting for that man!"

As she was devouring her abundant portion of seafood, Sally noticed that Fletcher had barely touched his fettuccini.

"Christian, what's wrong?" she asked. Fletcher's face had turned a ghostly shade of gray. "You don't look well," she added. "Don't you like your dish? Here, try some of mine. I'm stuffed and need to save room for dessert." She pushed her bowl toward him.

Fletcher took Sally's hand. He answered slowly, with great effort. "I hate to be a party pooper but I think I'm coming down with something," he told her. "I usually have an iron stomach but suddenly I feel quite queasy. Do you mind if I take you home? We can get your dessert to go."

"Of course," Sally said. "I'm sorry you aren't feeling well. Let's get you home."

Fletcher didn't wait for the check. On their way out, he pulled a wad of cash from his wallet and stuffed it into the maître d's hand. Fletcher put his arm around Sally's waist and rushed onto Bienville to hail a taxi. At the boarding house, he apologized profusely as he left Sally and walked stiffly up the stairs to his room. It was as though his stomach were about to explode, she noted, watching him.

Alone in her room, Sally paced the floor. Her anger swelled. She kicked the sheets that were still wadded up on the floor from her lovemaking session with Noelle earlier. In a rage, she picked up the phone and called New Orleans International Airport to see if she could get a flight out that night. As she waited on hold, Sally opened her doggie bag to nibble at her tiramisu. There was a midnight flight back to Houston, she learned, but it was fully booked. Her only option was to fly standby or to wait until morning. Sally was so pissed off at her husband that she hung up the phone and packed her bags.

In the large, airy attic apartment upstairs, something in Fletcher's gut was stirring. His mind began to unravel dark thoughts but he wasn't sure what to do about them. Yes, he knew this Nick Noelle was his little brother but it wasn't since he'd met Sally and learned that this brother and this lovely woman were about to carry on the family bloodline that his own sordid past hit him deeply. All the rage and shame he'd felt in his long, sordid life hit him like a hurricane. Fletcher felt as though he were in the middle of an emotional tornado with nowhere to go for shelter.

He unlocked a drawer in his desk and took out an old notebook worn with age. Fletcher sat in his most comfortable Victorian chair. Under the stark light of a fine Tiffany lamp, he opened the one notebook written in his mother's hand, the one notebook that his brother, Nick Noelle, had never seen. Christian had stolen it from Catherine's belongings when he'd finally found her at Saint Mary's Home a few years earlier. He hadn't read it since that day. Now, more than ever, he needed a reminder of the message it held.

Fletcher opened the notebook and read:

After Miss Kirkwood's letters from my hometown stopped, the scenes I used to enjoy in the streets of New Orleans seemed tarnished. Even though they were alive with people in the French Quarter, they looked sordid and grimy, but at least I fit in there. These were people like me. Some were lost or homeless and many seemed to be hunting for a new kind of life. I knew I was purposely trading my body for my soul because my soul belonged to my one and only son Brandon.

I felt like I was living in a beautiful prison, counting off the days until I could be released. What that freedom could be I wasn't sure but I knew one thing—I knew it would be shared with my boy, Brandon, who, by now, had probably long forgotten me. But I could never, ever forget him.

Some of the men I saw came from good homes and they paid me extraordinary tips. I spent my money wisely and went to school to improve my English and writing skills. Hoping for the day when I could be respectable. I must admit that I fantasized that one of these nights I might meet a nice man who would fall for me, ask me to be his wife and he would help me get back my boy. I knew this was a dream a lot of whores have, a dream that one day we will be respectable, that one day we will find a way out. But this silly fantasy kept me going.

God, I have become practical for my age and when I'm not feeling lonely or angry, I just feel numb and empty. I know the only good thing I ever produced that gave me pride was my son Brandon and I'm beginning to believe I may never see him again.

I don't mean to sound like one big, old pity pot because there is actually some blessing that I feel is about to happen. Most of the ladies of the night don't think it's a blessing and would call it a curse. And the Madame, well, she for sure don't think it's a good thing either. But I know from my own experience that the last time I felt these feelings, nine months later, Brandon was born. And that was a blessing.

Yes, God, I'm pretty sure I'm pregnant and I can't even say who the daddy might be. But I'm hopin' he's one of the nicer gentlemen I've laid with. Madame says I have to stop working in the parlor as soon as I start showing but she told me I can move down to the basement with the colored girl and help out with the house cleaning until my time comes. After that, I'm not sure what I'm going to do.

I know I don't want this new baby growing up in this house of ill repute, especially once the baby starts walkin' and talkin.' So, for now God, I just ask that You send me a healthy baby. I'd like a girl this time but I think it might be better that it be a boy. He'll have less of a hard life than a girl child will have with a mama like me. Well, God, I'll leave it up to You and Your wisdom.

There was a break in the writing, which started up on a fresh page. The script seemed different, shakier. Fletcher continued reading:

I haven't had time to write with the new baby and all but yesterday was one of those gray November days when nothing seems right. The sky had a greasy shine to it as it labored under bloated clouds. The whole environment around me gave me the creeps. People were swarming about as I walked slowly back to the house that I'm still calling home, unfortunately. The only thing that makes me feel "at home" in New Orleans is that the beggars walk side by side with the wealthy and the only fences between them are the fences they build in their minds. Pride is a frivolous thing and only useful for folks who can afford it.

As I walked back to Madame's place, I heard this old folk song in my head, "The House of the Rising Sun." The words kept repeating in my brain, "There is a house in New Orleans/ They call the Rising Sun/It's been the ruin of many a poor girl/ And God I know I'm one/My mother was a tailor/She sewed my new blue jeans/My father was a gamblin' man/Down in New Orleans..."

As I rounded a corner hearing that tune in my head, I almost tripped over a poor blind man on the sidewalk holding up his beggar cup and a sign. It read: "THIS IS THE WAY TO THE END OF THE WORLD. ENTER AND YOU WALK WITH JESUS. PASS ME AND YOU WALK ALONE."

I dropped some change in the beggar's cup and walked around him. As he smiled, I saw his toothless mouth and it made me think of the Reverend. I wished that the old Reverend would end up on the street like this poor, religious fool, with no pride — just blind, homeless and alone.

A few steps past the blind beggar, the sounds of a sad, melancholy saxophone came pouring out from a jazz joint. I noticed two men coming through the doorway. They were obviously rich because they were wearing fine clothes. The older one had an expression of shame on his face. The younger one seemed unfazed, unsullied. Rumor in the streets was that this particular club catered to the taste of men with the most extreme perverted sex appetites.

I passed by, reserving judgment, Lord, since who was I to cast the first stone. But I couldn't help look back and notice that one of them was very young. I was immediately struck by his good looks and strong presence which appeared tightly controlled. Maybe it was his eyes that gave me that impression. He had a very striking yet hard look for such a baby-faced kid. Like somebody who seen a lot.

He flashed me a charming smile. Even though he dressed like a wealthy gentleman, he couldn't have been more than 16. His eyes locked unto mine as this beautiful boy looked right through me. There was something so familiar that made me blush. It was the way Justin Morgan used to look at me.

After I walked away, I could not stop thinking about this man/child's haunting eyes. I wondered if I'd seen him before and thought that maybe he had been a customer where I worked. All the men I been with seemed to melt together in my mind after a while except for every now and then, when a teenage boy shows up. Usually their drunken fathers bring them to us whores to teach them a thing or two. Sometimes there was some sensitive young soul with lost eyes who appealed to me. I knew it was because he made me think of my Brandon. I couldn't help but wonder what was happening to my son--wondering now that he's grown. Was he happy? Was he sad? Was the Reverend and Mary kind to him? Was he struggling to earn a dollar? Was he a preacher? Or was he a sinner like me?

A few times, I even had young men wounded in the war. I had one once who came up to my room and ask me if he could just watch me touch myself. He said that was the only way he could feel something—with his eyes, by looking—since he was paralyzed below his waist thanks to that damn war. I didn't mind. It kind of brought me back to the lust that Justin had awakened in me. Justin was the only man that ever made me want to touch myself.

After I saw those two men in the street, I found myself thinking about the young one with the intense eyes. The very thought of him made me want to touch myself that same way I used to when I would think about Justin. It made me feel so ashamed. Here, I'd been a whore all these years and the thought of sexual pleasure made me feel ashamed.

With those crazy thoughts floating in my head, I sat in the parlor waiting for customers. All of a sudden, I look up and I see the same two men from the street: the rich, older one and the young fellow with the unforgettable eyes.

They entered the room and ordered drinks at the bar, taking their sweet time scanning the room for the ladies they wished to hire. After a bit, the older gentleman comes over to me. He told me he would pay me twice as much to take care of the both of them together. I felt really nervous, not because I had never gotten such a request, but because of how I had already pleasured myself thinking about that young man already. I had no good excuse to turn down such a good offer so I led them both up to my quarters.

The two fellows were pretty drunk and the old one did all the talking while the young one just kept smiling and looking innocent. It was the older man who asked me to start undressing in front of them while they watched. Then he told his friend to do the same. He kept his clothes on but kept touching and stroking his penis as he watched his young friend and me slowly undress.

I don't know why, but for the first time in years I felt so shy, like I did that very first time Justin tried to touch me. I guess there was something about this young man that reminded me of Justin, something so warm and charming and yet distant.

As soon as I was stripped down to my silk undies, the boy smiled at me. He was still wearing his undershorts. With those intense eyes, he studied me long and hard, scanning my body up and down. There was innocence and ice pouring through him all at once. He put one hand on my breast and slipped the other down my panties, exciting me with his fingers, gently probing me. As he did this, he turned to his friend and started to laugh and said, "Wouldn't that old Reverend be jealous as hell if he could watch me fuck this old whore?"

I snatched up my clothes and ran out of the room before the tears came. I knew I was getting older but until that second, I never thought of what I might look like to a young man. He was but a child, and for all I knew, he could have been my child. I ran to Madame and told her that she was going to have to send in another girl because I had become violently ill. Must have been something I ate, I told her.

I hid down in the basement and didn't know what had happened with them till the next day. When I inquired, Madame said, "Lucky we whores are interchangeable. Otherwise you'd be in big trouble for losing two clients." She assured me that the boy wasn't as pure as he looked. The girl who serviced them got a real kick out of watching the two fellas doing each other—and getting paid for it.

But I still couldn't get that remark he made about the old Reverend out of my head. Could it have been a coincidence? How did he know about me and the Reverend? It made me think long and hard about the possibility that the boy could have been my son Brandon. The thought that I almost had sex with him made me sick.

The shock of that night made me try harder to amend my ways. God, I pray that my baby boy Nick never ends up like that young man: a beautiful boy with no compassion. And God forbid if he was my son! Then I would know that I have committed the greatest sin by leaving him with Mary and that old Reverend.

So, God, if You get no more letters from me ever again, You will know I am in hell with the Devil.

Fletcher closed the journal, placing it carefully in his duffel bag beside an arsenal of tools used for his pleasure. He crept down the stairs and out the boarding house's back door to avoid being seen in the lobby. He jumped into the nearest cab. "Saint Catherine's Cathedral, please, and fast!" he cried.

Fletcher knew he would have to get to Father John first. When he arrived at the rectory, Mrs. Murphy answered the door. To his disappointment, she told him that Father John had gone out. Fletcher convinced her that it was crucial he find the priest since he was in grave danger and his friend Detective Noelle was also missing. Although Mrs. Murphy didn't like the looks of this fancy dandy, she thought it could do no harm to give Fletcher the address of the storefront where the women had their weekly meeting. Fletcher thanked Mrs. Murphy and hailed another taxi at the curb. The driver managed to get him to the gypsy store front shop quickly.

When Fletcher arrived, he found it exactly the same way Noelle had—with the broken display case and religious articles crushed on the floor. Like Noelle, Fletcher too searched high and low for clues. But unlike his brother, whose gut instincts hadn't been broken, Fletcher's were keen. He went through the place with a fine-toothed comb. He even broke the lock on a drawer behind the counter. Upon opening it, Fletcher discovered the secret place where Rose stashed her personal items. He went through each one meticulously.

An object of particular interest was a note from Rocco dated over a year ago. In it, Rocco gave Rose directions to an address where she was expected to perform her whoring for a small private gentleman's party. Something in Fletcher knew this note was an important clue. It excited Fletcher to think about how he too might possess the same sleuthing talents as his baby brother Nick Noelle. He remembered the address in Rocco's note and abruptly left the fortune teller's shop.

Fletcher had to walk a few blocks before he could find a taxi to take him out to the suburbs across town. If his hunch was right and he did find Noelle, and perhaps even the women there, he hoped it wasn't too late.

Several hours after Noelle had been abducted in the Cadillac, he woke up in a dark room, chained to a couch. He had a throbbing headache and couldn't open his eyes. Noelle felt a wetness around him and concluded that it was blood, probably his own. His eyes felt puffy and were glued shut. Noelle tried to move his arms but they were tied tightly to his body with ropes.

Sitting there helpless, Noelle knew he was the biggest idiot on the face of the earth. He realized what a stupid move he'd made, going to meet Rocco's henchman alone. Now he could do nothing to prevent the murders of Rose and Esmeralda. On top of that, he could only imagine how upset Sally must be. He was useless and beyond hope and Sally had every right to dump his sorry ass. As consolation, Noelle thought about his own demise and the fact that his murder might make things better for Sally in the long run. At least she'd be free to move on with her new life and their baby—maybe even find a new and better father for his child.

Noelle drifted in and out of his self-pity and consciousness. At one point, he imagined that he heard Rose speaking, but it was faint. It was like voices you hear when you're coming back into consciousness after anesthesia. Although it took a few minutes, Noelle realized that Rose was actually near him and he wasn't imagining her. Her voice was blurry.

"Nick," she apologized. "You never should have come."

Noelle tried to open his eyes but couldn't. His jaw ached when he tried to speak. Although the pain was unbearable, he managed to utter slowly, "I couldn't leave you and your mom with that…"

Suddenly, there was the sound of weighty footsteps. Noelle heard a door unlock and creak open. "Well, look here!" Rocco cackled. "I'm glad you came for dinner. I'm making mincemeat. Can you guess who's going to be the main course?"

Wincing through the pain, Noelle tried bluffing, "You don't think I was dumb enough to come without backup. The FBI should be breaking in right about now."

Rocco snarled, "Good try but even if it were true, Tucci would send the FBI on a wild goose chase. Before I serve you up, I'll let you watch me turn one of my whores into an appetizer first. I hope you like liver paté."

When Rocco paused, Noelle imagined he was looking at Rose and Esmeralda when he said, "Let's see, who should I start with? Rose's liver is cleaner than her mama's but Essie's will be juicy with all the fat she stores in there. It will yield more meat."

Rocco laughed and kicked Noelle in the ribs and left the room, this time leaving the door open. Noelle could hear Esmeralda chanting in some strange tongue, probably Creole. He heard Rocco's footsteps again and the sound of clanking metal. It sounded like heavy tools. Then he heard a struggle.

Noelle fought to pry his eyes apart only a crack. Through the swollen slits, he saw Rocco grab Esmeralda by the hair. She screamed wildly as he dragged her across the floor and out of the room. When Rose tried to get up to stop him, Rocco kicked her in the stomach. She collapsed from the pain.

In the adjoining room, Esmeralda shrieked fearfully in Creole. Rocco laughed wildly as he slapped a piece of duct tape over Esmeralda's mouth. Rocco yelled back at Rose from the other room.

"Your mother should know her hocus-pocus curses don't work on me. You bitches can scream as loud as you want because no one will hear you. This warehouse is soundproof and it's surrounded by an acre of dirt lot. Your bodies or what I leave of them will be eaten by the rodents before the police find what's left of you."

Noelle and Rose could do nothing as they heard Esmeralda cry out desperately from the other room. Noelle tried to move. He pushed his arms and legs in an attempt to loosen the rope but it did no good. He could hear things being thrown around in the adjoining room. There were clunks, knocks and blistering sounds. The awful cacophony went on and on.

Noelle's eyes had opened a bit and he looked down at his wrist. He was surprised to see his watch still keeping time after the beating he must have taken. He saw that it was eleven o'clock. Noelle tensed up when he heard the horrifying sound of an electric drill followed by Rose's muffled sobs through the duct tape on her mouth. He knew Rose was right, *'Rocco is the Holy Roller Murderer!'*

He felt a cloud of doom overtaking him as he saw in his mind's eye Rocco using a drill to cut open Esmeralda's chest. Noelle could only hope that the mother was already dead before Rocco started carving into the old woman.

After a few minutes that felt like an eternity, Noelle surrendered to their fate. He couldn't see who had entered the room but the footsteps he heard were not heavy like Rocco's. The shadow of a tall man approached from behind where Rose lay on the floor in a heap. There was an absence of sound—no more muffled sobs coming from Rose.

Then Noelle smelled chloroform and a wave across his eyes. Blackness followed.

Chapter Thirty-Three

Second Chances

When Noelle woke up he could hear Rose's voice but his eyes were still glued shut. Rose's body was so close to his that he wondered what had transpired between them. His first thought was that he'd been unfaithful to Sally, until his pain jarred his memory. Noelle tried to sit up but every muscle and nerve ached and burned.

Although his eyes were shut, Noelle could open his mouth. With his tongue, he felt a broken tooth lodged in his gum. He also tasted the sharp acid of blood in his mouth. Although his arms were bound, Noelle was able to move them enough to pick at the crust that sealed his eyes shut. After working the gunk out of his eyes, Noelle was able to open them slightly, but found that they were swollen so much, even when he tried to open them wide, he could barely see. Noelle struggled to speak.

"Rose, what's happened?" he choked in a dry voice. "You're not dead. What about your mother?"

At first, Rose didn't respond. For a split second, Noelle thought that perhaps they were dead and this conversation was happening in the afterlife. But when he felt the warm blood oozing from his mouth, he knew he was alive and all too human.

Rose gently wiped the blood away from Noelle's face with a wet towel.

"Your mother, what happened to your mother?"

Since she didn't answer Noelle assumed Rose was in shock. Finally, she was able to liberate him. She helped him sit up.

"We have to get out of here before anyone comes looking for us!" she whispered frantically. "Do you think you can stand?"

Noelle asked. "Where's Rocco? Why are we still alive?"

"I'll tell you as soon as Father John gets here but we have to move fast."

"How does he know where we are?"

Rose shrugged. "Before I passed out, someone whispered in my ear that Father John was on his way. And that he would take us to Saint Mary's. The voice said we'd be safe there. The nun is waiting for us."

"Sister Theresa?"

With Rose's help, he was able to slowly stand but he was unsure on his feet.

"Wait! Let me find a weapon," he said. "We might need one."

Rose screamed, "Don't go in there! Someone did a real job on Rocco and my mother saw the whole thing. She's in shock."

"Then she knows who the killer is!"

"I don't think so," Rose told him. "And even if she did, she's not talking."

"Where is she?"

"She's outside, waiting for us."

"*How* is she?"

"There's a patch of dried blood on her scalp where Rocco pulled out her hair when he dragged her across the floor but besides the trauma, she only has a few bumps and bruises."

Noelle took the wet cloth from Rose and used it to wipe the remaining crusted blood from his swollen eyes and mouth. He was able to pry his eyes open a little wider.

"Rose, I have to see this for myself," he explained. "There may be clues that can end this nightmare for all of us."

Noelle slowly made his way toward the adjoining room where the smell of blood and feces was overwhelming. When he entered, he saw Rocco's monstrous body splayed open. It had been split in half from his crotch to his skull by a chainsaw. Noelle was pretty familiar with the damage a chainsaw blade could do since he had seen more than his share, courtesy of Pamela and Howard. But Rocco's dismemberment was even more gruesome than the dead and dismembered ghouls of his nightmares.

Noelle stared down at Rocco's halved face and head, noting that his severed brain remained inside his skull. Noelle's eyes moved down the rest of Rocco's divided corpse. He took note that the heart and the liver were still there but that they lay in pieces beside Rocco's body.

From the next room, Rose insisted that they leave before any of Rocco's goons got there. When Noelle began to move toward her, he nearly tripped on the killer's tools. This gave him pause. He thought that perhaps this was not the same killer who committed the Holy Roller Murders. There was no message in blood and no missing organs. Noelle knew that assassin was far more meticulous than this one. That killer would never leave any evidence behind like his weapons, no matter how much of a hurry he was in. When Noelle saw a small switchblade lying on the ground, he grabbed it and slipped it into his pocket. He might need it later.

Rose yanked Noelle's arm, pulling him out from his investigative trance. She yelled, "Let's get the fuck out of here, NOW!"

Rose looked down at Rocco one last time and spat at his severed corpse. She turned to tug Noelle toward the door, mumbling something in a language he didn't recognize. Noelle could only assume it was Creole for something like "the bastard got what he deserved."

Although still wobbly from the beating he took, it didn't stop Noelle from playing Twenty Questions about who and where the killer might be. He wondered if he should call it in anonymously or just let Rocco rot there. Noelle knew that if Tucci found out where he, Rose and Esmeralda had been, he would try to pin the murders on them. This would bring a pat conclusion to the case and make Tucci a hero without actually solving the crime. Noelle was not going to let that happen.

When he and Rose made their way outside, the full moon was so bright it hurt Noelle's eyes. Esmeralda sat in a heap on the ground, still sobbing softly, rocking back and forth. Just as Noelle was ready to grab Rose's hand for support, Father John pulled up in Noelle's truck. The priest jumped out to help Esmeralda into the back of the Ford. Though aching and in agony, Noelle gave Father John a playful shove. "Hey, how did you get my truck?"

"Your skills are rubbing off on me," Father John suggested. "The truth is, I learned how to hotwire cars long before I became a priest."

Noelle slid into the back of his rig beside Esmeralda and let Rose sit up front with her lover/priest. Noelle watched as Rose leaned in close and rested her head on Father John's shoulder as they drove toward Saint Mary's.

She whispered to Father John, "I didn't tell Noelle but I think I saw who killed Rocco. The killer thought I was out from the chloroform but while he was slicing Rocco apart, I woke up."

"Who was it?" Father John gasped.

"I didn't see his face, but he was tall, slim and dressed in black. His clothes looked expensive. There was a large ruby ring on his finger. His hair was silver and longish but slicked back. And he had a black velvet hat which he put back on his head once he was done with the job. But as he walked away he suddenly seemed weary, like an old man who had used up every last drop of his energy on that kill."

Father John looked at Rose sternly. "You can't keep this from Noelle. He's the only one we can trust."

"I plan to tell him once he's less shaky," Rose promised. "I witnessed the beating he took from Rocco. He's lucky to be alive."

When they reached Saint Mary's, it was after midnight. Sister Theresa was in the empty reception area waiting for them. Without greetings or formalities, she quickly rushed the shocked and wounded to a hidden stairway that led to a secret room in the basement. As soon as Noelle made it down the stairs, he passed out. Father John carried him into a room furnished only with a pair of old sofas. He laid Noelle on the couch then tended to Esmeralda, who was still bleeding from her scalp. The priest placed her on the other couch facing Noelle. As Sister Theresa cleaned Esmeralda's wound, the old woman whimpered but didn't speak.

Father John watched the nun as she looked at Noelle and Esmeralda with compassion. The silent consideration the priest gave Sister Theresa spoke volumes. "We have our work cut out for us," she told Father John. "Dear God, please help us! It's not safe to bring them to a hospital."

"I know a doctor I can trust to come and examine them," he told her.

Rose was doubled over, holding her stomach. "If there's anything I can do to help, Sister, please tell me," she said. "I know it's risky for you and Father John to get involved with this mess."

"Rose, you don't look too good yourself," Father John told her.

"I'm fine," she stammered.

"Besides, we can handle it," Sister Theresa said. "Father John and I come from the streets too, you know."

Regaining consciousness, Noelle suddenly jolted awake. "I'm sorry, but I don't have time to wait for any doctor," he said wearily. "I have to get back to Sally." He stood shakily.

"Nick, are you crazy? You could be hemorrhaging internally or even worse. I don't think that's…"

"Once Tucci gets wind of his dead buddy, my wife and my friends aren't safe," Noelle cut Father John off. "But don't worry; before I went out I called my ex-partner, Juan López, in Houston. He's on his way to help. Sometimes my gut still guides me to make the right moves. I only wished I'd asked for his help sooner."

"What could he possibly do from Houston?" Father
John asked.

"Juan should be landing in New Orleans right about
now. I need to meet up with him at my boarding house. It's the
only address he has for me."

"Let me go with you," Father John demanded.

"You've got your hands full here," Noelle told him.
"Rose and Esmeralda need you. As soon as Juan gets to my
place, I'll take care of my wounds. I promise."

Noelle moved toward the door. "Father, please hold off
on calling your doctor friend. We can't risk letting anyone know
this location. I've got to get my wife to safety first. Sally has no
idea she could be in danger." Noelle who could barely stand up
straight, hobbled out the door.

While Sister Theresa tended to Esmeralda, Rose and
Father John spoke quietly to each other in Saint Mary's secret
room. It was clear they cared deeply for each other, more than
a priest and a call girl should. Sister Theresa noted this but said
nothing. Silently, she thought of Jesus and Mary Magdalene,
and smiled.

When Detective Tucci showed up at the warehouse
to meet Rocco as he had planned and found his defiled corpse
instead; he was shaken to the core. This turn of events was the
last thing he'd expected. Tucci and Rocco had concocted a plan
for Rocco to kill the two women then chop them up to make it
look like the serial killer had done it. He and Rocco had intended
to make Noelle look like he was the Holy Roller Murderer, but
now that plan was shot to shit.

In their foolproof scheme, Rocco would have given
testimony that he caught Noelle in the act and it was
unfortunately too late to save the women. Since the murder of
the archbishop had taken place on the same day Noelle had
arrived in New Orleans, Tucci knew he could plant evidence
plus get witnesses to say that Noelle was a mental case. His
heavy drinking and odd behavior was all the proof he needed. It
would be easy to get the authorities to believe that Noelle had
finally snapped after years of solving scores of sordid murder

cases—and drinking like a fish. Tucci himself would testify to seeing Noelle snooping around the crime scenes. Pinning the Holy Roller Murders on Noelle would be a given. All this would build an airtight case against Noelle. But now, Rocco's murder put a monkey wrench into Tucci's master plan.

Like Noelle, Tucci could also see that Rocco's killer didn't follow the rules he'd laid down in his previous murders because this time he was sloppy and left evidence. His bloody tools were still scattered on the ground, which really left Tucci perplexed. If the real killer's prints were on them, there would be no way to pin the killings on Noelle, that's if he could even find him now.

Tucci now feared for his own life, thinking that maybe these two Creole bitches really did have magic mojo and he was in for it. What scared him even more than black magic was that Tucci knew he now had to face the wrath of the mob family. If he couldn't prove he had no part in what happened to Rocco, Tucci would be a dead man too.

The detective decided to leave the scene and call in an anonymous tip so there would be no link to him. After that, Tucci went back to the station, shaking in his boots, while trying to figure out his next move.

While all of this murder and mayhem was going on, Sally caught a cab to New Orleans International so she could get on standby for the midnight flight back to Houston. She was so pissed off that she didn't even leave Noelle a note. In all her years of loving that man, she'd never felt such rage toward him. Sally chalked it up to maternal hormones, which made her decide to put herself above Noelle or anyone else, for that matter. She had a precious life growing within her. That baby was Sally's first and only priority. She didn't wish Noelle any harm, but she knew she was through with him after the stunt he'd pulled at Liuzza's. Sally did feel bad that she hadn't said goodbye to her husband but she figured she could do that in divorce court back home in Houston.

Noelle dragged his aching body to his room, hoping for some sympathy from Sally once she saw him. But instead, Noelle found Sally gone, along with her luggage. He looked for a note from her but found none. Noelle panicked. He imagined Tucci had gotten to Sally and was holding her as bait to get to Noelle.

Although it was very late, Noelle ran straight to Velda's room and pounded on her door. At first, she opened it slightly, peered through the crack and kept the inside chain latched. But when she saw it was Noelle, Velda opened up wide and greeted him in her pink foam curlers and unfastened bathrobe. Turning on her best faux Southern charm, she fluttered, "Why, Detective Noelle, where's the fire?"

Not in the mood for her questions, Noelle blurted out, "Where's my wife? Did you see her leave?"

"Why, no sir, I did not," Velda piped. "But I did see her in the lobby a while back with Mr. Fletcher. They seemed so chummy, those two. Perhaps you might find her up in his room. Although at this hour, I dare say...."

Noelle bolted up the stairs as Velda called after him, "I do hope that is not the case. I'd hate to see a scandalous gentlemen's brawl on the premises."

Noelle reached Fletcher's door and started to pound on it. After several minutes of getting no response, he decided to break in. Noelle remembered the switchblade he'd lifted from the crime scene and used it to jimmy the lock. The door popped open easily. He walked through all three rooms and stopped dead in his tracks when he caught sight of an old notebook on Fletcher's bed. It was strikingly similar to his mother's journals. When Noelle opened the book, he was shocked to find that in fact it *was* one of his mother's diaries. A letter addressed to him from Fletcher was taped to the inside cover. Noelle opened the note and read it quickly.

Nick, when you find this letter you will find the answers to all of your questions. And when you read the last entry of your mother's journal, you will know why I have done what I have done.

I have a very long story to tell but unfortunately, I will not be around to share it with you.

I know that you and Sally saw the letter from my stepmother Mary Garsett who wrote to Catherine about her son Brandon. Although you have been in the dark about it, let me confirm that I am indeed your brother. I changed my name when I left home and I've changed it many times since. Christian Fletcher has only existed since I returned to New Orleans a little over five years ago.

Long before that, after I killed the Reverend Garsett, I found I had a taste for blood, and as I matured, this obsession grew. I guess you can say addiction runs in our family. From what I've observed in you, I know you struggle with your own demons. But I think they're very different than mine.

I found that each new kill gave me a small degree of relief but that freedom from the hunger never lasted long. Because of it, I spent the better part of my life roaming from city to city and country to country, searching for new evil to stamp out in order to avenge our mother's—and my own—abuse.

It wasn't until I returned to New Orleans, my second time around that I finally found our mother Catherine. I think it might have been about the same time you placed her at Saint Mary's Home. By then, my blood lust had taken control and I no longer wanted to reunite with her. Instead, I was looking for answers as to why my obsession had only grown worse.

After breaking into her storage locker, I managed to find Catherine's journals. Like you I read them all but once I read this last entry, I knew she would be grossly disappointed in the man I had become. I left all of her journals where I found them. Except for this one. I kept it as a reminder of my own evil. Once you read it, you will understand why I was too ashamed to meet her face-to-face.

I'm sorry to say that I can't allow you to find me because if you do, it will be the end of me. For your brother, there is no redemption and I don't want to die in the electric chair.

You still have a reason to live, Nick. Sally has your child growing inside her and I hope her sweetness and love will be enough to wipe away the evil from our mutual bloodline.

*The only thing I ever got from my scumbag of a father was his
fortune—and in the end, that has been my undoing. Perhaps
if I did not have all that money, I might have grown into a
hardworking man like you.*

*This is my full confession that I am both the killer
and the brother you have been looking for. I am completely
responsible for the so-called "Holy Roller Murders" and the
death of that mobster Rocco who almost had you and those two
women on his chopping block.*

Sincerely, your brother,
Christian Fletcher (aka Brandon)

Trembling from shock and awe, Noelle folded his
brother's letter and placed it on the bed. He took a deep breath
and opened his mother's final journal. When he read about how
Catherine almost had sex with her own teenage son, it sent
chills down Noelle's spine. With complications from his beating
and from what he just learned, he felt physically ill. 'God!' he
thought, 'I need to find Sally. I can't deal with this alone.' But
with his next breath, his detective instincts kicked in and he
hoped he might still be able to find Fletcher and talk him into
surrendering. Noelle was truly at a loss about what to do.

Noelle had forgotten all about Juan and as he headed
back to his room, Velda was showing someone into the lobby.
"Oh, Detective Nick," she purred. "You have a visitor." Looking
worse for wear, Noelle rushed up to Juan Lopez and threw his
arms around him. "Man, if I ever needed a friend, it's now. You
are the answer to my prayers."

Juan was taken aback by Noelle's sudden burst of
affection and religion! "Well, I missed you too, Buddy."

"Things have gotten even crazier since I called you,"
Noelle told him. "Come to my room. We have no time to lose."

Safely in his suite with the door locked behind
them, Noelle gave Lopez the Readers' Digest version of the
nightmare he'd been living through since he got to New Orleans.
Noelle's words tumbled out of his mouth like a speed freak on
methamphetamine. In addition to getting his friends to a safe
house, he told Lopez that he also needed to find Sally, who

he feared was in mortal danger. Lopez laughed at Noelle's paranoia. "Slow down Boss. No need to find Sally. I know exactly where she is."

Noelle was stunned. "What?" he stammered.

"I ran into your wife at the airport," Lopez told him. "She was waiting to board the flight I just came in on. Sally was on the standby list for the midnight flight to Houston. I'm sure she's in the air by now, headed home."

"Thank God," Noelle gasped.

Lopez admitted. "Sally told me she was pissed off at you and heading for divorce court. I tried to talk her out of it but she wouldn't listen. This gave Noelle only a small comfort. He was glad Sally was alive but the ache of losing her gnawed at him. He was also in turmoil about his brother and conflicted about how he should handle that situation. Fletcher was a killer but he was also his flesh and blood. And what was thicker than blood?

Noelle and Lopez took off in the Ford and headed toward Saint Mary's to rally the troops. On the way there, Noelle told Lopez more details about the murders and how his own half-brother had confessed to the crimes. Noelle was a total wreck. He longed to connect to Brandon even knowing he was a crazed serial murderer.

Despite witnessing the horrible acts committed by Fletcher, Noelle somehow couldn't blame the man for the monster he'd become. He felt compassion—a new emotion he was trying on for size.

Lopez broke into Noelle's silent thoughts.

"Look, Boss, I really think the outcome is out of your hands. If ever there was one, this is a time when you need to trust in God."

Although Noelle looked at his friend with skepticism, Lopez continued anyway, "Hey, your wife trusts in Him, even if she does hate your guts right now. Anything can happen after that kid of yours is born. Have some faith, Boss!"

"I know, I know, lately I've been surrounded by more holy rollers than killers. I guess that Man upstairs is trying to get my attention," Noelle told him as they arrived at Saint Mary's.

One thing Noelle was not aware of: while he'd been in his brother's apartment: Fletcher himself was down in the rooming house's storage unit looking for his last will and testament. He needed to make some big changes.

Moments after Noelle and Lopez left the house, Detective Tucci rang the doorbell. Once again, Velda was disturbed from what she called her "beauty slumber." When she saw her pal Tucci at the door, she opened right up.

"Well, I'll be!" Velda drawled. "This has been one hell of a night! It's too much excitement for an old gal like me. What can I do for you, Detective?"

"I'm looking for Nick Noelle," Tucci told her dryly. "You just missed him," Velda said, leaning seductively in the doorway.

Tucci spoke up, "I don't want to alarm you, dear, but we have new evidence that suggests Mr. Noelle might be the killer we've been hunting."

Velda gasped and grabbed her ample chest in alarm. When Tucci dropped the thought into Velda's simple mind, it was like a professional hypnotist working his magic—the power of suggestion ran rampant.

"Let me remind you that Noelle arrived in town on the very day the first Holy Roller Murder took place."

"The archbishop!" Velda screeched. She tightened her robe around her thick middle and squealed, "Oh my God! How could this be? Mr. Noelle, an ex-detective with that sweet beautiful wife. Why Mr. Fletcher just told me they have a baby on the way? My word, what is this world coming to?"

"Don't worry. I've already placed a twenty-four hour guard around your house."

"Oh, my!" Velda yelped, "Why, Detective Noelle was just here and he met up with some smarmy-looking Mexican character. That was right after he practically broke down my door looking for his wife. You don't suppose that Mexican could be his accomplice, do you, Detective?"

"Whoever he is, you can rest at ease. No one will be getting in or out of here tonight," Tucci assured her. "If Noelle shows up here, he's going down. I assure you, Madame. I have one of my best men out front watching over you."

"What a relief!" Velda swooned.

While Tucci placated Velda in the lobby, Fletcher was trapped in the basement stairway, waiting out of sight until Tucci took his leave. Fletcher made sure that the nosy bitch went back to her room before he snuck out of the stairway. He had overheard the whole conversation and realized that he might need to protect his baby brother one last time before he disappeared forever.

Once the lobby was clear, Fletcher returned to his apartment to get a few tools. He slipped down the fire escape. Immediately, Fletcher spotted the unmarked police car in front of the rooming house, supposedly guarding the main entrance. He could see the cop dozing over his steering wheel. Fletcher hid behind the bushes and watched for a few moments, concluding that the policeman was definitely asleep. He snickered to himself thinking that the jerk was probably sleeping off one too many donuts.

Like a snake, Fletcher crept along the lawn until he got to the unmarked cop car. He crept up and opened the driver's side door. Before the sleeping officer could even open his eyes, Fletcher sliced his throat from ear to ear. He placed the cop's head back down on the steering wheel, closed the car door, and crawled back through the bushes and up the fire escape. Fletcher had enough killing for one day. He couldn't wait to get back to his room where he would run a luxurious bath and relax after a hard day's work.

Once back in his sanctuary, the flamboyant avenger prepared for his next adventure. Fletcher thought about how he had grown used to being a loner. But since he'd met Noelle and had gotten to know Sally, something had drastically shifted in him. A strange melancholy had fallen over Fletcher whenever he thought about how much he liked them both but could not have them in his life. He had never minded not having companions before because his mission was his passion. But now he felt empty, lonely.

Killing and the ecstasy he experienced from eating his victims' organs far surpassed the best sex or any form of intimacy he'd ever known. The only other thing Fletcher cared about in life was his comfort. When not out on the prowl, he was a homebody. He took great pride in the way he had transformed the shoddy, little attic rooms he rented on the top floor of Velda's boarding house into a palace.

Knowing that time was of the essence, Fletcher rushed into his bathroom and ran a very hot, cleansing bath. He poured his most fragrant bath salts into the steaming water. He went to his antique cabinet and opened his best French wine, a Chateau Latour, and poured a glass into his gold-trimmed, rose-colored goblet. For the last time, Fletcher played his favorite opera, swaying with great emotion to the opening strains of *The Marriage of Figaro*.

Back in his bedroom, he placed the goblet on the lace doily, which decorated his Chinese black lacquer end table. It also held a gorgeous vase of white lilies. Fletcher sniffed the flowers deeply, inhaling their aroma as if they were a fine line of cocaine. The Tiffany lamp overhead cast Fletcher's shadow on the floral print wallpaper. He circled his Louis V chair, still swaying with Mozart's music. Fletcher danced over to each exquisite item in the room, touching them affectionately as if he were saying goodbye to a dear lover.

When he was done, Fletcher removed his clothes and wrapped his silk robe around his body. He caressed its smooth texture and rubbed it over his soft skin. For an elderly gentleman with a voracious appetite, Fletcher somehow maintained a youthful, firm physique, except for the slightest bit of love handles at his waist. He knew the only thing that gave away his true age was his full, thick, shiny shock of silver hair. Fletcher thought he bore a striking resemblance to his favorite literary character, Oscar Wilde's *Dorian Gray*. If it hadn't been for the fact that he spent his life traveling, Fletcher believed he would have had a striking portrait of his young self, disintegrating in an attic somewhere.

The palms of Fletcher's hands itched. This happened just before he knew he was about to perform another holy sacrifice.

His heart pounded as he thought about what would happen next. The bath could wait for the moment.

Fletcher slid his almost-naked body under his billowy, down duvet. He touched himself until he was hard. It wasn't often that he liked to masturbate—it was a messy, nasty affair—but sometimes necessary. Fletcher discovered that it helped him relax whenever anxiety reared its ugly head. Oddly enough, he found himself fantasizing about his beautiful sister-in-law Sally, which both disturbed and delighted him.

Once he climaxed into a scented tissue, Fletcher went to get his sharpest knife, the one he had just used to slit the cop's throat. He took the knife into the bathroom where he washed the cop's blood off it and left it on the side of the sink. He carefully washed any droplets of blood from the porcelain. Fletcher checked his bathtub water's temperature. It was just to his liking. He breathed in the delightful lavender aroma of his bath as it rose up with the steam just before he stepped in.

At Saint Mary's Home, Noelle and Lopez were leading the endangered group from the basement into Noelle's truck. Father John sat up front with Lopez while Noelle and Sister Theresa squeezed into the back seat with the two other women. Moments after they drove away, Detective Tucci pulled up. He rang the doorbell relentlessly until the night security guard finally answered it.

On the way to the safe house, Father John turned and spoke to Noelle. "Mrs. Murphy got a message from Sally," he said. "She gave it to me when I called to let her know that I'd be gone for a few days. Apparently, Sally is staying at a hotel downtown. She never got a seat on that flight to Houston"

Noelle perked up. "Thank God. We can swing by and get her on the way to the safe house."

The priest continued, "I'm afraid not. She didn't say what hotel. Sally only called to tell you that she was concerned about her friend Christian. She asked that you check in on him as soon as possible."

"Why?" Noelle asked.

"All I know," Father John said, "Sally told Mrs. Murphy

to tell me to tell you that Fletcher sounded weird. She had just spoken to him over the phone and he told her something about adding Sally's name to his will. He told her you would understand and that he had hidden the will in his room, but to not tell you until after he'd gone."

Noelle looked hard at Father John. The priest turned to Rose.

"Now might be a good time to tell Nick what you told me about the killer…who you thought he looked like as he was saving your lives."

Noelle cut him off. "Rose, there's no need. I know who the killer is. I have a signed confession from him."

Rose blurted it out anyway, just to get it off her chest.

As soon as they reached the safe house, Noelle put Lopez and Father John in charge of the women. He instructed Lopez to do a search of all the downtown hotels to try and locate Sally. Noelle took off like a bat out of hell and headed back to Fletcher's apartment in the boarding house.

Rose's description of the killer she saw was a very clear confirmation that the confession Fletcher/Brandon made was true. Noelle didn't want to believe it, but more than likely, his brother was planning to disappear. But why would he put Sally in his will if he were planning to disappear? Noelle thought that maybe he better find the will Fletcher had stashed in his room before Tucci got there first.

Noelle parked the Ford directly behind the dead cop in the unmarked car. He didn't notice anything amiss as he rushed to the rooming house's front door and let himself in with his key. Noelle headed straight up to Fletcher's apartment. Since he had already broken the front lock, he was surprised to find it locked again, this time with the inside latch. He called out to Fletcher but got no answer.

Once again, Noelle used his knife to break the latch. Once inside his gut led him straight to the bathroom where he found another locked door. He pounded on it and called out his brother's name again and again. "Brandon, I know you're in there," he shouted. "Open up." No answer.

Noelle broke that lock, too. He shouldered open the door to find Fletcher luxuriating in a hot, steamy bath filled with bubbles up to his neck. Brandon opened his eyes weakly. In a thin voice, he uttered, "Baby Brother, I told you not to come. But you came anyway."

Noelle said, "Fletcher…or do you prefer I call you 'Brandon'? It's not too late. I can use my influence to keep you from the electric chair."

"No one can save me now, baby bro," Brandon sighed.

"Bullshit. I can arrange for you to live out your days in a hospital. I'd come visit you. Sally would, too. She really cares about you. She's the one who sent me here to save you."

"Oh, that's so sweet. I love her, too," Brandon said lazily, the hot water lulling him into a quiet place. "She's a keeper, brother. You better hang onto that one."

Noelle cut to the chase. "Look, I know what you did and I still love you. Nothing can change that! You're my brother, my blood. You're not a bad man, just a very sick one. We can help you."

"It's too late, brother."

Noelle was so focused on his brother's intense hazel eyes, the same eyes as his mother had, that he didn't notice the bubbles turning from pink to a deeper red all around his body. Noelle rushed to his side but Brandon raised his bleeding wrist out from the foam and in a split second, he slashed his own throat with the blade he'd been holding beneath the water.

"Noooo!" Noelle wailed. "Noooo!"

Blood spurting from Brandon's neck landing all over Noelle as Brandon's body convulsed in a horrific dance of death. In anguish, Noelle cried out, "Oh, my brother, why, why did it have to be this way?"

Noelle crumbled in a heap on the bathroom floor. Now he had nothing, no one, not even Sally. Noelle didn't know how long he lay there and he didn't care. When he was good and ready, he got up and removed all signs of his having been there. Noelle dragged himself to his truck to drive back to the safe house. He was hoping that by now Lopez had located Sally.

After he reached the safe house, Noelle learned that Tucci had ordered a raid on Saint Mary's just after they'd all gotten away. When Tucci couldn't find Noelle or Sister Theresa, he went ballistic. That's what the night watchman said anyway.

Noelle was relieved when Lopez told him he'd reached Sally at the Prince Conti Hotel in the French Quarter. Noelle immediately called her room. Gently, he told Sally how he had learned that Fletcher and Brandon his brother were one and the same man. Then he told her Fletcher could no longer live with his sins and took his own life.

Sally was silent on the other end of the line and Noelle knew she was crying. "I'm coming to get you," he said. "Is that okay?"

"Yes," she told him in a small voice. He warned Sally to be careful because there was an all-out manhunt for him. If Tucci and his men found her first, it could get ugly. Sally assured Noelle that she'd be fine. She planned to hide out in the lobby's ladies' room until Noelle arrived.

After he hung up with Sally, Noelle called his Houston cronies to see if they could get the FBI sent in. The feds were the only way to thwart Tucci. Noelle knew the crooked detective would stop at nothing to frame him. He was pretty sure that Tucci would try to make it look like he killed Fletcher along with all the others if he could.

Noelle drove his truck recklessly, rushing to reach Sally before anyone else did. He screeched to a stop at the Prince Conti's valet station then ran straight inside to the ladies' restroom in the lobby. Although he startled a blue-haired old lady putting on frosted lipstick at the mirror, he found no sign of his wife.

Next, Noelle bolted to the front desk and asked for Sally's room number but the desk clerk told him that she had just checked out. Noelle was in a rage and almost clocked the guy but he held back.

"Are you sure? I just spoke to her minutes ago," Noelle yelled. "She said she'd wait for me here."

The desk clerk just shrugged. "Sorry, sir. There's nothing I can do."

"Let me see her room," Noelle demanded.

When he flashed his Houston police badge, the clerk reluctantly gave him the key to Sally's room. Instead of waiting for the elevator, Noelle took the stairs, bounding up them two at a time as if he hadn't taken a near fatal beating earlier that night. His body was running on pure adrenalin. Fumbling with the key, he unlocked the door, rushed in and found nothing. Sally's suitcase sat on the bed, only partially packed. That scared the shit out of him.

Noelle was in a panic. He was pretty certain Tucci had sent someone from the mob to do a job on Sally. He didn't know where to turn. Just then, the phone rang.

Noelle picked up. A deep voice with a heavy New York accent said, "If you want to see your wife in one piece, I suggest you get over to Velda's now. My men are waiting for you."

By the time Noelle pulled up in front of Velda's, the scene was crawling with cop cars and flashing red lights. There was yellow tape around the perimeter of Velda's property. A flurry of cops were clustered around an unmarked car with a cop slumped over the steering wheel. He didn't look too good.

Velda was on the porch, pacing back and forth in her skimpy robe and pink curlers. She was flailing her arms, screaming, "Oh! Dear Lord! Why me, why me?"

As soon as Noelle got out of his truck, two officers were on him with drawn guns, shouting at the top of their lungs, "Get down on the ground! Get down!" Noelle had no option but to surrender. He lay on the sidewalk, his hands raised in defeat.

As Noelle was being handcuffed, Tucci sauntered over and pushed his heavy foot into Noelle's back. His partner Melville was right behind him. Tucci addressed his team.

"Did you read this scumbag his rights?"

The arresting officer laughed cruelly as he handed Noelle over to Tucci and Melville. As they yanked Noelle to his feet, he spat in Tucci's face.

"What have you done with my wife?" Noelle snarled.

"The shoe's on the other foot now, Detective, isn't it? If I were you, I'd cherish your right to remain silent." Tucci smirked at Noelle.

Noelle was like a wild animal trapped in a net. "If you've touched even one hair on my wife's head, you will pay. You may have the mob on your side, but I've got friends, too."

Noelle had no clue that Tucci had already made arrangements with his mob associates to take down Noelle. Once they moved him away from the swarm of cops and investigators, they'd make it look like Noelle had tried to run and they had no choice but to shoot him to stop him. Unfortunately, these boys shoot to kill.

Just as Tucci was about to put Noelle into the back of his Dodge, a whole new pack of unmarked vans pulled up, their red lights flashing. This time it wasn't the New Orleans PD but the FBI. With their guns drawn, they darted out of their vans. Melville looked frightened as he stepped aside. He pointed at Tucci. "That's him!" he shouted. The agents rushed Tucci and slapped handcuffs around his wrists.

Melville had long suspected that his partner was dirty but he was afraid of what would happen to him if he blew the whistle on Tucci. A dirty cop like Tucci could make even his partner disappear. But that night, Tucci had gone too far. Ordering Melville to abduct Noelle's wife was the last straw. Melville piqued the feds' interest by telling them that he had evidence of Tucci's involvement with the Carlucci family. It wasn't hard to convince them of this fact since they'd been watching Tucci for some time. With the cooperation of another officer on the squad, it was enough for the FBI to make an arrest.

As the federal agents released Noelle from his handcuffs, another unmarked car pulled up. One of the agents escorted a trembling Sally to meet her husband. Noelle was so grateful he almost kissed the ground—and the cop. He threw his arms around Sally and would not let go.

Over his wife's shoulder, Noelle saw the EMTs removing Fletcher's corpse from the rooming house and putting it into the coroner's vehicle. Velda and her remaining tenants stood on the lawn in shock.

"Oh my God, poor, poor Mr. Fletcher," Velda shrieked. "I just don't believe it. He was always such a gentleman."

Epilogue

Seven months later, Sally gave birth to a perfect eight-pound baby girl. She was beautiful, with fiery red hair and bright eyes. The newborn looked just like her grandmother.

Sally had used part of her inheritance from Christian Fletcher to pay for Noelle's ninety day stay at Hazelden, one of the best drug and alcohol treatment centers in the country. When Noelle came out, he was ready to start his new life.

He hadn't had a drink or gambled since the night his brother died. Noelle was overjoyed to be a new father, although he still hadn't found religion like his wife. The only time Sally could get Noelle into Saint Cyril's was the day Father Bruce christened their daughter Catherine Noelle. Her godparents were Maria and Juan Lopez. Also on the guest list were Noelle's friends from New Orleans: Sister Theresa, the ex-priest Father John and his new wife Rose, who was expecting their first child.

Saints and sinners alike rejoiced in the new lives of baby Catherine and Juanito, Maria and Juan Lopez's new son. To look at this group from a distance, no one could ever imagine the sins of their mothers and fathers.

Or that there was another murder brewing in Houston, bubbling just beneath the surface like a storm about to blow.

Nobody but Nick Noelle, that is.

CPSIA information can be obtained
at www.ICGtesting.com
Printed in the USA
LVHW021433281218
602058LV00001B/29/P